Redfire

by

Stephanie Pilz

Table of Contents

Viterlea

Planet Viterlea is the oddest and the oldest planet in existence to this day. Viterlea is located just out of Earth's universe. It's a planet full of many mysteries, magic, and wonders, but it's also dangerous. It's a dark and gloomy place, but still exquisite and exotic. Viterlea was created by two very different, but equally powerful beings. These two beings were so powerful that the beings, they created, thought they were gods. These two beings came from two different planets themselves.

They call one of these beings is Eleanor, and in the old days, when she would show herself to her beings on Viterlea, they would paint her image on the walls, and write stories about her. Most of the stories are only legends now and only a few still believe that she existed. The legends about her, quote she looked like an angel from the great heavens above, with rare blue gold skin.

One of Eleanor's powers was the control over the seven elements, and she bares their symbols on her blue golden skin. The seven different symbols were all in a different color. The colors represented each of the elements she controlled. The colors of these symbols were Green for Earth, Blue for Water, Red for Fire, Yellow for Light, White for Spirit, Purple for Thought, and Orange for Air.

Some portraits of her show her having a pair of blue wings coming out of her back that that shined gold in the sun. She also had white hair that had streaks of blue in it, and the blue streaks brought out the intensity of her icy dark blue eyes, which saw far into the furture.

The legends also say Eleanor always dressed in a white dress, and that she held a mysterious glowing blue scepter in her right hand. It is said she came from a planet called Witca, and it was once exquisite and magical, but dangerous to live on because it had a missive amount of poisonous plants growing everywhere and these plants could kill a person with a single touch.

They called the other one of these beings William, and the legends say he was once a mighty dragon warrior, but when he

6

betrayed his father, the king, for love, his father cursed him to be a half-dragon half-man creature, so he could never hold the woman he loved so dearly. When he wasn't in his dragon form, he had purple skin, horns, and red symbols coving his body that glowed and the symbols meant strength, honor, and loyalty, but only the symbols for strength remand on his skin after his betrayal. He always wore a battle suit, with a red glowing sword on his belt. In his dragon form, his scales changed to the color of charcoal, and he had wings that looked like the color of the blood he drank.

His long red hair was a darker shade than his wings, and he had a hypnotic, mesmerizing purple eyes. His hands were in the shapes of claws that could cut down his enemies with one swing. It is said he came from a planet called Darka, and it was true to its name, because it was a dark and fiery place, there was barely any life, making it seem like the planet was dead. It was hard to live on the ground, because of the many volcanoes, so most people on his planet lived in houses that floated in the sky.

A long time ago, before they fled to make a planet of their own, their planets were at war with each other. The war was mainly because of a misunderstanding, which led William's father to attack the people of Witca. Sadly, the violent and sudden battle between the two planets, ended with the destruction of both of planets, but

Eleanor and William had left their planets before someone had destroyed them, and they thought that they were the only survives.

They left just before the battle was over, because they were in love with each other, and they didn't want to die. They also didn't like the fighting and the hate that led to that battle, and they created a new planet with peace and harmony. So, they combined their powers to fashion Viterlea. They split the planet into two sides, so they could represent both their home planets on this one.

William's side is a beautiful place of night, dark as a moonlit sky, but without stars or a moon, instead there is a strange light that emanates forth, so it isn't as dark as Darka. There is a forest that's big and wide, that contains tall and menacing looking trees, that glow red to light the way through. There are also dangerous animals that live in the forest, like Mighty Dragons, Venomous Snakes, and Vicious Tigers.

The dragons ruled the sky, and they could breathe fire. They would also watch over those on the ground below, in case they were in trouble. William wanted some dragons to form a bond with the beings he intended to create. The Snakes stayed on the trees, not bothering anyone. That is unless someone invaded on the tree they were on. They would bite the intruder and poison them and then eat them, unless they brought the snake a gift, like a Nightspear Flower for their nest. The Tigers came in two colors. Some were black with red stripes, while others were red with black stripes, and they ruled the ground together. These Tigers are very vicious animals, but if you could beat them in a fight, and form a bond with them, they would be at your command, but if you lost the fight, they would devour you.

He made the rivers and the streams run bright red with blood, because that was what he drank, and that's what he wanted his beings to drink, and there were gardens of fresh food for his beings. He built houses and a castle for his beings to live in. He made the houses of Bloodstone and he made the castle of black moonstone. The most important thing he brought from his planet was the last Nightspear flower seeds. The Nightspear flowers are blue, orange, pink, and purple. They only bloomed at night, and all the colors shine bright in the dark. He brought this flower from Darka, because it was the first flower he gave to Eleanor when they first met. This flower symbolized their love because it was lovely and could heal anything, but it could also poison and destroy everything.

Eleanor made her side full of life and light. She made it so that three suns were in the sky shinning down during the day, and at night there were three moons that shined in the sky, with a lot of sparkling stars. There were fields of green grass that sparkled in the sunlight, and there were trees filled with all kinds of fruits, like sweet Tamila berries, which were her favorite fruit from Witca.

There were also flowers growing everywhere and, in every color, you could imagine. The trees on her side were alive and they could talk and move. She called them Guardians, since they protected all the things she loves so dearly.

She created wondrous animals, like Fairies in many colors, and they loved to play tricks on those who would cross their path. To anyone who could befriend one of these tricksters, they would be forever faithful. She also made magical, wild, yellow Wolves that were the gentlest creatures, and if they lost you, the wolfs would guide they to safety.

On her side, she made the rivers, and the streams run with clear shimmering water, that magically watered all the plants and flowers on the planet and helped them to bloom. She also gave the water healing properties. There were houses and a castle for her beings. The houses were out of ammolite; because of all the colors in the stone, it shone brightly in the sunlight. She made the castle of moonstone because she loves how it shines in the moonlight.

William made his beings that looked different, then himself. He brought them forth through a dark abyss he made appear on his side. His beings looked bewitching with long blond, shiny hair, and their skin was so pale it looked like ivory. Their eyes are a deep crimson, that seemed cold and empty, but they shined in a way you knew that they were trustworthy. He made his two beings have a mark on their backs of a Nightspear flower.

He gifted his beings with strength, speed, and the ability to control another's mind, and they could talk to each other with their minds too. They could talk to the animals that live in the forest, and if they formed a bond with an animal, the animal would become a part of their being. William called his beings Vampires. Despite their many powers, William gave them one weakness, the suns, which could ultimately kill them. He named the first two Vampires, Queen Deva and King Fontos.

Eleanor's beings differed from William's Vampires. She made her beings come down from the suns, and they were beautiful. They had skin that glows golden in the sunlight, and they had long golden hair to match. Their eyes differed from hers. They were an exotic blue that resembled a crystallized waterfall. She blessed her beings with magic, and a powerful amulet she had from Witca with an amuelet called the Redfire. The Redfire, was one of seven amulets from Witca that were called Fires. The Redfire is all powerful; it can do anything that the one who wields it wants it to do. Eleanor called her beings, Witches. She named the first two Witches Queen Dena and King Dolo.

William and Eleanor decided that the Vampires and the Witches shouldn't know about each other, not until the Vampires and the Witches started to make more of their own kind. William watched as Fontos and Deva made more Vampires by chanting to the abyss he made appear on the planet. After they did that, he saw more of his Vampires rise out of the blood. On Eleanor's side, she watched as Dena and Dolo made more Witches by praying to the sun, the ground, the water, and through the power of the Redfire made more Witches. She saw more Witches flowing down from the bright suns.

One day, the Kings and the Queens of the Vampires and the Witches went for a walk to see what was on the other side of the planet. On their walk, they ran into each other. William and Eleanor were watching them closely. They saw that King Dolo and Queen Deva wanted to fight each other. This made William and Eleanor mad, and just as they would interfere, and stop them from fighting. Queen Dena and King Fontos thought they could learn from each other instead of fighting. This made Eleanor and William thrilled, and they helped the Vampires and the Witches make a treaty of peace with each other. The main point of the treaty said that neither could cross the other's boundaries without having the other's permission first.

Before the Vampires and the Witches signed the treaty, Eleanor saw that a witch would end the peace on Viterlea one day, and she knew that she had to come up with a way to stop her. So, she added a hidden prophecy inside the paper of the treaty that the Vampires and the Witches didn't know about, and they would not know about until it was the right time. She put the prophecy in three parts, one in the treaty, the second part was in a book that the Vampires had, the third part was in a book the Witches had. But there was also a four part that contained the knowledge that the other three parts left out and only the one that would defeat this Witch would know. After they signed the treaty, William and Eleanor strangely disappeared.

Chapter One

Attack

Dylana sometimes hoped that maybe Witches, and Vampires were real, and hoped she would meet one in my life, and prove to herself they exist. The thing that didn't cross her mind was that she was a Witch, or that her boyfriend, Damien, would be a real Vampire, fangs and all. This new knowledge changed her whole life. At the same time, she found out that the world isn't as it seems, and that there's magic everywhere, even if others can't see it.

The first day she met Damien was on March Seventeenth. Dylana Volus was seventeen years old, at the time. Dylana had an all year tan, and she had long unnaturally colored black hair, and she had these eyes that were green, but the pupil part of her eyes was blue instead of black, and not just any blue, they were bright turquoise. No one seemed to know why they were like that though. Dylana's parents were no longer together, and they both remarried. She had just moved to New York a week ago from Kansas, with her mother, Debathena and stepfather Bob. She abhorred her stepfather so much; She didn't know what it was about him; She just felt like there was something wrong with him or unnatural, although she was never sure what it was. She thought Bob was just not a good person, and because Bob worked for the military, or something like that. Dlyana wasn't sure, because Bob was very secretive about his work, but whatever he did meant that they had to move around a lot.

Her mother was her world, and they did everything together, and her mother's eyes were even crazier than Dylana's. Her mother's eyes were a deep purple with blue spots here and there. They almost looked the same except her mother had golden hair that would shine in the sun. Her mother worked as an executive with a big company. Dylana didn't know what the name of the company was, because her mother never talked about work with her, but apparently her mother's company had offices all over the world. So that moving all the time didn't interfere with her mother's job. All the moving meant that Dylana had to switch schools all the time. It was annoying, and it also meant that she had no real friends, because she wasn't a school long enough to even make friends. She's been in about eleven different schools in the past seven years.

Her father, Russ lived in Maine, with his wife Jan. He worked at a lot of odd jobs. He never could stay at one job for longer than a week, but her father didn't need to work, because he had money from his family that passed away years ago, she guessed that he just wanted something to do. Her father had golden hair like her mother, and he had a all year tan. Jan was a housewife, and she came from Greece to be with Dylana's father. When Dylana first meet her, she thought Jan was nice, until the day that Dylana dropped a plate on the floor, and Jan yelled at Dylana for about an hour and a half of what Jan yelled wasn't even in English. Dylana also had a little half-sister named Melissa, who was about seven years old.

On March Seventeenth, Dylana was trying to sleep in, but she scared awake at 6am by her alarm clock, that was blasting music from some radio station. She rolled over to shut it off, but the alarm clock just kept playing music. She was getting fed up with the alarm clock, so she grabbed it and threw it against the closed door of her room. On impact it smashed into pieces. After about a minute, music started to play from the smash clock, and she thought something must haver possessed it. She just stared at it with amazement and wondered why it would not die. As she thought that there was a knock on the door.

"Yes," Dylana asked as her mother opened the door, and she looked at the dying alarm clock on the floor.

"So, what did your alarm clock ever do to you?" Her mother asked joking with her.

"It went off, and it refuses it shut up. So, I tried to kill it, but the freaking thing refuses to die." Dylana told her, and they laughed, as the music finally stopped.

"I see, well since you're up, why don't you get dress. You have school today." Debathena told her, and Dylana thought to herself, great I get to go to another new school, and be that new girl that anyone stares at and whispers freak behind her back.

"Do I have to, why can't I just make up the last three months of the school year, being homeschooled? I hate always being the new girl, and when I make friends, we have to move again to somewhere else." Dylana asked her mother.

"Honey, I'm sorry for all the moving around, but you have to go to school, and I don't have to time to homeschool you. I have some good news. I think we'll be here until you graduate high school. So, you'll have time to make friends." Debathena told her, but as her mother said that, she knew that it was a lie, because she knew they'd have to move again soon, to make sure that her mother didn't find her and Dylana.

"Do you mean that?" Dylana asked her, as she hoped that her mother meant it, because she told Dylana the same thing, when they were living in Kansas.

"Yes, we will stay in New York." Debathena said, as she thought maybe.

"Okay, I guess I'm getting dressed then." Dylana said, and then her mother left the room. Dylana climbed out of bed and she walked over to her closet and tore though her suitcases, she still hadn't unpacked, because she didn't know when she'd be moving again. She had to move all her books, to get to her clothes, and then she grabbed the first things that her hands touch, which were a red t-shirt and a pair of black jeans. After she got dressed, she sat on her bed as she put on her favorite pair of boots she got from her mother. Dylana, then headed to the kitchen for something to eat before school.

"So, mother, what's for breakfast?" Dylana asked her.

"Well, my darling, I have eggs, bacon, and toast for you." Debathena said, as she put a plate of food in front of Dylana.

"So, where's Bob?" Dylana asked, as she started to eat her food.

"He had to go out early this morning." Debathena told her daughter.

"Really, I didn't hear him this morning." Dylana said, because Bob liked to make as much noise as he could just to make Dylana mad.

"I told him to be quiet, so you could sleep a little longer." Debathena told her.

"Thanks," Dylana told her.

"Your welcome, sweetie now eat, and I'll walk with you to school," Debathena said, being protective.

"Mom, I'm not a kid, I don't need you to walk me to school. I'm sure I can find the school all by myself. Using the GPS on my phone. what's the name of this school again?" Dylana asked, because she wasn't paying any attention when her mother told the school name last night.

"You weren't listening to me at all last night, were you?" Debathena asked.

"I remember the part where you say that New York City could be dangerous at night, and that you wanted me home before it got dark every night." Dylana said to her.

"Well, at least you listened to something I told you. So, the school's called Blake High School," Debathena told her, and as she said the school's name, Dylana was typing it into her phone's GPS.

"Okay, it's in the phone, and now I'd better hurry, so I get there on time. Bye Mom, I'll see you later." Dylana said, and then she hugged her mother goodbye and grabbed her schoolbag and left. Dylana walked to where the elevators were and hit the button for the elevator. She was standing there impatiently waiting for the elevator doors to open.

When the doors opened, she saw that there was someone already in there. As she walked onto the elevator, Dylana couldn't help but stare at him, because she thought that he was the hottest guy she'd ever seen. She thought he had this beautiful porcelain skin, and she figured he worked out because she saw that he was muscular, and he had black eyes and dark brown hair. She thought he must be a model or something.

"What floor are you going to?" He asked her.

"I'm going down to the lobby." Dylana said, and he reached over the hit the button for her.

"Are you new to this apartment building? I haven't seen you before." He asked her.

"Yes, my mom, stepfather, and I just moved in about a week ago, how long have you been living here. I'm Dylana, by the way and you are?" She asked.

"It's nice to meet you Dylana, I'm Damien, and I had an apartment here for years, but I spend most of my time traveling. Hey, I don't do this, but if you need help to get around the city, just let me know." He said, as the elevator stopped, and the doors opened.

"Well, I guess that we ran out of floors. I'll see you around." He said as he walked away from her and headed outside. She just stood there watching him walk away, when she remembered that she had to get to school. She quickly walked outside, and then she took out her phone to see what way she had to go, but when she did that, she also saw the time and if she wanted to make it there on time, she knew she'd have to run. As she ran to school, all she was thinking about was Damien.

It took her about half an hour to get to school, because she made a few wrong turns, and as the school came into view, the bell rang for classes to start, and she thought fuck, now I'm late. She walked into the school and went to the office to get a late slip. As she walked into the office, she knew that her being there was bothering the lady in the office. They quickly wrote her a late slip and told her to get to class.

The school day was a bore to her, because at her last school she was in all AP classes, so she was ahead in all her classes, and as she was answering most of the questions that the teachers were asking. She started to hear the other students whisper, "Know it all, or teacher's pet." Walking through the halls was even worse for her, because some people in her classes pushed her into lockers, or just making fun her for the way her eyes looked. Dylana was just trying to ignore all of it, because this wasn't the first time she had to deal with this kind of thing. She wondered to herself why do other kids have to be so cruel.

At 3pm the bell rang for the end of school, and she practically jumped for joy and ran out of school and down the street just to get away from all the nasty kids before they could pick on her some more.

As she was running, she heard a few guys from her school chasing after her, and they were getting closer and closer to her, and then one of them grabbed a hand full of her hair and pulled her down. She fell hard on the sidewalk. As they were talking about what they were going to her, she saw someone walking, and she said, "Help."

"No one will help you. This is our neighborhood outsider." One guy said to her, and when he grabbed her, she heard someone say, "Let her go." the guy dropped her, and she turned away to see Damien, and she thought he must have heard her say help.

"What if we don't want to? What are you going to do about it?" Another one guy from her school said.

"You really don't want to find out." Damien said, and one of kids tried to punch Damien, but Damien moved out of the way of the punch and threw a punch of his own and hit the kid on the left side of his head and the kid went down and then the other two grabbed their friend off the ground and run for it.

"Are you okay Dylana?" He asked her, as kneel next to her.

"I think so, just a few bruises. Thanks for saving me. I don't know what would have happen if you didn't come along." She said to him.

"I do, I've seen those guys before, and what they do to girls it's not good." He said, and Dylana didn't want to ask more, because

23

she really didn't want the answer. As Dylana tried to stand up, she fell over when she put pressure on her right ankle. Damien caught her before she hit the ground.

"Is it your ankle?" He asked her.

"Yeah, I think it's twisted." She told him.

"Do you think you can make it over to that bench?" He asked her, as he pointed to a bench that was a few feet away.

"Maybe if you help me." she said, and he told her to put her right arm around his neck, so he could take the weight off her right ankle, and he half carried her over to the bench.

"Have a seat, and I'll look at your ankle." He said.

"Are you a doctor or something?" She asked him.

"No, but I'm good at first aid. I've had to patch up some of my wounds in the past, because I don't like doctors." He said, as she watched him take off her boot and pulled up her leg of her black jeans. He put pressure on different parts of her ankle, and he asked her to tell him when something hurt. After he looked at it, he said, "Well, I have good news."

"Really, so what's the good news, Doc?" she said, trying to be funny.

"It's not twisted but I should put ice in it when you get home. I think I might have something in my bag that should help you." He said, as he looked in his bag, and pulled out a small ice pack, and he put it against her ankle, and he wrap some gauze around it to keep it in place, and she asked him if he always had first aid stuff in his bag.

"Yes, I usually have something with me, for first aid, I like to fight a lot. So, does that feel better, with the ice on it?" Damien asked her.

"A little but, thanks for your help again." She told him when his phone rang. He reached into his front pocket of his jeans and answered the phone.

"Hello, Debathena." He said, and Dylana looked at him confused, because he just said her mother's name.

Chapter Two

Soulmate

"Is that my mother on your phone?" She asked him.

"Yes," he said to her, and then said to her mother, "Yes, she's all right, yes, I'll get her home safety, bye."

"Why did my mother call you? And how do you know my mother, if we just moved into the apartment, because she never mention meeting you?" She questioned him.

"It's a long story. Plus, there's a lot of things that your mother doesn't tell you." he said.

"What do you mean by that, because I'm not going anywhere with you until you tell me what you know." She told him.

"Fuck, well here's the true, your mother and I have known each other for a very long time, that's how she had my number. She called me, because she saw that I was with you, and she knew that your phone was dead, from you not charging it enough. She wanted to find out if you were okay after being attacked by those guys. Your mother also wanted to curse me out for being here, because she thinks I will bring trouble to you and her." He said to her.

"Wait, what do you mean she saw us together? Why would she think you'll bring trouble to us? Another thing my phone's not dead." She ranted to him, as she reached into her bag for her phone, and saw it was dead.

"So, what's your battery at?" He asked, smirking at her.

"So, my mother was right about my phone being dead. I'm still not going anywhere until you answer my questions." She said.

"I shouldn't be the one to tell you this." He said.

"Why not?" She asked curiously, and he thought if he tells her the true, Debathena will really kill him.

"I think I should get you home and then we should have a talk with your mother, because if I tell you anything, she doesn't want you to know, she'll kill me." He told her.

"No, you're going to answer my questions, because if you're right about her reaction, there's little chance she'll tell me anything." She told him.

"Okay, but if your mother kills me, I'm taking you down with me. So, here's the short version on how I know your mother. Debathena and I have known each other since we were kids on Viterlea." He said, and then Dylana laughed at him.

"You think I'm joking?" He asked her.

"Yes, because there's no place called Viterlea." She told him.

"Yes, there is, it's just not a place that can travel to unless you have magic. Viterlea, is a planet that's located just out of Earth's galaxy." He told her, and she laughed harder. "So, what you and my mother are freaking aliens from outer space?"

"I hate that word, I'm not a fucking alien. Please stop laughing, because you're from that planet too." He said to her, and she said, "How can I be, when I was born on Earth, smart guy?"

"Yeah, you were, but your parents weren't born here." He said.

"Wait, are you saying that my father is from this imaginary place too?" She asked, laughing some more.

"Yes, and this isn't supposed to be funny. Now focus Dylana, your mother knew I was with you, because she is a powerful Witch, and she saw it, and you're a Witch too." He said, and she thought her mother being a Witch would explain a lot of things.

"Okay, that is the first thing you said that made sense." She said, still nonbelieving that there was a planet called Viterlea.

"So, you believe that your mother's a Witch, but the rest?" He asked her, and she told him no.

"What if I could prove it?" He asked her.

"How could you do that?" She questioned him.

"What, if I could show you a creature, from the planet?" He asked her, thinking about his dragon.

"What kind of creature?" She asked him.

"You'll have to wait and see." He said to her.

"Why do I have to wait?" She asked him.

"Because I haven't told you what I am yet." He told her, and she asked, "So, what are you?"

"I'll get to that later," He said.

"Okay, so why does my mother think you'll bring trouble to us?" She asked him.

"I'm not going to lie to you, I've done bad things in my life, that part of me enjoyed doing. The person I've done these things for is after your mother and her power. Debathena knows I'm here on her orders." He said.

"What bad things have you done?" She asked.

"I've murder Witches and even some of my kind. Most of it was when we were at war with the Witches. Or I was just order to kill someone." He said.

"I'm surprise that you're telling me all this, and honest after what you just said, I don't feel afraid of you. So, I'm just guessing that you're not a Witch?" She asked me.

"Maybe you don't feel afraid, because I have no intention to hurt you. To answer you question, I'm half-Witch, half-Vampire." He told her.

"You're shitting me, right? You're a fucking Vampire?" She asked.

"Yes, I even got the fangs to prove it." He said, as he extended his fangs and he flashed a smile to show her his fangs.

"That's so cool." She said, and he looked at her a little surprised.

"You're taking this well. I wonder why your mother never told you any of this," he said, as his phone rang again. He answered it.

"Hello, yup, okay, we'll be right there." He said.

"Are we in trouble?" She asked him, because she had a feeling it was her mother on the phone again.

"Yup, but at least she's madder at me than you. Do you think you can walk?" He asked me.

"I think so, just let me put my boot back on." She said, as she grabbed her boot and put it on, and then she tried to put pressure on her ankle, but it still hurt a lot.

"Okay, I don't think I can walk that far. Maybe we can get a taxi." She said.

"I have a faster way." He said.

"Do you now?" She asked wondering what he was talking about.

"I'll show you, hop on my back." He said as he kneeled to make it easy for her to get on his back.

"I must be crazy for doing this." She said, as she got on his back, wrapped her legs around, and put her arms around his neck.

"Hold on," he said, and then he ran, and he was going so fast, that Dylana felt like she was flying. As Damien got closer to the apartment building, he started to slow down and then he stopped.

"You okay back there?" He asked her.

"Yeah, can we do that again sometime?" She asked him.

"Maybe, if your mother doesn't kill me," he said.

"I'll just have to protect you from her wrath." She said, as she got off his back and looked at him for a moment. In that moment she knew that she'd do anything for him, and that he would do anything for her.

"I guess that's only fair love. I safe you, and now you get the save me. We should go up, before Debathena comes looking for us." He said.

"Yeah, right," she said, as she grabbed his hand and they felt spark that started in their hands and then shot through their hearts, that formed a bond between them.

"What the fuck was that?" Dylana asked.

"We just experience a soulmate spark. It happens when soulmates touch hands or kiss for the first time." He said, not sure of how she would react.

"So, we're soulmates? Did you know this? Is this why you're here?" She asked him.

"Yes, it appears so. Someone told me, you were my soulmate, but I didn't know for sure until now. And yes, that's why I'm here. I wanted to find you and find out if it was true or not." He told her.

"What if I don't want to be with you?" She asked him.

"That's your choice, but you will never find another love like me," he said, smiling.

"Is that so?" she asked him.

"Yes, now come on," he said, and he led her inside and to where the elevators were. He watched her hit the button, and the doors opened within seconds. They walked in and Damien hit the button for the seventh floor.

"Do you even have an apartment here?" She questioned him.

"Yes, I'm on the thirteenth floor, and I also own the building." He said, and it shocked her, he wasn't lying to her about anything.

"Oh, so, how mad was my mother, when you talked to her?" She asked him, but before him could answer the doors opened and they saw her mother standing there waiting for them.

Chapter Three

Trouble

"Hi Mom," Dylana.

"In the apartment both of you now." She yelled at them, and then they followed Debathena to their apartment and she opened the door for them, and they walked in, with Debathena right behind them.

"Dylana, go to your room. I need to talk to Damien alone." Debathena said as she slammed the doors closed.

"No, I want to know what else you've kept from me." Dylana said,

"No, it's better if you don't know." Debathena said. Before Dylana had to chance to say anything else Debathena waved her arm, and she used her power to do a spell to make Dylana forget anything that Damien just told her, and replaced her memories, to made Dylana think Damien was just a normal guy that lived upstairs, that your mother asked to look after her. When the spell was complete, Dylana felt dizzy, and Damien caught her as she stumbled.

"You okay, love?" Damien asked her.

"Yeah, I just got dizzy, for a second. I don't think you should call me love; we hardly know each other." She said.

"You're right, sorry. Do you want me to help you to your room? That is if you're still dizzy." He asked her, and he knew the Debathena was glaring at him.

"Yeah, I am, but I think I can make it there by myself thanks." She said.

"Okay, feel better." He said. He watched Dylana leave the living room and go into hers and she closed the door behind her.

"Really, Damien, my daughter?" She said, because she knew that they were soulmates, so she knew that there was no way to keep them apart.

"You of all people should know that, Vampires and Witches don't have a choice in the people we fall in love with. With us, it's always an act of fate or destiny. Just like it was with you and Russ." He said to her, and she flinched when he told her love's name.

"Fine, I get it, but we need to talk about something first." She told him.

"Ask away," he said to her.

"Who am I talking to? Are you really Damien, or are you Michael?" She asked him, and he smiled at her.

"Does it really matter?" He asked her grinning, because he was sure she knew that he was Michael and not Damien.

"So, it's Michael then, and why did my mother sent you here?" She asked, as she was getting ready to fight him, if she had to.

"Well, you should know that Damien did have control for a little while, that was until Fantos find him. Lilith had Damien tortured to give me back control over his body. When she told him who he's soulmate was, he gave control back to me. I came here to show him she wasn't lying, and honestly, I was curious if it was true. You know what Debathena, as long as I'm in control of his body, his never get to talk to her or actually be with her." He told her.

"You're terrible, that's so cruel to do that to him." She said.

"I know, and I so enjoy bring pain to him." He said laughing.

"I hate you; did you also tell Lilith that I'm here?" She asked.

"I didn't tell her where you were. She already knew where you were, she was the one that told me where you were." He said, because Lilith always knew where daughter was. Lilith's power of sight was much more powerful than Debathena's.

"Does it matter where I run to?" She asked him.

"I don't think so, I mean that golem, that you made isn't doing his job, and if he was, then I wouldn't have been able to find you, even if you were standing right next to me." He said.

"I can't believe I will ask this, because I know how you are, and I know I can't keep you from Dylana..." She said.

"What are you trying to ask me?" He said.

"I know I shouldn't trust you, but will keep my daughter safe?" She said to him, hoping that she was making a bad decision.

"You don't need to worry about Dylana. I'll keep Dylana safe, but we both know that you will die soon, and there isn't anything you can do about that, if I do hurt her, and I knew that Lilith has plans for her." He told her.

"So, you know that I foresaw my dead. Is that why Lilith stopped asking me to help her? She's waiting for the Redfire to pass to Dylana." She said to him.

"Yes, that's the plan, but it must be her choice, on which side she joins. She will have a join a side, be it the Vampires, or the Witches." He told her, and she knew that a war would start between them soon and that if she wasn't there to fight, her daughter would have to.

"I have another question for you. What does it say in the prophecy that my mother has?" She asked him again.

"Do you really want to know?" He asked her.

"Yes, and since I will die soon, who am I going to tell." She said to him.

"Okay, you make a good point, plus this part has already come to pass. The part that Lilith has talked about me and Niculus and a spell that Lilith cast on Jane. Lilith cast a spell to steal one of Jane's children, but the of spell want wrong and it split Niculus's soul in half and make two of him and it went into Damien's body, and my soul is the other half of Niculus's." He told her.

"Are you telling me that in a way you're Niculus?" She asked him.

"Yes, in everyway I am Niculus, but I'm the opposite of him, and because of this we are one, if one of us dies, then we both die, along with Damien." He told her.

"Should I be on the lookout for an attack?" She asked him.

"I wouldn't be too worried if I were you, until your death gets closer. I just don't know if the attack will be from Lilith or Niculus." He told her.

"Has Lilith ordered you to report to her?" she asked.

"No, she told me she has nothing for me to do until you die, sorry if that comes out harsh." He said.

"I think I'm used to you being bluntly honest. If you want to get to know Dylana, I need your word you will watch out for her and keep her safe." She said to him, because she knew that she had his word on this, that she wouldn't have to worry Dylana being with him.

"You have my word. I will keep her safe." He told her, as he thought, that is until you die.

Chapter Four

Rome

Dylana's mother had lied to her once again, because their stay in New York only lasted about seven weeks, and then her mother told her they were moving again. Dylana was glad she didn't have to pack much, because it wasn't like she did any unpacking, in the first place. In those seven weeks in New York, she started dating Damien, and they become inseparable. Dylana knew that her mother wasn't Damien's biggest fan, but Debathena saw how much he cared for her.

The next place Debathena picked for them to move to was Rome, because Debathena knew that was where fate was taking her.

Dylana was happy to go to Rome, plus her mother told her she could do online school from now on, so that meant no more being the new girl at school. Damien was sad that she was moving, so he moved there to be close to her and to keep his word and keep her safe.

When they were in Rome for three and a half months, Debathena felt like her dead was coming sooner she thought it would happen, and that she knew that she'd be dead within a few days. And she knew that Dylana would feel lost without her. So, as she sat at the kitchen table, she wrote a letter to Dylana telling her want she needed to know.

"Is it time to wake her?" Bob asked as he appeared in front of her.

"You love doing this, don't you?" She asked him.

"Yes, I like how mad she gets, and I have nothing else to do, unless someone attacks us." He said.

Dylana was trying to sleep in when she heard Bob coming up the stairs in a hurry, but it sounded like he was thundering up them. She didn't know that he just like to scare her, because there wasn't anything else that brought him joy. She suddenly heard him slam her bedroom door wide open. Bob slammed it so hard that it whacked into the wall. Dylana just rolled to the other side of the bed, because she didn't want to look at his ugly face this early in the morning. She then heard him walk into her room. He stomped around to the other side of the bed, then he got as close as he could to her face, and then he shouted at her, "Get up, girl."

"What's and the matter with you, Bob?" she shouted back at him, with anger in her voice and it also showed in her eyes. She just glared at him, and she thought he was such an asshole, and she wonders why he was always doing things like this to her. She didn't know what she did to him, to make him treat her like this all the time. She hated him so much this morning. Dylana wondered to herself, why her mother married him, and why she let him do this to her.

"Your mother wants to take you shopping for something, so be downstairs in thirteen minutes' girl." He explained rudely to her, and loudly. She watched him run of the room. She then heard him thunder back down the stairs before she could reply to what he said to her. So, Dylana forced herself to get out of bed. While she did this, she suddenly got a bad feeling in the pit of my stomach. To her it felt as if something bad would happen soon. She thought it was an odd feeling to have. She'd experienced nothing like it before, and deep down this feeling was making her feel worried that she would lose someone, she cared about, like her mother or Damien.

"Dylana, will you hurry, sweetie?" She heard her mother say to her from the kitchen. So, she quickly got dressed in a red and white tee and a pair of jeans, and then she went down the stairs. When she walked into the kitchen, she still had this feeling that just didn't seem to want to go away, and she felt it getting worse. She figured that she should eat something light. So, she had a piece of toast and a glass of orange juice before they left to go shopping.

They went shopping, all along the Via Condotti street, but the whole time they were together, Dylana and her mother didn't say much to each other, Which was odd in its own way, because her mother was never this quiet. She got the feeling that there was something that her mother wanted to tell her, but her mother didn't know how to bring it up. Dylana didn't know why she was having this feeling either. She could just tell that there was something on her mother's mind. It proved the feeling her was having right when her mother said, "Dylana, Bob and I have a dinner party to go to tomorrow night, and I know that its last-minute sweetie. I was wondering if you'd like to come with us."

"I would love to come, Mom, is that why we're shopping for dresses? Why didn't you mention it to me sooner? Will Damien be there?" She asked her, cheerfully and unsurprised, because Damien told her about this party a few days ago, and was planning to bring her with him, and he would ask her mother today, if it was okay if Dylana went to the party.

"Yes, that's why we're shopping for dresses, and Dylana the reason I didn't ask you this sooner is because my boss just mentioned the other day to us, we could bring our kids to the party with us. I wasn't sure how I would ask you, and I'm sure that Damien will be there, since he was an intern at my job. You seem unsurprised, did him tell you already?" Her mother said to her, with a smile, and Dylana told her that Damien told her about it a few days ago and that he would ask her if Dylana could go with him.

"I see, so you were already planning to go," Debathena said.

"Yes, if it's still okay?" She said.

"Yes, I knew that he would ask you, but I'll be watching him." She said, she rolled her eyes at Dylana, and then she told Dylana that they should head home. So, they got back in the car, and then they headed home. They got home around three o'clock in the afternoon. Dylana put the green dress that her mother got her, in her room so it wouldn't get wrinkled. After she did that, she went to one of my bookcases to grab a book to get lost in. She went through each shelf, looking for just the right book to read. The book she finally picked was Inkheart. She then sat on her bed and read the book.

As she started the third chapter, she had a feeling that someone was watching her. she got the sudden urge to look up from the book. So, she looked out her window, and she saw that there was this odd and mysterious man outside looking up at her. As she stared back at him, she was wondering why he was out there. She couldn't see his face because he had the hood of his coat up, but she could see that he had these peculiar glowing ruby red eyes. As he was just staring at her, she felt a chill that down my spine. This chill made her look away from the man, and when she looked back out the window, he was just gone, like he just disappeared into thin air.

As she started to wonder where this man had gone to and why he was out there. She got another chill up her spine. Just as she got this second chill, she heard someone ring the doorbell. The sudden sound scared her and made her fall right off her bed and onto the hard-wooden floor. She knew that she hit the floor hard, and she was in a lot of pain from the fall. She didn't know why she hit the floor that hard, like she did. Her bed wasn't that high from the floor. She slowly got up from the floor and she rubbed the side of her leg she fell on, because it hurt a lot. As she pulled up the leg of her jeans, she saw that there was a big bruise on my leg. She thought she should put some ice on it, so it wouldn't get worse. She went downstairs to get some ice and as she did this, she completely forgot that someone rang the doorbell.

Dylana thought her mother must have heard her coming down the stairs, because just as she was about to go into the kitchen to get some ice, her mother asked me, "Dylana, could you see who's at the door for me?" she did as Debathena asked, and she turned away from the kitchen, and she walked the short distance to the front door. She didn't know who could come over now, because they didn't get many visitors, plus they hadn't been living in Rome that long. If they had someone coming over, they would know about it, because her mother always told people to call first. She opened the door, and she saw that it was the man that was staring at her though her window. She started to freak out a little, and she slammed the door shut in his face and ran into the kitchen.

"Mom, there's a weird guy at the door, and before he rang the doorbell, he was staring at me though my window upstairs." She told my mother franticly.

"Dylana, calm down sweetie, I'll go tell him to go away okay." Debathena said to her. Before Dylana could tell her not to, her mother was already heading to the door, so she followed her. Dylana tried to tell her to stop, because she was getting a bad feeling about her opening the door. She was too late, because when her mother opened the door, but there was no man on the other side, and in his place, there was this red and black tiger standing there instead, and it was growling at them. Her mother backed away from the tiger, as it got closer to her, but it just walked pass her. It then looked at Dylana, and then it started to run straight at her.

Dylana ran up the stairs to get away from the tiger. As she got to the top of the stairs and turned around and saw that the tiger had the same red eyes of the guy she saw. She closed her eyes and screamed as it was about to attack her, but then she heard a loud bang instead. She opened her eyes, and she saw that Bob was standing there next to her, with a baseball bat in his hands, and saw that the tiger was dead at the bottom of the stairs, or it looked like it was.

"Thanks, Bob," she said, as she looked at the dead tiger, and noticed that there was no blood on at all on the floor. She then watched as the tiger just seemed to fade away into thin air. Her mind was racing, and she didn't know what was going on. Like how did that tiger just disappear? And where did Bob come from? She thought he would not be home until seven like always. She thought maybe he just got home early, or he just appeared at the top of the stairs?

"Girl, run, when you see a tiger like that." He barked at her. When she turned around to look at him, he disappeared. She wondered where the fuck did, he go to? She also wondered what he meant by a tiger like that. How could that tiger and the guy have the same colored eyes? She looked at my mother, and I saw that she

49

looked worried about something. She looked as if this was normal to her.

"Mom, how did that tiger just disappear like that, and how did Bob just appear at the top of the stairs and then the next second disappear like that?" She asked her.

"Dylana, it was probably just a magic trick, and that guy you saw was probably just playing a joke on us, to scare us for you slamming the door in his face." Her mother told her, as she looked at Dylana.

"Okay, but what about Bob appearing, and then disappearing?" she asked her.

"What are you talking about? Bob's not home yet." She said to Dylana, but Dylana knew what she just saw. She knew that her mother was trying to lie to her. She knew something she didn't want Dylana to know about.

"Mom, why are you lying to me? Bob was here. I saw him." She said to her mother, and the look she saw on her mother's face was a shock and showed that she was hiding something from Dylana. Debathena didn't answer, and Dylana watched as she pulled something out of one of her pockets. Dylana couldn't see what it was, and then Debathena walked up to Dylana and she put her hand to Dylana's head. Dylana didn't know why she was doing this, but Dylana then heard her mother tell her to forget about Bob, the tiger, and the man.

"Mother, what are you doing? Why are we just standing on the stairs, and why's the front door open?" She asked her mother.

"Nothing baby, why don't you go back upstairs and read," She said to Dylana, as she went to shut the door, and Dylana went back to my room, and I fell asleep while reading, forgetting she wanted to put ice on the bruise on her leg.

Chapter Five

Party

The next morning, Dylana was having a bizarre dream. The dream she had didn't feel like a dream to her. Instead, it felt like her mind was trying to get her to remember about the tiger attacking her. She woke up screaming when she saw the man's glowing ruby red eyes in her mind, because those eyes scared her to her core.

As she got out of bed, she noticed that her right leg was killing her. As she got to my feet, she wondered what she did to it. She pulled up the leg of her pants, and she saw a swollen big black and blue bruise. As she looked at it, she realized that she didn't remember how or when she got this bruise. She knew that she had to put ice on it now to make the swelling go down, so she could dance with Damien tonight. She went downstairs slowly, because every step she took was painful. As she walked into the kitchen, her mother was already cooking up a storm in their little kitchen, because her mother's boss volunteered her to cater the food for the party, because before she worked for the company she works at, she used to be a chef.

"Hey mom, can I some ice?" She asked her.

"What do you need ice for sweetie?" She asked Dylana.

"I need it for my leg. I must have fallen last night when I was sleeping or something. I have this big, swollen, black and blue bruise on my right leg." She said, as she walked over to her mother to show her.

"Wow, that looks terrible, Dylana have a seat I think I have something that'll work better than ice." She said to Dylana, and she took a seat at the table. Debathena then left her in the kitchen by herself, as she went upstairs to get something. When she came back into the kitchen, she was carrying a vial with some strange blue liquid in it.

"What's that?" Dylana asked her, but Debathena didn't answer her, she started to pour the blue liquid on the bruise on

Dylana's leg, and then she started to rub it in. As the blue stuff touched her skin, it felt cold to her and before her eyes, the swelling started to go down within minutes, and the black and blue colors started to turn yellow.

"Okay, Mom, what is this stuff, and why is it working so fast?" Dylana questioned her.

"It's magic," she said.

"Magic's not real," Dylana told her.

"Really, then how do you explain how fast this stuff healed your leg?" she asked me.

"I don't know," I said, as she thought this blue stuff was amazing.

"Dylana, why don't you just relax, and keep your leg up, so it can heal the rest of the way." She said, as there was a knock on the door.

"Do you want me to get the door?" Dylana asked her.

"No, baby I'll get it, it's for me anyway, and you should just go into the living room and read until we have to get ready for the party." She said to me, and she got up and went to the living room, and she read a romance novel I had on the table by the couch. As she was reading, she was wondering who was at the door and why her mother wanted to talk to them in private.

By seven P.M., her mother told her she should go get ready for the party. As Dylana went upstairs, she was so glad she had her own bathroom, because her mother takes forever. She got in the shower and noticed the blue stuff left a blue stain on her skin, and she had to scrub it off her leg. When the blue stuff was all off, she looked at her leg and saw she didn't have a bruise anymore, and it was just gone. She then thought maybe my mother used magic.

She put the thought out of her mind as she got out of the shower, and she started to work on her hair. Her hair was so long, it went down the length of her back. So, she decided that it would just be easier to braid it. She grabbed the dress she got yesterday. It was not just green, but it was a bright green, and it had a reddish silk at the bottom. As she started to put on the dress, she was having a hard time getting the zipper up. She finally won the fight with the zipper, after a few minutes of fighting with it. Though she almost fell over. She headed downstairs after getting dressed and saw that her mother and Bob were already down there waiting for her.

At about nine, they started to put all the food that her mother made in the back of her mother's black van. After everything was in the van, they got in and Bob drove to where the party was. As they

55

were driving, her mother and Bob were chatting about something all the way to the party. Dylana wasn't paying any attention to what they were saying to each other. Her mind was only thinking about seeing Damien tonight, because she hadn't seen him for about a week because he was working a lot.

When they finally got to where the party was. Dylana looked out the window, and she saw a building that looked like a castle from the middle ages. It even had a tower and everything. The odd thing Dylana had noticed was that someone had broken all the windows. She also saw that the doors looked like they were rusting off their hinges.

"Hey mom, are you sure we're at the right place?" Dylana asked her, as they got out of the van.

"Yes," her mother said, but Dylana still had her doubts about it. To her the building looked like it was about to collapse any second.

"Dylana could you get the door?" her mother asked her. Dylana walked over to the door and opened it for her mother, so she could bring the food in. She just stood there as they took about three trips each to bring all the food in. When Bob brought in the last tray of food, she followed him inside the building.

She walked in and started to look around the place. She thought it looked a little better, then the outside did at least. inside the building, black-and-white tiles covered the floors, which glowed from the candles that were lit all around the place. There were three tables set up, with seven chairs for each table, and a small table with two chairs for the company's president and his son. On the right side of the room there was a long table that had all the food on it.

There were only Twenty-three people at the party, and some of them were sitting, and the others were standing around talking. Dylana was looking around to see if Damien was there yet. She didn't see him but saw someone she wished that she hadn't seen. The person she saw was Markus Smith. He was the son of the president of the company that her mother worked for. Dylana didn't like him at all, because from the first time she met him, he just seemed weird. He would just stare at her, just like he was doing right now. Another thing that bothered her about him was the fact he was always trying to ask her out on a date. He didn't know what the word "no" meant, and he just kept on trying. He didn't seem to care that she was already dating someone else.

It still shocked her that her mother let her date Damien, because he was about seven years older than her. They never wanted to be apart, and when she moved to Rome, he followed her there. Her mother even helped him get a job as an intern with her company.

She looked over at Markus again and she was wondering why Markus just didn't give up. She would never like him, and she wished that he would stop staring at me, because it was freaking her out. She wished that Damien was here already, that should hopefully get him to stop staring at her.

As she was thinking about how much she wanted Damien to be here already. She saw him walked into the building, and he was wearing a very nice black suit, with a red shirt, that Dylana thought it looked so good on him, and fit him so perfectly. She watched as he started to walk in her direction. She thought Damien was the hottest guy she'd ever met or dated. She loves it when he puts his strong arms around her. He always makes her feel so safe. She could get lost in his black eyes, which seemed to glow red sometimes. she didn't know why they did that, but she loved it. He was also strange, but she loved him for that too. Damien was a bad boy, but he was still caring. He could always make her smile, even if she was sad and about to cry. When he got over to where she was standing; He put his muscular arms around her, and he kissed her on her forehead.

"Dylana, love what's wrong?" Damien asked her. He always knew when there was something wrong with her. She liked that about him too, but it can annoy her sometimes. She didn't even have to tell him what was wrong, because at the same time they noticed that Markus was staring at them.

"Damien, why does he have to stare at us like that?" She asked him, and Damien took a step back and put his hands on her shoulders.

"He stares at us because he has no life, and he's also dick." He whispered into her ear. When he said that she started to smile, he was still staring at her, and it was still bothering me. He's staring bothered her because she thought he was creepy.

"Is it still bothering you, love, that he's just staring at us?" he asked her, as if he were reading her mind. She didn't know what to say to him, but she didn't have to say anything. She knew that he saw in her eyes it was still bothering her. He then grabbed her hand, and he kissed it.

"Dylana, love, I'll be right back." He said to her, as he let go of her hand, and he smiled at her like he would do something bad. As he walked toward Markus, she knew that he would beat the shit out of Markus. She didn't want to watch Damien beat Markus to a bloody pulp, and she went into the bathroom until it was over.

Just as she got into the bathroom, Dylana got a feeling like the one she had yesterday. The feeling was stronger than it was before. She just knew that her mother would die tonight, and a lot of other people too. She thought Damien getting into a fight was the least of her worries now, because he was always getting into fights,

59

so that wasn't a shock. As she was wondering how she knew that her mother and other people would die tonight? She suddenly heard windows breaking, chairs and table being thrown into walls, and she heard people screaming for help. She didn't know what was going on in the other room. She stayed right where she was, plus she felt that there was an invisible force keeping me in here. She listened as the screams for help started to get louder, and louder, and at this point she was so scared, that she couldn't move, and she expected someone to crash into the bathroom and kill her too.

After what seemed like an eternally, there were no more sounds at all. After a few more minutes of silence, she got the courage to move. She got to her feet, walked to the door, and pushed it opened. As she stepped into the room, all she saw were dead bodies lying all over the floor. It looked like everyone was at the party was dead, and the sight of this bloody scene made her want to scream herself.

The sight of all the dead bodies made her fall to her knees, onto the bloody floor, because she was so shocked by what she was looking at. Suddenly she felt someone touch her shoulder, so she turned around, and before she saw who it was, she knew that it was my mother. Debathena looked like she was bleeding badly out of a wound on her right side, like someone plunged a knife in it. Dylana saw bones sticking out of her mother's leg, which was bleeding badly too. She grabbed Dylana's hands in hers, and she put something in her hands.

"Dylana, take this, and keep it with you at all times. The note with tell you about it, and what you are my beautiful girl, I love you now and always." She said to Dylana, as she stopped breathing.

"What is this, and what do you mean, what I am? Mother, Mother?" She said, as she was screaming her name, because as she was talking, her mother fell back onto the floor. Dylana pulled her into her arms franticly trying to get her to wake up, but it was too late, and Dylana just held her mother in her arms. She didn't know what else to do, so she just sat there on the bloody floor, holding her mother's limp, cold, and now dead body in her arms, and she cried. She tried to think maybe this was just a nightmare, that would wake up any second now, and her mother will be alive.

As she sat there, it was sinking in that this was all real, and her mother was dead. She then started to cry more, and she thought about who could have done this to my mother and the other guests? She suddenly thought about Damien, and she was wondering if he was okay. She didn't see him anywhere, and to her that could mean that either he was with the people that attacked them, or maybe they took him. She noticed that Bob was missing too, and she thought asshole probably ran out to save his own skin. She looked at the other bodies, and she thought this was a horrible way for anyone to die, and that none of them deserved to die like this. She felt sad for all of them, and as she thought this, she suddenly heard someone breaking down the doors. She got up to see who it was. She saw that it was the cops, and two of them came toward her, and they grabbed her by the arms, and they pulled her outside.

"Did you make the 112-call miss?" One of them asked her, in Italian, and she just looked at him with a blank face.

"What, I don't understand what you're saying. Could you speak English?" She asked him.

"Yes, I can speak English. Would that be better?" He asked her, in his Italian accent, and she nodded in agreement. He then repeated what he just said, but in English this time, and she told him no.

"Do you know what happened in there, miss?" He asked her, as his partner went over to tell the other cops about all the dead bodies inside the building. While he was waiting for her answer, they saw Damien limping toward them, and he looked like a car had hit him.

"Dylana, are you okay?" he asked her, with a weak voice.

"What happened to you, young man?" The cops asked, as they looked at him, and Dylana was thinking the same thing as they were, what happened to him?

"I got beat up." Damien said to them.

"Did you make the 112-call young man?" The cop asked him.

"Yes sir, I did." Damien replied, and then the cops told them to stay right where they were, as they went to call an ambulance to help Damien, and to check out the crime scene inside the building.

"Love, are you okay?" Damien asked her after they had walked away.

"No, Damien, I not okay. My mother is dead, I'm cold, and I'm freaking out about seeing all those dead bodies in there." She said, as she cried again. He then pulled her into his arms, and for the first, it didn't make her feel any better, because right now the only thing that would make her feel better, would be her mother alive, or killing the person who killed her.

"I'm so sorry about your mother, love," he said to her, and then he let her go, and he put his jacket around her to keep her warm, and then he kissed her.

"First things first, kids, what are your names?" One cop asked them when they came back over to them. She told him that her name was Dylana Volus, and that his name was Damien Red Dragon.

"Well, Dylana, Damien, I'm officer Tad, and this is my partner Valentino, and we need to know what you know about what happened here tonight." Tad said.

"I didn't see what happened, but I heard windows breaking." She said, as Valentino pulled out a notepad and a pen, so he could write what she said.

"Where were you when you heard this?" Valentino asked her, and she told him, that was in the bathroom.

"Did you hear anything else?" Tad asked me.

"I heard things breaking and screams for help, and it made me too scared to move." she said, and then they turned toward Damien.

"So, young man, what did you see?" Valentino asked Damien, and Damien was getting annoyed by being called young when he was older than these Humans.

"Well, I was standing by the windows, arguing with some guy about something, when suddenly someone crashed through the windows behind us. One of them pushed the guy I was talking to out one of the other windows." Damien said, and he started laughing in his head, because he was the one that really pushed Markus out the window, and he enjoyed killing that prick.

"Damien is that the guy, that you were talking about over there, by side of the building?" Valentino interrupted Damien, as he pointed to the body was on the ground by the side of the building. Dylana saw it was Markus's body on the ground, and she started to cry again, because she thought even though he was a freak, he didn't deserve to die like that, she that it looked like he was torn apart, then she looked back at Damien.

"Yes, sir, that's who I was talking to earlier." Damien said.

"We will need you to identify the body when we're done talking here." Tad said.

"Yes, sir," Damien told him.

"Now please continue what you were telling us about what you saw, young man." Tad said to Damien.

"Right, so, after the person threw the guy out of the windows, twelve more people came crashing through the windows.

Two of them went to lock the doors, so that no one could get out of the building. Two of them started to beat viciously, and at one point I got hit hard on the head, and then I fell to the floor. I think I blacked out after that, and when I came to. I saw that they were still killing people, and it looked like there were about thirteen people still left alive. I saw the doors open, so I took a chance, and I ran for the door. I went through the doors, and I ran to the nearest phone, that I could find to call for help." Damien said, and as he was talking, Dylana put the thing that her mother gave her into a pocket in Damien's jacket.

"Damien, why didn't you use your cell to call for help?" Dylana asked him, when they left them to fill in the other cops on what they said.

"My phone kind of got stepped on." He told her, as he pulled out his phone, that was bent in half. After he said that, the ambulance pulled up. Tad helped him walk over to identify Markus's body. He then brought Damien over to the ambulance so that the medics could have a look at him. She saw that the medics had stopped the bleeding, and it turned out he had broken his leg, when he was running to find a phone, and she heard someone said that he needed a doctor.

"Dylana, is there someone I could call to come and get you?" Tad asked her, with concern in his voice.

"No, the attackers killed my mother, and I don't know where my step-father went to, and my father lives in Maine." she said to him, as she started to cry again.

"You should call your father and tell him what happened," he said, as he handed her a tissue, so she could dry her tears.

"Can you give me a ride to my house? I'll call my father when I get home." She asked him, and he nodded, and opened the car door for her, and she told him her address. The two cops drove her house. When they got there, one of them opened the door for her, and she got out of the police car and went inside the house.

Chapter Six

Note

As she walked into the house, it seemed so empty and cold without her mother there. She couldn't help thinking; Without her mother here, this house just didn't feel like home to her anymore.

She suddenly looked down and noticed there was blood all over her dress, and it was dripping all over the wooden floor. She looked behind her and saw bloody footprints on the floor too. She first pulled off her shoes, and just left them on the floor, and then her took off Damien's jacket and she threw it away from the bloody puddle that was forming on the floor. She then ripped the dress off herself and dropped it on the floor too. She then saw dried blood on her arms and on the rest of her skin, too. So, she went to the bathroom that was downstairs to wash all the blood off.

When she got in there, she got out of the rest of the clothes, and she got into the shower. She scrubbed herself until she got all the blood off herself. After that, she went upstairs to put on some dry clothes. When she dressed, she went into the kitchen to grab some gloves, a garbage bag, and something to clean the floors with? She put the bloody shoes and dress in the garbage bag and scrubbed the floors until they were all clean.

She then went up to her room, to call her father, and on the way up there she thought it's probably a good thing she unpacked nothing, except for her books. She thought packing will be easy, because she knew that she would have to move to Maine, to stay with her father, because he was the only family she had now, and she knew that she couldn't stay here. It would be too painful for her; she'd always be thinking about her mother. She also knew that her father wouldn't let her stay in Rome by herself, even if she wanted to. She walked into her room, grabbed the phone, and called her father.

"Hello," her father said, in a tired voice, because she must have woken him up with the phone call.

"Daddy, it's me Dylana. Something bad happened to Mom." She sobbed into the phone, as tears started to fall from her eyes once more, and she felt them roll down her cheeks.

"Dylana, calm down sweetie, what happened to your mother? Dylana are you still there?" He asked her, with concern in his voice.

"Yes Daddy, I'm still here. Someone killed her. My boyfriend and I were the only two people left alive from the attack." She told him, as more tears fell from her eyes.

"Baby, please don't cry." He said to her, and she thought to herself, why should she stop crying? She just lost her mother.

"Daddy, why should I stop crying? Mom died right in my arms. Daddy, I feel so alone. Can you come and get me?" She asked her father, as she said that she knew that it was true, without her mother, she felt alone, because she was everything to her.

"Yes, baby. I'll come and get you. I'll take the first flight out." He said.

"Ok, bye Daddy, I love you." she said, as she was still crying.

"Bye, I love you too, baby." He said, and then she hung up the phone. She started to pack up her books into the boxes she still had in her room. Just as she grabbed the first book, she remembered that her mother handed her something. She remembered that she put it in Damien's jacket, so she wouldn't lose it. She went downstairs to go it out of Damien's jacket, and she brought it back upstairs with her. She put the thing that her mother gave her on the bed, as she opened the letter was with, and it said,

Dylana, I should have told you this secret of what you are years ago, or maybe I shouldn't have taken your memories away from you, when Damien told you the truth. Dylana, if your memories haven't come back to you by the time you read this, here's the truth, you're a Witch, just like I was. I didn't want you to find out like this though. I wanted to tell you this myself in person when you came of age. I wrote you this letter yesterday because I knew that I would die; I knew that there was no spell that could change my fate. So, I knew that I had to write you this letter to prepare you my darling. Dylana, I gave you an amulet called The Redfire. The people that killed me wanted me to use The Redfire, but I told them I would never use The Redfire for what they wanted me to use it for. Another thing is that when I see things, they aren't the clearest, and I didn't see who killed me, but whoever they are, they work for the people that wanted me to use The Redfire. They might come after you now, and try to use you, since you're the next in line to use The Redfire. You have the same powers as me, and so much more. You will know when something bad will happen, which I think already awakened, and you probably knew that I would die. You'll be able to tell if danger is around you. You can use The Redfire to fight these people off. In my room, there is a trunk that's in my closet. I want you to press the middle of The Redfire. Three knife-like keys will come out of it, and I want you to pull them together, and then stick them in the keyhole, and stand back. You'll see a green light fill the room, but don't panic. Inside the trunk, there are potion ingredients, a steel cauldron, potion vials, and books of spells I've made, and some books to tell you about your enemies, and a few of the books will tell you how to fight them. The Redfire has seven elements in it. The main four elements are Fire, Water, Air, and Earth. You can use them in any of their forms. The other three are Spirit, Light, and Thought. Spirit will give you the power over someone's soul. Thought will give you the power to control someone's mind. Light will give you the power to light the dark. The Redfire will keep you safe until you can use it properly. Be safe, my darling. I love you, and if you need my help, you can always summon me.

P.S. BE CAREFUL WHO YOU TRUST,

Love Mom

She was shocked when she first read the letter her mother wrote her. She couldn't believe what she was reading. She looked at her bed and picked up the thing that her mother called the Redfire, and she saw it was gold along the edges, with a gold chain attached to it. She saw that the seven elements were in a circle, and each of them had their own symbol and color. What her mother said about a trunk made her curious.

So, she walked into her mother's room, and being in there made her a little scared at first. She opened the closet and found the trunk, that Debathena mentioned. She pulled the trunk out of the closet and pressed the middle of the Redfire. She watched as knife like things came out of the bottom, and she pulled them together and pushed them into the keyhole of the trunk. She stepped back away from the trunk, and like Debathena said, a green light filled the whole room. After a few minutes, the green light seemed to disappear.

She suddenly started to feel a little strange. She thought the green light went inside her; If possible, she also felt like her mother was there with her. She started to wonder why her mother wanted her to be so careful, and she was wondering where Damien fit in all this. Was he a Witch too? Dylana knew that when she learned to summon her mother, she must ask her. As her thoughts passed, she opened the trunk and started to go through it. All the things that

Debathena told her were in there. She found another letter in there to but decided that she'd read it later. She grabbed the Redfire, and shut the trunk closed, and she figured that she could go through the rest of it later and went back to my room.

She walked back into her room, and stopped in the doorway, and for a moment. She thought about all the things that had happened to her early tonight. She thought tonight was a night she would never forget. It will take her a lot of time to get that bloody scene out of her mind. She made a promise to herself that she would find out who killed her mother and that she would kill them for taking her away.

She went to sit back on the floor and started to pack her books into an old container, when one title made her stop. The title of the book was 'Vampires are out There', and as she was reading the title. She remembered that Damien told her he was a Vampire. She figured that this was the start of her memories coming back, as she was pondering this thought. She suddenly got a chill up my spine, and she knew that there was someone outside the house, and then she heard someone banging on the door downstairs. She immediately dropped the book on the floor, and she ran as fast as she could back to my mother's room to get the trunk, because she thought if her mother knew something would happen to her, that there might be weapons in there. Dylana didn't realize that with the Redfire she was a weapon herself.

As she was pulling my mother's trunk into her room, the banging stopped. Her first thought was that was odd, and then she thought maybe her mother bewitched the trunk keep her enemies away, or Dylana's enemies now. She tried to put these thought away, as she started to go through the trunk once again.

She started with the books, the book she grabbed was, "How to Harness your Powers." This book had spells in it that could help her control her new powers. She then grabbed, "How to Fight Your Enemies." This book was about different fighting styles and different weapons, but it had nothing about who her enemies were. The other books just had the word spells written on them.

The potion ingredients were strange; there was Nightspear nectar, dragon blood, and snakeskin, and this stuff was in jars or bags. There was also a map and some crystals, and at the bottom she found another book, but she couldn't read what was on it. She read the note she found earlier, but it was just her mother telling her to be careful again. She wished that her mother would have told her, who these people were in one of her letters. As she was putting the stuff back in the trunk, she thought she would have to talk to Damien about what she remembered, and then she cried herself to sleep on the floor.

Chapter Seven

Lost Memories

At about three o'clock in the afternoon, the sound of someone knocking on her front door woke Dylana up. She got up, and on her way out of her room, she grabbed a bat that was lying on the floor, and she went downstairs to answer the door. She opened the door, and she was so happy to see that it was Damien. She dropped the bat on the floor, and she heard the bat hit the floor, as she hugged him. She then showed him inside the house.

"Love were you going to hit me with that bat?" he asked her, with a smile.

"No, I would not hit you, it's just…" She told him, and he let go of her, as she stopped talking.

"It's just what love? Did something else happen last night? Is that why you're answering the door with a bat in hand?" He asked her, and she didn't answer him back right away, because she didn't know where to begin.

"Love are you okay? Tell me what happened last night?" He asked me.

"Damien, I'm not okay, not at all. I cried myself to sleep last night, and every time I closed my eyes, all I see was my mother's dead body in my arms, or all those other dead bodies. The reason I answered the door with a bat in my hands is, because I heard someone banging on the door last night, it scared me, and I thought the people that killed my mother were coming here to kill me too." She told him, and he pulled her into his arms, and he kissed her on the top of her head.

"I'm so sorry, love. I should have been here with you last night, but I couldn't leave until this morning, and you don't have to worry tonight, I'll stay here with you, and I'll keep you safe. I won't let anyone, or anything hurt you." He told her, and after he said that she kissed him on the lips, because she knew that he meant every word he said.

"So, love, have you eaten anything since yesterday?" He asked her, and she told him no. After she said that, he took her hand, and he led her into the kitchen. She sat at the table and watched him as he made her some eggs to eat. As she was eating, they didn't say much to each other, and she was thinking about how to ask him if the things she remembered were true. She kept losing her train of thought because Damien kept playing with her hair. It was so distracting and made it hard for her to eat. She started to feel safer that he was here with her. When she finished eating, she said to him, "Damien, there's something I have to talk to you about."

"Okay, what's up?" He asked her.

"Well last night, I remembered things I think you told me before, and conversations I overheard between you and my mother." She said to him, and she saw that he didn't seem surprised.

"What do you remember?" He asked her.

"I remember that you told me you were a Vampire, and I remember you and my mother arguing about telling me that truth or not." She said.

"Is there anything else that you remember?" He asked her.

"The rest is all in bits and pieces. Wait, so you really a Vampire?" She told him.

"Yes, and you're a Witch. Do you want me to show you how to get all your memories back?" He asked her.

"Yes," she told him.

"Okay, all you have to do is hold the Redfire in your hand and will your memories to come back." He said.

"It's that easy?" She asked him.

"Yes, why don't you try it." He told her, she motioned for him to follow her up to my room, where she left the Redfire. When they got into her room, Damien sat on her bed as she grabbed the Redfire off the floor. As she touched it, the Redfire glowed Purple and she did as Damien said. She focused her mind on what she wanted to happen and used all of her will to remember. As the memories hit her, she fell backwards, and Damien caught her before she fell.

"Dylana, are you, all right?" Damien asked her.

"Yeah, I'm fine, that felt so weird. What the fuck." She said as she caught her reflection in her wall mirror. She saw that her eyes were bluest purple, and they sparkled, her black hair was now blonde with red steaks, and her skin was now reddish.

"Damien, what the fuck just happened to me?" She asked him, as she was staring to panic a little.

"Dylana, calm down, it's just the glamor that your mother put on you is disappearing, this is what you really look like." He told her.

"Well, how do I put the glamor back up, I don't want to look like this?" She asked him, because she like the way she looked before with the glamor. He told her that imagine what she looked like before and then bring the image to the surface to cover what she really looked like. She closed her eyes, as she did what he told her, and when she opened her eyes again. She saw in the mirror that her skin was back to being tan, and her hair was black, but there were still a few red steaks, and her eyes were still bluest purple.

"Damien, it didn't work. My eyes are still bluest purple and there's still red in my hair." She said.

"It's okay, you're just new to this. You'll get better, and the eyes of a Witch are hard to change the color of, because they show others of our kind what we are." He said.

"Oh really, and what does my eye color show others?" She asked him.

"A Witch with bluest purple eyes shows you're powerful and not to mess with you." He told her.

"I don't feel powerful." She said.

"You just don't know how powerful you really are, especially with this." He said, as he grabbed the Redfire out of her hands, and he put it around her neck, and he told her not take it off, and that if she wears it, she'll be safe.

"So, this will probably be a stupid question, but does your leg still hurt?" She asked him, laughing.

"No, there was nothing wrong with it to begin with, and the cuts they saw healed before they got me to the hospital." He told her.

"Why didn't you just leave?" She asked him.

"I tried to, but someone injected me with something, and I passed out, until this morning and then I put back on my bloody clothes and run out of there." He told her.

"Why didn't you get here sooner?" She questioned him.

"I went home to change my clothes, and I needed something to eat," he said.

"Do you mean you needed blood?" She asked him.

"Yes, but Vampires need more than blood to survive. I eat food too, I'm not undead or anything. I was born just like you were." He told her.

"I guess that there's a lot I don't know about you." She said.

"So, do you want to talk about last night, because there're things I didn't tell those stupid Humans." He told her.

"Why do you talk like that?" She asked him, and he smiled at her and said, "I'm sorry love, but it's true, Humans are stupid creatures. I also hate it when children called young man, when I'm so much older than them." She didn't know how to respond to that, so she just changed the subject, "So, what didn't you said to them?"

"Well, you should know that Bob isn't real, your mother made him with magic, so when she died, he disappeared." He said, and she was glad she didn't have to deal with Bob anymore, and if he wasn't real, it would explain him appearing and disappearing act.

"Okay what else, because in the letter my mother gave me, she told me she knew that she would die, and I think I knew that it would happen too." She said.

"There was that, and we knew that it would happen last night, that's why she wanted you there, so I could protect you. She didn't know if they'd come after you here, if you were home alone. I'm sorry that I wasn't here last night, but at least the crystals in your mother trunk kept you safe." He said.

"How did they keep me safe?" She asked him.

"If you're close by them, they form a kind of force field around you." He said, and she thought the banging stop when she was right near the trunk.

"Okay, so do you know who these people are?" She asked him.

"Yes, it was Vampires that attacked us last night." He said.

"Why did they attack us?" She asked him.

"They were after your mother, but I guess someone ordered them to kill everyone, they even attacked me, until they realized who I was." He told her, and he saw that she was thinking about killing them, because he saw that her eyes were shining red now.

"Dylana, if you're thinking about going after them, it's pointless, because the Vampires that attacked us are probably dead." He told her.

"Why makes you think?" She asked.

"They're probably dead, because they attacked me, and by doing so, they attacked their king, my brother. We're cursed in a way that if you hurt one of us, and other one gets hurt to. Dylana once I find out who killed your mother, I'll tell you, and I'll help you kill them." He told her, and she wondered if she'd be able to kill your mother's killer.

"So, love, where are you going to?" Damien asked her, as she cuddled up next to him on the bed.

"I will live with my father in Maine." She told him.

"Why are you going there, love?" He asked her, with disappointment in his voice, because he wanted her to stay in Rome with him.

"I have to go to Maine, and live with my father, because he's the only family I have left, and I know that my father won't et me stay here in Rome." She told him.

"Love, but why can't you stay with me? You can tell your father I can take care of you." He asked her.

"I know that you can take care of me. I want to stay with you, but I just can't be here in Rome. It'll be too painful for me, and

84

I'll be thinking about my mother all the time. Damien, can you come to Maine with me, instead of me staying here?" She asked him, and she knew that his answer would be yes, from just how he was looking at her.

"Yes, love, if that's what you want me to do." He said, with a loving smile, and she kissed him on his lips.

Chapter Eight

Maine

Her father arrived in Rome three days after her mother died. When he walked through the front door of the house, he pulled her into his arms and hugged her as hard as he could. She felt like she would pop. As he was hugging her, he told her he brought tickets for the flight back to Maine, and that they had to be at the airport in about seven hours, and that he rented a moving truck. He also told her he knew someone here in Rome that would ship all her stuff for free.

"Do you need any help packing?" He asked her, as he let go of me.

"No, Damien and I finished the packing the other day. There really wasn't much to pack; it was mainly just books." She said to him.

"Who's this Damien?" Her father asked me, and as he said that she just knew that her father already knew who Damien was. It made her wonder if her father and Damien would get along or not.

"He's my boyfriend, Daddy." She said nervously, because she didn't know how this would go.

"I didn't know that you were dating anyone sweetie. When can I meet this boyfriend of yours?" Her father asked, kind of sarcastically, at the end.

"You can meet him now if you'd like, Daddy. Damien's just upstairs." She said nervously again, because she had a feeling that when they saw each other they would yelling at each other.

"Okay," he said to her. she went upstirs to get Damien, and told him that her father was here, and that he wanted to meet him. When she told Damien that, he didn't look happy about seeing her father. Before they went downstairs, she told him to be nice. Damien told her that he would try, and grabbed her hand, and they walked downstairs.

"Daddy, this is Damien." She said, and she noticed a strange look in both of their eyes.

"It's nice to meet you, sir." Damien said, as politely as he could, but she could tell that he was cursing under his breath and he didn't mean a word of what he said.

"Same here," her father said, and she noticed that he didn't mean it either. After they shook hands with each other. She asked her father to help Damien bring the boxes down from her room. Meanwhile, she went to the garage to get her car out, and she parked it next to the moving truck that her father rented. She then went back inside to see if they needed help, but they said that they needed nothing. She pulled her mother's trunk downstairs and put it by the other boxes. She saw that the two of them were putting the boxes into the back of the moving truck.

"Dylana, are you sure that this is everything?" Her father asked as he looked over at her.

"Yes, Daddy," she said, as she checked that everything was on the truck.

"What are you planning on doing with your car?" Her father asked her.

"I was planning on bringing it with us to Maine, is that okay?" She told him. He told her that it was fine with him. Her father put three of her bags in the trunk her car. Damien got in the driver seat Dylana's car. While Dylana and her father got into the truck, and Damien followed her father to the place where her father was going to drop off her boxes to get shipped to Maine. The guy that her father knew lived about seventeen minutes down the road from the house that she was living in. They pulled into this guy's driveway, and her father got out, and he knocked on the front door. The guy that opened the door looked very sketchy. They had a very quick conversation, and then they shook hands, and then her father came back.

"Okay sweetie, my buddy says he'll have no trouble shipping your things to Maine, so let's get in your car, and head to the airport." Her father told her. After he told her this, she thought this was weird. She thought the guy that her father knew looked like he was on something, and she was wondering how her father knew this guy. She also thought, how does her father know that this guy isn't going to just sell her stuff on eBay, or something? But she said nothing, because she was trying to have faith in my father. Instead, she just got in her car with her father and Damien, and then they headed to the airport.

They got to the airport in perfect time, and when they got there, her father unloaded her three bags on to a luggage cart. They had to use two carts for her bags. When they got inside, they had to head to the right gate, and then her dad had to check in all three bags, because they were too heavy, due to the books that she had in them. After they got through security, she kissed Damien goodbye. He told her that he was going to be on the next flight out, and that he would be staying with his brother Christopher, who happened to live in Maine, which Dylana thought that was kind of a coincidence. As they were saying goodbye, Dylana saw her father talking to someone on his phone, and he told her that he had arranged for her car to come to Maine by boat.

Dylana and her father then got onto a small plane that had about twenty other people on it. They took our seats next to this monstrous man, but it could have been a woman, it was hard to tell. This person had about five chins and not much neck at all. Dylana couldn't tell where his legs were, when he was sitting down, because his waist dropped down so far. On the other side of them there was this woman, who was as skinny as a toothpick, and Dylana thought that if she turned a certain way, she would be invisible.

They were on the plane for about Nine hours, but to Dylana it felt like it took much longer. She slept most of the way, but when they were landing there was so much turbulence, that it woke her up, and her felt like she would throw up. When they finally passed through the turbulence, they landed, and it was about eleven o'clock at night. She was so exhausted from the trip. Her father left her in the terminal, while he went outside to bring his truck around from the parking lot. As he did that, she went to get her things. She got her three bags off the conveyor belt, but she had a lot of trouble trying to carry all three over to the door. When She finally got the doors, she saw that her father was waiting for her. Her father came inside, and he took the bags from her, and he put them on the back seat of his truck.

"So, before we leave to go home, we should go around to the back of the airport, to find out when your car will be at the house." He told her, and she thought that was odd, that he had to ask the people here about her car. She thought that it was coming here by boat, or at least that's what her father told her.

They got into the truck, and then they drove around to back of the airport. she just kept on thinking that this was weird. Her father got out of the truck, and he told her that he'd be right back. As she sat there in the truck, she watched her father go up to a booth that was back here. She didn't know what the guy said to my father, but it looked like my father was angry at the person in the booth. For about the next twenty minutes, she watched her father and the guy in the booth arguing with each other. She then saw her father walk back to the truck, and he got back in, and he told her that her car should be at the house in the next three days.

"Hey sweetie, are you hungry?" He asked her.

"I could eat," she said to him, and he told her okay, as they started to drive away from the airport, and headed to his house and her new house. She thought they would stop somewhere close by, to get something to eat, but it seemed like they were driving for about an hour before they stopped. They stopped at this little twenty-four-hour diner to eat. Dylana got a veggie burger and some fries, with a glass of water. Her father just got a coffee and a piece of pecan pie.

"Well, Dylana, I forgot to tell you, when I was getting my truck, my buddy texted me, and he told me that your stuff should be at the house, by tomorrow if we're lucky." My father told her.

"That's great daddy," she said, as she thought that was fast, and that it was odd that it would only take a day. She thought her father's buddy must be a Witch or something too. When they finished eating, they were back on the road again, and she thought they drove for another hour, before they finally pulled up to her father's house.

As they drove up all she could see were yellow and white lilies, and pink, red, and white roses, but it looked like they were starting to die. They pulled up a two-story house, and it was painted yellow and white, it was also surrounded by trees.

Her stepmother Jan and sister Melissa came out of the house, when they heard the truck pulling into the driveway. They stood outside the house waiting to greet us. She saw that Jan had a gray coat on with green pants, and Melissa had on an all pink outfit. Just as she got out of the truck, Melissa ran up to her, and she hugged her legs so tight that, Dylana almost fell over onto the ground. She thought that Melissa was so cute with her blonde curls. Dylana picked her up when Melissa let go of her legs, and they hugged some more. She then put her down and Melissa grabbed her hand and they walked over to where Jan was standing. While they were standing there by Jan, she saw that her father was bringing her bags inside the house.

"Dylana, how are you doing? I'm so sorry about your mother." Jan said to her.

"Thanks, I'm doing okay, I guess." she said back to her, but she was still a mess, and she just missed her mother.

"We should all go inside, it's getting late" Jan said, and Melissa and Dylana followed her inside. As they walked in, Jan

93

asked her to help Melissa take off her shoes and her coat. Dylana did what Jan asked, and helped Melissa take off her coat and shoes, and she took off hers. As they walked into the kitchen, they saw Jan put some water in a kettle and put it on the stove, so they could all have some hot chocolate before bed.

They all sat on the kitchen table talking about the trip here, when the kettle started to steam. Jan got up and started to make the hot chocolate for all of them. As she was putting a cup on the table for each of them, there was a knock on the door. Her father jumped out of his seat and ran to the door to see who it was. Jan also ran to the door, but first she told Melissa and me to stay in the kitchen until she got back. After she said that, Dylana first thought was, what the fuck, but before she could ask Jan anything, or think of something to comprehend what was going on, and why her father and Jan both had to go running to the door, her sister handed her a book.

Melissa asked her to read it to her. The book she handed Dylana was the one she saw sitting on the table. It was, 'The Little Mermaid', as Dylana turned to the first page of the book, Melissa told her to just read the ending of the book. She thought what Melissa asked was strange, but she did as Melissa requested. As she finished reading the ending to her, Jan came back in.

"Who's at the door?" Dylana asked her.

"Nobody's at the door silly goose." She said, as she looked Dylana straight in the eyes. When she said that, Dylana was wondering if Jan thought she was stupid or something? That she can't see she's lying to her, and that she's hiding something, and so is her father. She didn't know what they were hiding, but she would find out what it is they're not telling her. Just as Dylana would say something to Jan, Melissa said, "Mommy, Dylana read me a story."

"What story did she read to you, sweetie?" Jan asked her, with a very sweet voice.

"Dylana read, 'The Little Mermaid', to me mommy, can I watch the movie before I go to sleep?" Melissa asked Jan, as she started jumping up and down.

"Yes, sweetheart you sure can, but when the movie's over you go right to sleep." Jan said to her.

"Okay, Mommy," Melissa said.

"Dylana, would you watch it with her?" Jan asked her, and she said that she would, but Dylana just couldn't shake the feeling that Jan just wanted her out of the room. Melissa and Dylana grabbed our cups of cocoa and they headed upstairs. On the way to Melissa room, she showed Dylana where her room was.

As she looked inside the room, she saw that it was a big room, with black and red paint on the walls. She thought the colors went together so nicely, but she was wondering why her father painted the room with those colors? It also looked like someone just painted the walls. It just seemed odd, like he knew that she would come to live here with him, before she called him, and then she remembered that he was a Witch too, and she thought he probably knew that what would happen to her mother.

As she was thinking, Melissa suddenly grabbed her hand, and she pulled Dylana out of her train of thought. They walked down the hallway to Melissa's room. Her room was nothing but pink, she had pink walls, pink blankets, and the floors were painted pink, with all the pink, it was scary. She watched Melissa get the movie and then she asked Dylana to put it in the DVD player. She put in the movie, and she pressed play, and then she sat down next to Melissa on the floor as they drank our cups of cocoa. They watched the movie for about an hour. Before the movie was over, Melissa had fallen asleep, so Dylana picked her up, and she laid her on her bed.

After she put Melissa to bed, she went back downstairs to see what her father and Jan were up to. When she reached the last step, she saw that her father was still standing by the door. She saw that he was talking to someone that looked just like Damien. She noticed that the only difference between this guy and Damien was the hair color, and that this guy had tattoos on his arms. She thought maybe this was Damien's brother Christopher, because she knew that it wasn't Damien, because he was still in Rome, but she wasn't sure. One thing she knew about Damien is that he doesn't have a tattoo of a black rose with thorns around it, on his left arm, and that he doesn't have a tattoo of a red tiger on his right arm, and Damien doesn't have blonde hair.

There was also a woman at the door with this guy, and she had the same tattoo on her left arm. When she looked at this guy's eyes, it shocked her to see that they were ruby red. As she looked at his eyes, she knew that he was at her house in Rome. He was the guy that was staring at her though her window in Rome. She started to wonder who is this guy? She started to walk toward her father to ask him who they were, when Jan stepped right in front of her.

"It's late, and you had a long trip. You should go up to bed and get some sleep Dylana." She said to her, as Jan said that the guy looked at her and he winked at her.

"Okay, Jan, goodnight." She said, and Jan said goodnight to her. she had no choice but to go back upstairs to her new room. As she got in there, she started to look around the room more. There was a brown desk in the corner, and there was a twin bed, and her three bags were sitting by the closet. That first night there, she couldn't get any sleep. She also cried all night long, and she just

97

kept wondering why Jan didn't she want me to know anything? She was also wondering if that guy was Damien's other brother, that he told her about. She was also wondering why he was here to talk to her father.

Chapter Nine

Damien's Brother

The next day, she woke up with the sun nearly blinding her; The sun woke her from a dream she was having about a pair of red eyes staring at her. The dream freaked she out a little. When she opened her eyes and woke up completely, she heard her father and Jan talking about something downstairs. She couldn't tell what they were saying though, because their voices were low. She went downstairs to find out what they were talking about. The moment she stepped into the kitchen, they stopped talking instantly. It was all quiet for a second, and after that all she heard was Melissa singing a song from, 'The Little Mermaid'.

"Good morning, sweetie. I think the moving truck should be here at about noon." My father told her.

"Really? That's great, Dad." She said with a lot of shock, because she couldn't believe that it would only take one day for my stuff to get here, and it just seemed odd. She thought okay, her father's buddy is a Witch.

"Yup, but I have leave now, but I'll be back around noon to help." He said, as he got up from his chair.

"Okay, I'll see you later than." She said to him.

"Yup, bye Dylana, bye honey, I'll see you later tonight." He said to her and Jan. Jan kissed him goodbye, and then he kissed Melissa on her head, and then he went out of the kitchen, and out the front door. She heard him start up his truck and then he drove off to work.

"Dylana, what do you want for breakfast?" Jan asked her.

"Anything's fine with me. I'm not too picky." She said to Jan.

"Okay then, eggs it is." Jan said, and she told her that was fine.

"Do you want some eggs too sweetie?" Jan asked Melissa in a sweet voice.

"Yes, Mommy," Melissa said. So, Jan made us scrambled eggs with toast and bacon. She made a small plate for Melissa and a bigger plate for Dylana. While they were eating, Jan was telling Dylana that she and Melissa were going into town to do some shopping, and that they wouldn't be home until about two. So, when Melissa finished eating, they put on their shoes and coats, and then they were out the front door in a flash. Then she was all alone in her father's big home.

When she finished eating her food, she put a plate in the dishwater. She then went back upstairs to her room to change her clothes. She put on a shirt with a pink bunny on it and a pair of black pants she got out of one her bags. She then started to put away the rest of the things in the three bags. She put the clothes in the dresser and in the closet. She also put some things on the desk, like some of her books.

As she went to have another look at the thing that her mother gave her, she heard the doorbell ring, she then looked at the clock, and it said that it was ten in the morning, so she knew that it wasn't the moving guy. She went downstairs to see who it was. She opened the door, and she was so relieved to see that it was Damien. She kissed and hugged him, and then she showed him inside the house, and they went up to her room.

"What are you doing here? Not that I'm not glad to see you. How did you get here?" She asked him when they walked into her room. He told that he had his dragon flew him here.

"What, so you really have a dragon? How long did it take to get here?" She asked him curiously.

"Yes, I really have a dragon. It took Fury about an hour to fly here. She was taking her time, so she could yell at me." He told her.

"What was she yelling at you about?" She asked him.

"She thinks some things I do are stupid." He told her.

"I see, so how long have you been in Maine?" She asked him.

"I got to Maine late last night, why what happened?" He asked me.

"Do you know why your brother was at my house last night?" She asked him.

"What are you talking about? Christopher wasn't here last night." He said to her.

"I didn't say that it was Christopher," she told him.

"Did he have blond hair, red eyes, and marks like these?" He asked her, as he took off his coat and rolled up his sleeves. She saw that Damien had a tattoo of a red rose with thorns around it, on his right arm and black tiger with red stripes on his left arm.

"Yes, but he's marks as you call them were different. He had a black rose with thorns around it, on his left arm and a red tiger with black stripes on his right arm." She told him.

"I wonder why Niculus was here. Did you hear what they were talking about?" He asked her.

"No, I heard nothing, their voices were too low, and Jan wouldn't let me go near them to find out anything. As Jan was telling me to go to bed, he looked at me and winked." She told him.

"Was there anyone with him?" He asked her.

"Yup, there was this woman with him, and she had a black rose on her left arm too. Who is she?" She asked him.

"She's Niculus's wife, Trinity. Did anything else happen?" He told her.

"Damien, there is something else. I didn't tell you about this when we were in Rome, but I saw Niculus the day before someone killed my mother. He was standing outside my house looking at me though my window. I know that it was him because of his red eyes, and at my house there was this tiger too." She said to him.

"I had a feeling that he was there. I felt his energy. What did he have his tiger do?" He asked her.

"He must have told it to go after me, because it came into the house and went right for me. That was until Bob whacked it and it went down." She said, and then Damien laughed.

"What's so funny?" She asked him.

"I find it funny you were afraid of an astral projection of a tiger. It wasn't really there." He said.

"Oh, I didn't know that was a thing." She said.

"Yup, that's one of many forms of magic that Niculus can do." He said, and then we heard the door downstairs.

"Who's here?" Damien asked her.

"It's probably my dad. He said that the moving truck would be here today, and he came back home to help the guy bring the stuff in." She told him. As she finished what she was saying there was a knock on the door, and she said, "Come in," and her father walked through the door.

"Hey Dylana, I'm back, and I think the moving truck will be here in about a half an hour. I will take the downstairs door off its hinge to make it easier for us to bring your stuff in. Oh, hey there, Damien. I didn't see you there. Are you here to help us with the moving truck?" My father questioned Damien.

"Sure, why not?" Damien said to my father.

"So how did you get here? I saw no extra cars in the driveway?" Her father asked him.

"I walked here from brother's house." Damien told him, and her father just nodded his head.

"Oh Damien, could you move my truck by the garage for me?" Her father asked Damien.

"Sure," Damien said, and she watched her father handed Damien the keys to the truck, and Damien headed outside to move the truck. She heard Damien go through the front door, and just as she heard it shut her father turned to look at her.

"What were the two of you doing up here with the door closed?" Her father asked angrily, but she noticed that he didn't look mad.

"We were just talking dad, that's all." She said, as she tried to explain it to him.

"Did Jan know that he was up here with you?" He asked her, and she told him that Damien didn't get here until after Jan had left to go shopping with Melissa, and that she didn't know that he was coming over.

"Dylana, I don't know what your mother's rules were about boys in the house, but in my house if he will be over here, keep the door open, okay, sweetie? See you downstairs," her father said to her.

"Okay dad, I got it, keep the door open. Hey dad before you go, I was wondering what you and Niculus were talking to last night at the door?" She asked him, as he was about to leave the room.

"Oh boy, so you know the truth. We'll talk about this later." He said to her.

"When later?" She asked him.

"I don't know. I have to summon and talk to your mother First." He looked her straight in the eyes, and then he shut the door behind him as he left, before she could ask him anything else. She was just left in the room by herself, wondering why he had to have a talk to her mother first. As she got down there, she saw that they were sitting on the couch talking about something.

"What are you two talking about?" She asked them.

"Nothing, just sports, Dylana, I think the moving truck should be here soon. While you were upstairs, Damien helped me take the door off its hinges." Her father answered her, and then moving truck pulled in the driveway, just as her father stopped talking, and he went outside to meet the driver. Damien and Dylana went outside to help her father. She wasn't much help, so she watched Damien and my father bring everything in and put it in her room. After everything was in her room, they put the door back on and then her father left to go back to work.

Damien then helped her unload the stuff was in the boxes, and they put everything away and it only took them few hours, which was amazing because she had a lot of stuff. Damien looked at her as he put the last thing away on my desk, and he asked, "So, did you ask your father why my brother was here?"

"Yes, but he wouldn't tell me anything. He told me he'd tell me later, after he talked to my mother." She told him.

"I see, well if he won't tell us, I'll ask Niculus why he was here." He told her.

"Your brother really scares me." She told him.

"Don't worry love. I'll protect you from him, but also as long as you wear that he can't touch you." He said to her as he pointed to the Redfire.

"So, Damien, why haven't I ever seen your rose and tiger marks on your arms before?" She asked him.

"The reason you couldn't see them before is, because you didn't know that you were a Witch." He told her.

"Dylana I have to go now, but I'll talk to you later okay love." Damien said, as he was walking out of the room.

"Damien," she said.

"Yeah," he said.

"How can I get in touch with you? Didn't you break your cell phone?" She said to him.

"Right, I guess that I have to get a new phone, until then if you really need me just say my name, and I'll be there." He told her.

"How will you hear me?" She asked him.

"Vampire hearing. I could hear your call even if we were worlds apart." He said.

"Okay, I'll see you later than." She said.

Chapter Ten

Van Trap High

It's been about a week since Damien and Dylana last talked. She knew that she could call him any time, but she figured she'd give him time to talk to his brother. The whole week her little sister was keeping her very busy playing games, reading and watching Melissa favorite movies. As the week was ending, Jan took her shopping Friday to get clothes, because she had to start her new school on Monday, which she was used to, but this time she was still nervous about it, and she didn't know why.

The first day of school, she had to get up at five in the morning, and Dylana hated getting up that early, but her father said that she had to. Plus, her father wanted her to be there early on the first day, and it shocked her he was letting her drive herself to school. She got out of bed and she got dressed. She got dressed in a white skirt, with a black shirt and these hideous white socks that had black strips on them. She had to wear this uniform because her father enrolled her in a private school called Van Trap High School. Dylana thought the school the named of the school was strange. She wondered why her father would do this to her.

She went downstairs to grab something to eat before going to school. Her father was the only one that was up at six in the morning. When she walked into the kitchen, her father was sitting at the table, and she saw that he was reading the newspaper, and she could hear him mumbling about something under his breath. As soon as he saw her, in the corner of his eyes, he put the paper down and he asked her, "You ready for school."

"I think so, why?" She asked him.

"Nothing, it's just that some teachers are strict." He said.

"Really," she asked him.

"No, I'm just messing with you, Dylana." he said, with a little laugh.

"Thanks for trying to scare me on the first day, Dad." She said.

"Dylana you should get going or you will be late for school." He said.

"Okay, I'll see you later than." She said, as she grabbed her bag and then walked out the door. She got into my car that had just arrived at the house a few days ago because of bad weather or something. Her car wasn't the coolest, but at least it ran. It was a ninety-seven, rusty red colored Mustang. It didn't take long for her to get to the high school, because it was about seven miles away. As she got there, she saw that the school was three stories high. The windows all had bars on them. Dylana saw the school was a gloomy gray color that looked very depressing. There was only one set of doors into the high school, and it looked like there were chains on the ground by the doors. She figured that once you were in the high school you couldn't get out, and that seemed a little extreme. When she pulled into the student lot, which only one other car parked there.

She got out of her car, grabbed her bag, and she headed to the doors of the high school. She saw that here was a girl about her ago standing right by the doors reading. Dylana thought the green car in the parking lot must be hers. She was in the same ugly uniform as Dylana and she had a black jacket on. She had the hood of her

112

jacket up, but Dlyana could see that under it she had hair like gold. She also had this skin that glowed in the light, just like her mother's. She walked up to this girl, and she asked her where the office was in the high school. She also asked her why no one else was here yet. She didn't answer Dylana; She just went on reading her book, like she didn't hear or see Dylana there at all. She walked closer to her, and poked her in the arm, and then the girl looked up from her book, and then she looked at Dylana like she just woke her up.

"What do you want? Can't you see I was trying to sleep?" She said in a sleepy voice, and she lowered her hood. As Dylana and the girl looked at eachother, Dylana noticed that they had the same color eyes, but she didn't say anything about it.

"Really, because it looked like you were reading a book," she said to the girl.

"You're new here, aren't you?" She asked Dylana.

"Yeah, how did you know that?" Dylana asked her.

"You just look a little lost, that's all. Also, most people at this school don't talk to me." She said to Dylana.

"Why don't people talk to you?" Dylana asked her.

"They don't talk to me because they know I'm different from them, and most of them are scared to talk to me." She said. Dylana had a feeling that this girl was just like her and she was a Witch too, and she knew exactly what she meant about others knowing that they were different, because of how other people treat her.

"Oh, okay, well since you're awake now, can you tell me where the office inside the school?" Dylana asked her.

"Sure. It's through the front doors, and it's the first door on the left." She told Dylana, and she thanked her.

"So why aren't the other students here yet?" Dylana asked her, and the girl told her that school didn't start for another hour.

"I didn't realize that I was that early. Are the door unlocked now?" Dylana asked her, and then she started to wonder why her father made her leave so early.

"I don't know if the doors are unlocked yet or not. You could go try them." She told Dylana, and she went over to the doors, and she tried to open them, but they didn't budge. Dylana heard the girl ask her if she had any luck, and she told her no. Dylana then walked back over to the girl, and they talked about the school for the whole hour they were waiting for the school to start. From what the girl told her about the school, it seemed even weirder. She thought she'll wait and see if the school was that weird, as she thought this the school doors opened. Dylana turned her back to for a second, and when she turned back around the girl was gone, and it seemed like she just disappeared. Dylana thought to herself okay so the girl, she just met was a Witch like her.

She walked into the school, and she saw that the inside looked just like the outside; it was gray and depressing. She walked to the office, and it seemed to feel welcoming, and the only other person was in here was a woman. She was sitting at the most beautiful desk Dylana'd ever seen, out of a kind of dark wood. She walked over to it and the woman behind it said in a sweet voice, "Hello, can I help you with something, dear?"

"Hey, I'm Dylana Volus, I'm a new student, and I need my school schedule, and maybe a map." She told the women.

"Sure, thing dear, just let me find you in my computer." It took about thirteen minutes for her to find Dylana in the computer. Then she printed out her schedule and handed it to her. She also gave Dylana a hall pass, because classes were about to start. She told Dylana that there were maps on the table by the door. She went over to the table, and she grabbed a map, then she walked out of the office.

She looked at the class schedule, and she saw that her first class was History, and that classroom was in Room 5B. She looked at the map, and she saw that the class was upstairs. She tried to take her time going to the classroom, but when she got to the stairs, she got a sudden urge to run up them. As she got to the last step, she didn't notice that there was this big gate blocking her way, and she ran right into the gate. As she crashed into the gate, she saw that there was a hall monitor standing there laughing at her.

"Where do you think you're going?" She asked Dylana, as she kept on laughing at her, and all she could say was to class.

"What room is your class in?" She asked Dylana, and she told her that the class was in 5B. She then unlocked the gate, and she pointed out where the room was to Dylana. She walked toward the room and walked into the classroom. As she walked in, the teacher asked her, "Are you the new student?" She nodded yes. She took the pass, and handed Dylana a textbook, and told her to sit in the back of the third row.

The seat the teacher had an assign to her, which had been right next the girl she had met outside, but she still didn't know her name. She walked to the back of the classroom, and she took her seat. As she sat, the teacher resumed talking. The History teacher's name was Miss Flang. She was tall, and kind of wide, with light brown hair, which was curly, and a mess. She was wearing a bright red shirt with a black skirt. She listened as Miss. Flang was talking about the First World War.

After a while Dylana stop paying attention to what the teacher was saying, because she looked around the room, and all the other students in the class looked like they were all just so amazed by what Miss. Flang was saying. It was like they were hearing this stuff for the first time, which was weird. She then looked at the girl next to her, and she seemed different from the other students. She looked like she had when she was outside. Dylana saw that the girl's eyes open, but it looked like she was in a different world entirely. The rest of the class was on page two hundred, but her book was just turned to some random page. It was as if she just opened her book, and then she fell asleep again, like she did outside. Just as she was wondering how she could do that; the bell rang for the end of class.

She looked at her schedule again to see what her next class was, and she saw that it was Math, and the classroom for Math was in the room next to this one. As she was leaving, she noticed that the girl next to her was still in her sleep trance thing, so she shook her awake and the girl asked, "What?"

"The bell rang." Dylana said to her, and she said thanks. They then walked to their next class, which they also had together. The math teacher had Dylana sit next to her. The math teacher looked normal, but his name was odd, because it was Mr. Patard.

The girl and Dylana talked through the whole class and she finally found out that the girl's name was Jade. She told Jade that her name was Dylana. They talked about their families. Jade told Dylana that she lives with her mother and that her father died a month before she was born. She didn't have a lot of family, but she had a few aunts and an uncle, but she hadn't seen them in years. Dylana told her she just lost her mother, so she had to move here to live with her father.

They were talking so much that before they knew it; it was lunchtime. Jade and Dylana sat at a table away from everyone else, and she noticed that everyone was staring at them, so she asked Jade, "Why is everyone staring at us?"

"I think it's because of me, sorry I guess you will be an outcast like I am," she told Dylana.

"I guess it could be worse. At least I have one friend, that's more than I've had at the other schools I've been to." Dylana said to her.

"That's sad. Why was that?" She asked Dylana.

"I moved around a lot with my mother. I was never in one place long enough to make friends." Dylana told her, and Jade said I see. After she said that, she started to ask Dylana questions about well everything, like who her father was, and she told Jade that my father was Russ Volus. After she said that Jade just stared at her, and then she asked Dylana, "That's your father?"

"Yeah, why?" Dylana questioned her.

"It's nothing, so who's your mother?" She asked Dylana, and she told Jade that her mother was Deb Volus, but then she asked Dylana what her full name was and what her maiden name was. Dylana answered Jade by saying that her full name was Debathena Flower.

"Oh, my goddess," she said, as Jade fell back in surprise.

"What?" Dylana asked her.

"Nothing, it's just that it's a small world, and that explains the color if your eyes and the fact you see things that the humans don't." She said, and Dylana asked her what she meant about it being a small world.

"It's a small world, because your mother is one of my aunts, and you have eyes like the rest of our family." She told Dylana.

"What, my mother's one of your aunts? What do you mean I have eyes, like the rest of our family?" Dylana asked her.

"Well, all Witches are born with blue, green, yellow, or purple eyes. Our family has always had bluest purple eyes, because our lines the most powerful. Didn't you notice that mine are the same color as yours?" She asked.

"Yes, I did notice your eyes before, I just didn't say anything about it. Before my mother died though, my eyes were different. Why's that?" Dylana asked her.

"Our eyes take their true color when we get to full power." She said.

"I see, I didn't know that. Knowing that I'm a Witch is still new to me, I only found out when my mother died." Dylana asked her.

"I'm sorry about her mother, how did she die?" Jade asked her, as she changed what they were talking about. Dylana told her Vampires murdered her and that she died in her arms. Jade then asked Dylana if her mother gave her anything when she died. She told Jade about the letter, and the Redfire. She didn't know why she was telling her all this, but there was just something about Jade, and Dylana knew that in her soul she could trust her. She thought maybe she could help me figure out all this Witch stuff, because she was family and probably knew more about magic then Dylana did.

"Does your father know anything about any of this?" She asked me, and Dylana said her father and her hadn't really talked about it. Jade then said that's a good thing, and then she started to read her book for real this time. Jade and Dylana said nothing else for the rest of the school day. The other classes she had were very boring. School day ended at three in the afternoon. As she started to walk to her car, she saw that Damien was standing by her car waiting, and she walked up to him.

"Hello Damien, so what have you been up to? I haven't seen you for about a week. I've missed you." She asked him, as she hugged him. Seeing him made Dylana realize how much she missed him.

"I missed you too love. So, I went to talk to my brother Niculus. I wanted to find out why he was at your house for." Damien said.

"So, why was he there?" She questioned him.

"Well, he told me that your father is doing some work for him, and that's all I could get out of him. Love, I want you to promise me something, okay?" Damien asked her, and she said okay.

"Say nothing to your father, okay." He said to her, and she couldn't help but wonder why.

"Why, Damien?" She asked him.

"You can't trust your father. If anything happens, anything at all, let me know love. You can call me anytime now." Damien said.

"Does that mean you got a new cell phone?" She asked him.

"Yes, and here's the new number." He said, as he handed her a piece of paper, with the number on it.

"I have to go, now, I'll call you if I find out anything else." He told her and kissed her on the top of head and then he took off running through the woods by the school.

Chapter Eleven

Aunt Misty

Dylana's been in school for about a month now, and her life has been boring lately, which was nice. She would get up and go to school, where she still only had one friend, who was also her cousin. Some days they would talk all day, and other days they wouldn't talk at all. She would then go home and do her homework, or she would play with Melissa, and then her father would come home, and then they would eat dinner. After that, she would call Damien and talk to him until she fell asleep.

When she woke up this gloomy Wednesday morning in October, she knew that it would be a weird day. She had a strange feeling was like the one she had the day before her mother died, but it felt different. She thought this feeling was telling her that today she would meet Jade's mother. She didn't know how she felt about meeting her, as she got up and got ready for school. At six, she left for school, and as always, she would meet up with Jade early before school started.

When she got to school today, however, Jade wasn't in her usual spot by the door. Dylana thought maybe she was absent from school today. When the bell rang at seven, she walked upstairs to her History class. In class today, Miss. Flang was talking about some other war, or something. Dylana wasn't paying any attention to what she was saying. It was just blah, blah, and blah to her. She was wondering where Jade was, because she wanted to know if she was right about this feeling. As she sat there, this class felt like it would never end, but when it finally did, Dylana thought thank God.

On her way to math, she must have not been looking where she was going, because she ran right into someone. She was so thrilled, not because she ran into someone, but because it was Jade. Then they walked to class together, and she saw that Jade seemed distracted throughout math class. The look on her face told Dylana that she was contemplating something she wanted to say to her. She tried to get back to the math she was working on.

When they finally got to lunch, Jade asked her to go outside with her. Dylana followed her outside, and Jade asked her, "Dylana, so do you remember the first day of school, when I told you that your mother was my aunt?" Just as Dylana was about to open her mouth to say something, Jade told Dylana to let her finish.

"Well, I finally told my mother about you the other night, and she wants to meet you and to see if you're your mother's daughter." She said to Dylana.

"I had a feeling this morning I would meet your mother today. What do you mean by my mother's daughter?" Dylana asked her.

"She just wants to see if you can do magic like your mother. But you can if you knew what I would ask you today." She said.

"I didn't know that having these feelings was magic. I already figured that the sleeping thing you do has something to do with magic, but I don't how you do it though." Dylana said to her.

"The feelings as you called it is really the power of knowing, and if you didn't have magic, you couldn't do that. And your mother also knew things just like you. She could even know what anyone would say before they said it. The sleeping while awake is a meditation that takes me to another world." She said.

"What was the amulet that your mother gave to you again, I just want to make sure I heard you correctly, when you told me the first time." Jade asked her, and then she stopped for a second and said, "Don't say it out loud. You never know who's listening out here. Here, write it on this." And then she handed Dylana a piece of paper and a pen. On the piece of paper, she wrote, _Redfire_, and then she handed it back to Jade.

"Do you have it with you now?" Jade asked her.

"Yes, in the letter, my mother told me to keep it with me at all times." She told her.

"Good. Did your mother ever tell you she had other family?" Jade asked me, and Dylana told her no

"Well, that explains why you were so shocked when I told you that your mother was my aunt. Did she tell you about your father?" Jade asked Dylana.

"No, but I know that he's a Witch too. Is there something else I should know?" Dylana asked her.

"Well, your father's been working with our enemies, and they're after that amulet, and the one that wields it. At least that's what my mother told me." She told her.

"I see," Dylana said, and she was wondering if Jade was talking about Niculus.

"What are you doing after school?" She asked Dylana, and she told Jade that she wasn't doing anything.

"Can you come over to my house after school? So, that you can meet my mother tonight, that's if you want to?" She asked Dylana, and she told Jade that she would. Jade and Dylana spent the rest of the day talking. Jade was telling her all about her mother. She told Dylana that her mother was always doing magic around the house and that she was very in tune with nature. From what Jade told her about her mother, Dylana thought Jade's mother sounded cool, but Dylana was wrong to think that.

At three, they left school, and she followed Jade to her house. Her house was in the woods, and it looked like a small cabin. It had moss covering it. As Dylana got out of her car she said nice place, to be polite, but she thought it was a creepy place, like something out of a horror movie. Jade must have thought Dylana meant what she said, because Jade said thanks. she then followed Jade up some stone steps, and though the front door.

"Mother, I'm home, and I brought a friend." Jade said to her mother, and then Jade's mother came out of one of the other rooms. She wore the oddest thing that Dylana had ever seen. It was a dress that could pass as a tablecloth.

"Jade, who it this?" Her mother asked her.

"Mother, this is Dylana. You know that girl I was telling you about the other night." Jade said.

"Yes, I remember, so this is the girl you think is my sister's daughter." Her mother replied.

"Mother, Dylana is Aunt Debathena's daughter. She told me she has the Redfire," Jade said.

"She does?" Jade's mother asked, and then Jade said yes to her mother.

"Did you see it?" Her mother asked her, and Jade told her mother she hadn't seen it.

"How do you know that she has the Redfire, if you haven't seen it yet Jade?" Her mother questioned her.

"She told me she had it, and I believe her." Jade said, as she was getting defensive towards her mother.

"That means nothing. She could have lied to you, Jade."
Jade's mother yelled at her.

"You wouldn't lie to me right, Dylana?" Jade asked, as she
looked at me

"No," Dylana said, as she finally got into the conversation.

"If you're not lying, then show us the Redfire." Jade's
mother turned toward Dylana, as she said that. Dylana didn't know
if she should show it to them or not, there was just something off
about Jade's mother.

"Dylana, it's okay, just show it to her, it's not she hasn't
seen it before. You're safe here. We will not bite you. You know."
Jade said to Dylana, and Dylana thought, okay so Jade just made
a vampire joke, she started to smile. She knew she could trust Jade,
so she grabbed the chain of the Redfire that was around her neck
and pull it out from under her shirt to show them and she saw
Jade's mother's eyes light up at the sight of the Redfire.

"Why are you she just staring at it like that?" She asked
them.

"She hasn't seen it in so long that's all." Jade said.

129

"I'm sorry about your mother." Jade's mother said, as she took her eyes away from the Redfire, and looked at me, and Dylana told her thank you.

"Why don't you two come in here with me, and we'll all have some tea," Jade's mother told us. They followed her into the other room she came from, and as they walked in, three cups and a pot of tea just appeared on the table. they all took our seats at the table.

"Dylana, if you like, you can call me Aunt Misty," Misty said, as she poured the tea into the three cups.

"Mother," Jade said.

"Yes, Jade, what is it?" Misty asked her.

"I think Dylana might be a little confused." Jade said, and Dylana thought Jade was right about her being confused, by the magic that Misty was doing. Before she could say anything, Misty asked her, "What are you confused about, Dylana?"

"It's just that this is all still new to me. Enjoy seeing all this magic you're doing. I just have a lot of things on my mind like why my mother never told me any of this before, she died." She said.

"What do you mean? That you're a Witch, or just the magic thing?" Jade asked me.

"Well, I guess both have been on my mind, but I think I've accepted that I'm a Witch. I just don't understand how the two of you are doing magic. Another thing I keep thinking about is the fact that my mother never told me I had other family besides my father." Dylana said.

"Well, Dylana, your mother probably didn't tell you about Jade and me, because your mother and I didn't get along well, and she doesn't talk to the rest of our family either. Another reason is to protect you. She knew that someone was after her. That's why she left your father, and she disappeared so that no one could find her or you. You see your father was working for our enemies were after her." Misty said.

"Who are these people?" She asked them, because she wanted to find out if it was Niculus that they were talking about, or if it was a different person.

"Our enemies aren't people at all, they're Vampires." Misty said.

"Okay, so are you talking about Niculus?" She said, and the looks that Misty and Jade had on their faces told her they didn't expect her to say that.

"Yes, but how do you know who Niculus is? Who told you about him?" Misty asked her.

"My boyfriend told me about him, and I know that my father doing something for him. I just don't know what it is." She said.

"Who's this boyfriend of yours?" Misty asked.

"I know, she's talking about Damien," Jade said, and it should have surprised Dylana that they knew him, but it didn't.

"What, no, you need to stay away from him, he's a fucking killer and he'll end up killing you too stupid girl." Misty yelled at her.

"I know he's killed before, but he's a different person now, and he's my soul mate. Plus, he's done nothing but make sure I was safe. So, fuck you, I'm out of here." She said, as she walked out of the room, and as she got to her car, she heard Misty yelled, "A tiger can't change its stripes." After that she got in her car and got out of there as fast as she could. She pulled into her driveway, and she got out of her car, and she went inside. She saw that her father and Jan were sitting on the couch watching some romantic movie on TV.

"Hey, Dylana, where have you been?" My father asked her.

"I was hanging out with a friend from school." She told him.

"Did you have fun?" He asked her.

"No, not really, her mother's crazy." She told him.

"Oh, I'm so sorry sweetie, do you want to watch this movie with us? It just started?" He asked her.

"No, I think I'm just going to go to bed, but thanks anyway. Night." She said, and he said goodnight to her. She went upstairs to her room, and she sat on her bed, and then she grabbed her cell phone, and she called Damien. It took Damien forever to answer the phone, and she was getting worried.

"Hello," Damien said, and all she had to say was his name, and he knew that something was wrong.

"Love, what's wrong?" He asked her.

"I just need to talk to you. Can you come over?" She asked him.

"I'll be right there in a little while, love." He said, and then they hung up their phones. She was just lying on her bed when she heard a tap, tap, and tap on her window. She went over to the window, and when she opened it, she saw Damien in the tree next to her window. She backed away from the window, so that Damien could come in, and he jumped into her room without making a sound.

"So, what do you want to talk to me about, love?" He told me.

"Well one thing, why didn't you go to the door?" She asked him.

"I don't want your father to know that I'm here." He said.

"Why not?" I asked him.

"It's a long story okay, so what's wrong, love?" He said, after he said that she thought, so there is something between them.

"Okay, well I have other family besides my father. Well, I guess I knew that since the first day of school I had other family. Today though I met my aunt that my mother never told me about, but you know that, already don't you?" She asked him.

"Love, you're rambling a little, but yes, you're right. I knew that you had another family that lived here in Maine. So, how is Misty these days?" He asked her.

"She's crazy, and she really doesn't like you. She said that I should stay away from you, and that if I didn't, you'd kill me." She told him.

"Good old Misty, it sounds like she's still off her rocker. Dylana, know that Misty's been out of damn mind for years." He told her.

"Really, is that why my mother never told me about her?" She asked him.

"Yes, and no. Your mother just wasn't close to her family, and the ones she was close to, she couldn't trust them, or they got killed." He told her.

"Did you find out anything else about what my father doing for your brother?" She asked him.

"I found out your father been working for my brother for a while. I still don't know what they're doing, my guess is that your father a spy of some sort for Niculus. I think how Niculus found out you and your mother were in Rome. Niculus has some powerful spell on your father, that he had Trinity cast, or maybe they did a spell together." He said.

"There something else that you're not telling me isn't there?" She asked him.

"It's not really something I'm not telling you, but maybe if you talk to Niculus, maybe you could get the information out of him." He said.

"Okay when," she asked.

"How about tomorrow after school?" He asked her.

"Okay, are you going to pick me up, or am I going to meet you somewhere?" She asked him.

"Well, this isn't a place you have to drive to, after school, go to the back of your house. There's a trail right behind your house. I want you to follow that trail until you see me. Love. Tomorrow's the first day we came to Earth, and Niculus likes us to meet there every few years so all of us could catch up on we've been up to." He told her.

"Okay, so how long have you been on Earth?" She asked him.

"A long time, I don't remember the year. I'll see you tomorrow then love and do me a favor. Don't bring the Redfire with you." He said.

"Why don't you want me to wear it?" She asked him.

"Niculus has been asking me if you have it, and I've been lying to him, to keep you safe. If he finds out I've been lying to him, he'll be piss at me and he'll think of it as betrayal." He told her.

"Well, I'm still wear it. I'll keep it out of sight. So, you don't get in trouble." She told him.

"Okay, that'll work. I just hope that Trinity isn't there tomorrow." He told her.

"Why's that?" She asked him.

"She's a Witch too, and she'll feel the power coming from the Redfire." He told her.

"I see, I guess we're just going to hope that she won't be there." She said.

"I guess so, night love, sweet dreams." He said, then he kissed her on the forehead, and then he went out the window, and she watched him run out of sight.

Chapter Twelve

Forest

Dylana woke the next day thinking it would be a good day, but it also felt like it would be a day like no other. She got up and got ready for school, and she ate breakfast and then drove to school. She didn't see Jade when she got there, and Dylana was happy about that, she didn't want to see her, anyway.

As She walked into History class though, she saw Jade, and Jade waved to her, but she didn't wave back at Jade. Dylana just took her seat, and for the first time she was paying attention and she was so bored at what Miss. Flang was saying.

"Dylana, are you mad at me?" Jade asked her, and Dylana told her no, and she thought it wasn't Jade's fault that her mother was bat shit crazy. They talked for the rest of class. Toward the end of the school day, Dylana started to feel like something bad would happen tonight if she went to meet Damien and his brother. She saw that the Redfire was glowing red through her shirt.

"It glows red when it senses that you're going into a dangerous situation. I think you should wear it around your neck, when you go into the woods tonight." Jade said to her.

"How do you know about that I was going into the woods tonight?" She asked Jade.

"I just saw what would happen to you if you don't wear it, that's how." Jade told her.

"I was planning to wear it, but you can see things?" Dylana asked her. She told Dylana that was her main power. Dylana wanted to ask her more about it, but the bell rang, and Jade disappeared. So, Dylana went back home, and she dropped my things off inside my room. The Redfire was still glowing red, when she walked outside, and she walked around to the other side of my house, to where the trail was.

The trail was easy for her to find, and she started to walk along it. The trail started was wide, but then it started to become small and narrow; It also had some broken glass and nails on it she tried not to step on. Trees surrounded her, and as she was walking the trees started to look like they were decaying. She finally came to an opening, and she saw Damien. She ran right for him and he put his arms around her.

"Niculus, I hope you don't mind, but I invited Dylana to meet us here? She wanted to talk to you about something." She heard him said.

"It's fine she's here. I want to talk to her too." Niculus said.

"Dylana, can you make that stop glowing?" Damien whispered into Dylana's ear.

"I don't know how to." She said back to him, and then Trinity said to something to Niculus about the power she felt coming off Dylana, and Trinity told Niculus that Dylana had the Redfire.

"Damien?" Niculus said.

"What," Damien said impatiently, and a little nervous, because he knew what going to happen next.

"Dylana has the Redfire," Niculus said to Damien, as he pointed at Dylana.

"I know that she has the Redfire, Niculus. I knew that she's had it since we were in Rome," Damien said.

"If you knew that she had the Redfire, then why didn't you tell us it passed to her, after her mother died, brother?" Niculus asked Damien.

"I didn't tell you, because I love her, and I didn't want you to hurt her Niculus, or tried to use her." Damien said, as he held Dylana closer in his arms.

"Damien, you still should have told me regardless, and what makes you think I want to hurt Dylana?" Niculus asked him, and Dylana was getting annoyed by the two of them were talking about her.

"Will you two, stop talking about me, like I'm not here?" She yelled at Niculus and Damien.

"Well, look who has a temper? You're just like your mother." Niculus looked at Dylana, when he said.

"Love, I think you should get out of here." Damien said to her calmly. She didn't listen to Damien, she wanted to know what

141

her father was doing for Niculus and now she wanted to know why Niculus care so much that she had the Redfire.

"Hey, Niculus, why do you care if I have the Redfire?" She said, as she looked at Niculus. Niculus started to smile at her, and then he said something to the other three people, and they walked into the woods away from them. She watched as Niculus sat down on a tree stump.

"I like you, Dylana. I bet that you want to know more than that, you probably what to know why I was at house talking to your father, because I saw you staring at me with curiosity from the stairs." He asked her, as he laughed a little, and she told him yes.

"Okay then, little one, come over here, and I'll tell you." As she started to walk toward Niculus, Damien grabbed her arm, and he told her to stay away from him.

"I'll ask you again, brother. What makes you think I want to hurt Dylana?" Niculus asked Damien.

"Well, maybe it's because you've hurt girls I've been with in the past, or you turned them against me," Damien said.

"Brother, that's true, so true. But, brother, Dylana's very different, your past girlfriends. Dylana's your soulmate plus she has the Redfire, and I'd be stupid to hurt someone who wears that."

142

Niculus said. After he said that, Damien and Niculus just stood there looking at each other, like the two of them had an understanding, and then Damien let go of her arm. Dylana walked over to where Niculus was, and she stopped a foot away from him. she didn't want to get any closer to him.

"Please sit on my lap, little one." He said to her, and she turned around to look at Damien, with a face that read, "Is your brother fucking serious?" But the look that Damien's Black eyes told her that Niculus was for real, so she sat on his lap. Being this close to Niculus was making her very uncomfortable. As she sat on his lap, she started to shiver, because his body felt freezing cold.

"So, Niculus, what does my father do for you?" She asked him.

"Well, he does odd jobs for me, like keeping track on where you and mother were living. And I'm sorry for your lost. We were friends at one time, that was until she found that I was using her. I hate to say it, but I'm the reason she left your father." He told her, and she was a little confused.

"What, so, you used my father to spy on us? And what do you mean you're the reason that my mother left my father?" She asked Niculus, and Damien felt her anger rising from where he was standing.

"Yes, I had Trinity put an obedience spell on him, and he'll do whatever Trinity and I tell him. And Debathena left when she found out about the spell." He told her.

"You're a monster, you know that? So, are you planning to use me too, because I have the Redfire now?" She asked Niculus.

"Oh, little one, you may think I'm a monster, but there are others that are worse than I am. I don't want to use you, but I need your help, and if you don't want to help me willingly, my sweet Dylana. Then I will force you help me, and you don't want me to have to force you little one, do you? What do you say, will you help me?" When he asked that, she didn't know what to say. She was getting a little scared of Niculus and she knew that his threat was real, and the look in his eyes scared her. She tried to run back over to Damien, because she knew that she would feel safer with him holding her, but Niculus pulled her back against him so fast she didn't even see his hands move, and he had a very strong grip around her.

"Wrong answer, little one." She heard him whisper into her ear. Damien then started to walk in their direction, but before Damien could get to her, Dylana heard Niculus say, "Christopher, Selene, go hold our brother in place." She watched as they came running out of the woods toward Damien. Christopher and Selene slammed Damien onto the ground, right at Dylana's feet. She looked

144

at Damien, and she saw that his eyes were different, because they looked like two swirling black holes in his eye sockets, and she watched as his canines grow into a part of fangs.

"Now, Dylana, that's what an anger Vampire looks like." Niculus said to her, as he flashed a smile at her, with his own set of fangs, and she saw that both of his eyes were red, and she also saw a faint green tint in his eyes. She saw the Trinity come out of the woods, and Niculus asked Trinity to help him restrain Dylana, because Dylana was trying to get away from him. As Trinity got closer to them, the Redfire started to glow red again, and a force threw Niculus backwards away from Dylana, and into a tree with so much force, that the tree fell over, and the same thing happened to Trinity, but she went into another direction, into a different tree knocking it down.

She saw that the two of them were recovering quickly from being hurled into the trees. They both got up, and they ran at Dylana again. Just as they did that, Dylana put her hands up, and she saw flames coming out of her hands engulfing them. She didn't know why at that moment she put her hands up, and she didn't know why the flames didn't burn her. She watched them running away, and as were running away, Dylana thought they looked like two balls of fire.

She then fell backwards onto the ground because she noticed that Damien's skin was burning, as if she had set him on fire. She watched as Damien hurled his brother and sister about ten feet into the air, without exerting much force at all. Damien then got up, and he ran away from her. After a few minutes, she saw him coming back, and she saw that his skin was healing itself before her eyes. He walked up to her.

"Are you okay, Damien? Did I hit you with my flames too?" She asked him.

"No, but whatever happens to Niculus, happens to me. I'm fine. Are you okay, love?" Damien asked her.

"I'm fine. I didn't know I had that much power." She said, as they heard the others back.

"Dylana, run, I'll talk to you tomorrow." He told her, and she ran as fast as she could back to her house.

Chapter Thirteen

Possessed

When she saw her house coming into view, she looked behind her and saw that someone was following her. She kept on running, and she ran inside the house and closed the door behind her. As she ran inside, she saw that her father and Jan were on the other side of the door which she thought was weird. At first, she was glad to see that it was them, until she remembered that Niculus could make her father do anything he wanted.

"What's wrong?" Her father asked her.

"Nothing much, Damien's brother attacked me because I have the Redfire. And I think someone was chasing after me." She said, and after she that, her father and Jan laughed at her, like she just told them a joke.

"What's so funny, I'm telling you that truth." She said to them.

"I know that you're telling the truth. I just think it's funny you came back here, to the two people under my control stupid girl. I'll just have them keep you busy until I get there, because I know that you won't hurt them. See you soon Dylana." She heard her father said, but it was Niculus voice. She was shocked to hear that, and then she noticed that her father and Jan's eyes looked white. She started to back away from them when she saw that they had baseball bats in their hands, and they swung the bats at her. Her father and Jan seemed to knock her unconscious. She wanted to hurt them, but then the Redfire glowed blue and ice came out of her hands. She watched as her father and Jan froze there them were in solid ice. As she stood there frozen in shock at what she just did, someone opened the door, and she thought it was Niculus, but it was Jade.

"Jade," she said, with relief in her voice, that it was Niculus.

"Dylana, are you okay?" Jade asked her.

"No, I have Niculus after me and I just froze my parents." Dylana said.

"I see, we have to get out of here. It'll be safe at my place. Vampire can't go there." Jade said.

"Okay, but what about them?" Dylana asked her.

"I can fix that." Jade told her, as she waved her arm and Dylana watch her parents defrost.

"Are they going to be okay?" Dylana asked her.

"They're breathing, so I think they are fine, but we need to go now, they're coming." Jade said.

"Okay, let's get out of here." Dylana, and then they run outside and got in Jade's car and slammed on the gas, and as Jade was driving, Dylana felt someone following them, and she just knew that it was Damien making sure that Niculus didn't get to her. When they got to Jade's house, they rushed inside, and then Dylana fell to the floor, because the Redfire drained her of all her energy. The last thing she remembered, before she passed out, was Misty coming toward her.

Chapter Fourteen

Misty's Story

Dylana woke up in what it seemed to be morning, because the sun outside was blinding me, and as she looked around, she realized that she had no clue where she was though. The room she was in she didn't recognize. Dylana thought the room was a colorful room. The walls were yellow, blue, purple, red, and pink, and it looked like a rainbow. The floor was wood, and had green paint, and looked like real grass. As she was looking at the floor, Dylana started to realize that she didn't know how she got here. Dylana remembered nothing about last night at all, and the last thing she remembered was her mother dying in her arms. Just as she was thinking about that awful night, she heard voices in one of the other rooms. She recognizes the voices, but at the same time she wasn't sure who that were, and she thought maybe they could tell her how she got here.

Dylana got out of bed, and she walked out of the room to ask them. She found the room they were in. She looked at them, and she seemed to recognize them too, but she still couldn't remember who they were, but she knew them from somewhere.

"Come on in dear and have a seat and eat something." Misty said to her. Dylana did what Misty said, and she sat down in one of the other seats at the table. Dylana then grabbed a piece of toast was on the table.

"Dylana, so tell us what exactly happened in the forest last night? I only saw you were running away from something, so that's why I went to your house." The younger one asked her, and Dylana did not understand what she was talking about.

"I don't mean to be rude, but who the hell are you people? I do not understand what you're talking about. I don't remember what happened last night, and I was wondering if you could tell me how I got here?" Dylana asked them.

"Mother, why doesn't she remember last night, and why doesn't she remember us?" The younger one asked.

"She's probably blocking out what happened last time. My only guess is that what happened must have been too much for her to comprehend. Jade, could you get the memory crystal?" Jade's mother said to her, and Jade left the room to get a memory crystal, as Dylana thought these two are out of their minds. After a few minutes went by, Jade came back into the room, and she was carrying a blue crystal in her hands. She put the blue crystal on the table right in front of Dylana, and then she sat back down in her seat.

"Dylana, I want you to hold this crystal in both of your hands, and try to think of last night, and who we are." Jade's mother told her. Dylana thought, okay she'll try it. So, she picked up the crystal, and she held it in her hands. She started to feel silly doing this, and that it will not work, but as I thought, the crystal made her feel like her mind was spinning around and around. Her memories of what happened last night came swirling back to her, and she started to remember who Misty and Jade were. She then wished that she didn't have her memories back, and she was so mad at Niculus for what he did, that she threw the crystal at a wall, and it shattered on impact. She looked at Jade and Misty, and she walked outside, because of all the rage, that I was feeling toward Niculus. She also didn't want to break anything else of theirs.

Dylana was sitting outside for about an hour, just thinking about that she had to talk to Damien and asked him to get his brother to leave her alone. She was also thinking if her parents were okay, as Jade came out of the house and she sat next to her and asked, "Dylana, do you want to talk about what happened to you last night?"

"Not really, but I need to talk to someone about it. Or I think I'll go mad. I thought I could go there and talk to Niculus and find out what my father was doing for him. And I found out he was using and controlling my father to get information on my mother and me." Dylana said to her.

"I know all about that. That's why I said not to tell your father anything." Jade said.

"Why didn't you mention that to me, before I went into the woods?" Dylana asked.

"If you knew beforehand, I knew that you would still have gone to meet them?" Jade asked her.

"Okay, I see your point, and you're right I would have gone either way." Dylana said.

"So, why did Niculus attack you?" She asked me.

"Well Niculus asked me if I would use the Redfire to help the Vampires with something, and he said that if I help them willingly, that he'd force me to help him. I didn't answer him, and when I tried to get back to Damien. He grabbed me and told Christopher and Selene to hold Damien in place. And they slammed him to the ground by my feet. He then told Trinity to help him restrain me, and I use the Redfire to hurl them away from me, and when them came back, I engulfed them in flames. After that, Damien helped me get away." Dylana told her.

"I guess maybe you were right about Damien, maybe my mother's wrong about him. Maybe he has changed." Jade said.

"How long have you known him?" Dylana asked her.

"I've known Damien and his family a long time, and honestly I've been keeping things from you. Please don't be mad, but I just had to be sure of who you were. I knew that you'd be coming to Maine, because I saw it, and I knew what school you'd be going to, so I enrolled myself in the school, and then I waited for you to find me. We're drawn to each other through blood. I'm about a hundred years old. I've had a lot of problems with them living so close." She told Dylana.

"So, you knew that I was coming? Did you know why I was coming to Maine, because you seemed shocked what I told you that someone killed my mother?" Dylana asked her.

"No, I didn't know why you were coming here. I only knew that you were family, and I wanted to know who you were. I never knew that Aunt Debathena even had a daughter, and I never sensed you before she died. She hid you well from the Witches and the Vampires." Jade told Dylana.

"I see, wow you're old." Dylana said, mainly because she didn't know what else to say.

"So, I guess that you're not mad at me then?" Jade asked Dylana, as she smiled.

"No, I'm not mad at you, and thanks for being honest with me," Dylana said to her.

"Well, since I'm being honest with you, I should tell you that Damien and his brothers and sister are part of the Royal Vampire line." Jade told her.

"Wait one Fucking second. Are you telling that Damien is fucking royalty?" Dylana asked Jade, as she was laughing.

"Yes, Dylana he is, you didn't know that, did you?" She asked Dylana.

"No, Jade I didn't know that." Dylana said to Jade.

"I guess that there's a lot you don't know about them, Vampires I mean?" Jade asked Dylana.

"Well, I know that they have dragons, they're fast, strong, and unlike the myths I've read the sun doesn't seem to burn them." Dylana said to her

"Well, that's a start, I guess, but there's a lot more to learn about them. Come back inside, and I'll tell you all about them." Jade told me.

"Jade wait," Dylana said.

"What?" she asked Dylana.

"Do you know if my parents are okay, or not?" Dylana asked her.

"After I brought you here, I went back to your house to check on them, and they're fine." Jade told Dylana.

"Okay," Dylana said, and then she followed Jade back into her house. She told Dylana to have a seat in the tearoom. Dylana did as Jade told her as Jade went into another room to get some books on Vampires. The books that Jade came back with weren't little books, no these were giant books, and all of them had some weird writing on them that Dylana couldn't read. Jade put the books on the table in front of Dylana, and she turned the pages to a chapter was in the same language that Dylana couldn't read, so she asked Jade what language it was in.

"It's written in Greek," Jade told her.

"Since I can't read Greek, can you tell me what this says about Vampires?" Dylana asked her.

"Well, Dylana, this chapter has a list of Vampires that are the biggest threat to us Witches. The Vampires listed here are far more dangerous than the Vampires you would see in movies or on TV. I know that you don't want to hear this, but Damien and his brothers are killers. Damien must love you if he's willing to go against Niculus. Our biggest threats are Damien and Niculus. The two of them have killed more Witches than any other Vampire. Also, Damien and Niculus are threats to each other." She told Dylana.

"Why would you say something like that?" Dylana said to her.

"I know that Damien and Niculus have had a lot of problems with each other. They have a long history of trying to hurt each other in any way they could. I'm sorry to tell you this, but they hate Witches. Also, for more years than I can even put a number on, the

Vampires have been trying to wipe out all the Witches, under Niculus's rule." She said to Dylana.

"What do you mean, when you say under Niculus's rule?" Dylana asked her.

"Oh right, I forgot you don't know, well just so you know Niculus is the Vampire King." Jade said, and Dylana didn't know what to say to that, so she just stayed quiet.

"Also, Dylana, in this chapter it says how many Witches, each Vampire, has killed, and the last time I looked at this, I think it said that Damien killed a good hundred Witches." Jade said.

"Oh, come on Jade, that can't be true." Dylana said because she wanted to believe that Damien was more than just a killer.

"Dylana, it is true, but I think it was way over a hundred." Misty said to Dylana, as she walked into the room in a haze.

"I can't even believe that," Dylana said as she looked at Misty with a disbelieving look on her face.

"Well, if you don't believe what I said, why don't you ask him yourself?" Misty said in a very nasty way. So, Dylana told her, "I'll do that."

"Jade, how can Damien go in the sun and not get burned by it? Or is the thing about the sun just a myth?" Dylana asked her, as she looked back at Jade.

"That's a good question, and it's not a myth about the sun burning and killing Vampires. The answer to how they can go into the sun. The Vampires in the royal family have special rings that allow them to go into the sunlight. The rings they have give them an advantage, because the only thing that can kill a Vampire is sunlight. The one sun on Earth, however, isn't as strong as the three suns on Viterlea, so if they didn't have their rings on Earth, the worst thing that could happen to them would be a terrible sunburn and killer headache" Jade told Dylana.

"Okay, so what about garlic, silver, holy water, or what about a wooden stake through their hearts?" Dylana asked them both, and Jade laughed at her. When she stopped laughing, she told Dylana that all that stuff was a myth, and that it does nothing. She said that a Vampires' skin is way too hard, and that a wooden stake wouldn't even go through their skin.

"Dylana, do you want to know our history?" Misty asked me, and then she said, "And, just so you know, our history has a lot to do with Royal Vampires. Dylana, Jade, a long time ago on Viterlea, The Witches and the Vampires were at war with each other. But as the Witch Queen and the Vampire Queen started to have children, they made their kings sign a treaty. They made the treaty because they didn't want their children to get hurt or killed." Misty said, and then paused and said, "My grandparents were King and Queen of the Witches. They had two girls named Jane and Lilith. The Vampires had two boys, and their names were Dmitry, and Marcus. On our planet, time works differently, and a day on Viterlea is a year on Earth. It was a peaceful time for about three hundred years. That was until my Aunt Jane secretly married the Vampire Prince Dmitry. The two of them had three boys and a girl. Their children are Niculus, Your Damien, Christopher, and Selene." Misty said, and then she took a break.

"What, so how old are they, really?" Dylana asked Misty.

"They're actually older than the Earth itself" Misty told her, and then Dylana replied really.

"Yes really, are you going to let me finish?" She asked Dylana coldly, and she didn't know why Misty said that so coldly to her. It was just a question, but Dylana told her yes.

"Now, as I was saying, Jane and Dmitry had four children, and when the Witches found out that Jane had not only married a Vampire, but that she also had children with one, the Witches attacked the Vampires, for taking Jane away from her own kind. To stop the fighting, Jane went to see her sister Lilith, with Damien.

Lilith also married, but she married another Witch, and they also had four children. Their children were three girls and a boy. There was your mother Debathena, our sister Serena, me, and our brother Fantos." Misty paused and then said, "And we are just as old as the Vampires, if you were wondering, Dylana. Oh, if you haven't guessed it yet, we are also royalty, because Lilith is the Queen of the Witches, and she's your grandmother."

"Wait, are you telling me what I think you are?" Dylana asked, as she was stuttering.

"Yes, Dylana, you're a Witch Princess, and by birth you are next in line to be the Queen." Misty told her.

"What?" Dylana asked.

"Too much information?" Misty asked her.

"Yes, just a little too much. Please continue with the story." Dylana said.

"Okay, so when Jane came to see my mother, my mother killed her for her betrayal, and then my mother dragged her head outside and put it on display for all the Vampires to see. There was nothing they could do to stop it from happening, because of the suns and the Vampires had to wait for the suns to set before they could retaliate for Jane death." Misty said.

"After that happened, a huge war broke out, so my sisters and I came to Earth so we could get away from the war. I think the war has stopped, for now at least," Misty said, with a wicked smile, because she wanted the war to start up again. She then left the room as she was laughing at nothing. Dylana thought about Misty little story, and some of it just made little sense to her. There had to be more to it. Dylana thought what was wrong with her. and what the hell was with her smiling and laughing like that? Dylana thought now it means that she has a lot more things she must ask her mother when she learns how to summon her. As she was thinking about this, there was a knock on the door, Jade and Dylana just looked at each other.

Chapter Fifteen

Trinity

"Hey, Mother, I'll get the door." Jade said, as she answered the door. At the door was the girl was at Dylana house the other night. She was also the other girl was in the forest; it was Trinity.

"Can I help you with something?" Jade asked her rudely when she saw who it was.

"Yes, I think you can, cousin." Trinity said, as she was mocking Jade a little.

"I'm not your cousin. I don't even know who you are or what you want, and I think you should leave." Jade said to her.

"You are my cousin, Jade. Another thing is if I wasn't, I wouldn't be able to find you. You know that blood calls to blood." Trinity said to Jade, and then she started to look at Dylana, and then she smiled.

"Oh, hey there, Dylana, how are you? Sorry about attacking you last night." Trinity said to her.

"What do you want, Trinity?" Dylana asked her.

"Well, Dylana right to the point, well I came here for you." she said, as she was still looking at Dylana.

"Why are you here for me?" Dylana asked her.

"Oh, I think you know why I'm here." She said, in a devilish voice.

"You're Serena's daughter, right?" Jade asked Trinity.

"Yes," Trinity said.

"Why are you on the Vampiures side, They're killers." Jade said.

"I'm on the Vampires side, becasue the night my mother was killed by someone that we trusted, Niculus saved my life for you infromation. Also, I lve him, just like Dylana here loves Damien. Another thing you should know, the Vampires aren't the only killers here. The Witches are killers to. Did you ever ask your mother how many she's killed?" Trinity asked her.

"So, what, I bet that they were all Vampires, and aren't we at war with the Vampires?" Jade said to Trinity, and then Jade turned to Dylana, and she asked Dylana, "Dylana, do you?"

"Do I what?" Dylana asked her.

"Do you really love Damien?" Jade asked, and Dylana told Jade yes.

"Now to what brings me here, Dylana, the thing is that Damien wants to see you," Trinity said to her.

"Where is he, and why didn't he come here himself, instead of sending you?" Dylana asked Trinity.

"Well, your lover boy is about ten miles down the road from here. That was as far as he could get to this place. That's why he asked me to come here and get you." She said.

"Why's that?" Dylana asked her, and then Trinity looked at Jade.

"It's because we have a spell around the house, to keep Vampires away from here." Jade answered.

"Dylana, just so you know, Damien made Niculus promise to leave you alone until he could talk to you," Trinity said.

Dylana told Trinity to take her to see Damien. Dylana followed Trinity to her car, and they both got in. While Trinity was driving, they didn't talk. Once they were out of the woods around Jade's house, Dylana saw Damien sitting by the road. Trinity stopped the car, and Dylana got out and walked over to where he was.

"Hello love, I'm so happy to see you." He said to her, as he looked up at her. He got up, and he walked toward her, and he wrapped his arms around her and kissed her on the lips.

"What happened after I left?" She asked him.

"Niculus tried to follow you, but I attacked him and by the time Christopher got me off him. You were already at Jade's house." He told her.

"So, Trinity said that you make Niculus promise to leave me along. How did you do that?" She asked him.

"After you were at a safe place, Selene made Niculus and me talk about what happen, and I told him you didn't agree or disagree with him, that you just wanted to get back to me. He admitted that he shouldn't have acting like that. He didn't mean to hurt you, he under a lot of pressure as King. Also, Trinity must have misspoke, he didn't agree to leave you alone, but he gave me his word he won't try to hurt you again, or try to threaten you, that is unless you threaten him." Damien told her.

"Why would he think I would threaten him?" She asked Damien.

"Love, if you wanted to threaten him, you could. You're more powerful than his is, and I know that he only threatened you, because he's afraid, and he sees you as a threat." Damien said.

"So, he's afraid my power?" She asked him.

"Yes, so, what happened at your house?" Damien asked her.

"It was weird. I think Niculus possessed my father and told me he was using my parents to keep me busy until he got there. I kind of froze my parents." She told him.

"How did they get unfrozen?" He asked her.

"Jade unfroze them for me. Is there anything else you wanted to tell me?" She asked him.

"Yes, Niculus wanted me to ask you something," he said.

"Okay, what does his highness want?" She said, as she almost laughed.

"I see that Jade has told you a lot. So, the King requests that you summoned your mother. He has something he wants to ask her." Damien.

"Tell him I'll ask Jade about how to do it tomorrow, and he can send Trinity to ask questions for him." She told him.

"I'll tell him, but I know that he wants to ask the questions himself. Either way, Trinity will come over to help you two summon your mother. I must go now. I love you Dylana, I'll see you tomorrow." He said.

"Why do you have to go?" She asked him.

"Niculus is calling me." He said.

"I didn't hear your phone ring." She said.

"We can talk with our minds. I hear him in my head telling me to come back home." Damien told her.

"Bye," he said, and he kissed her on the lips before leaving. She then got back into Trinity's car, and she drove her back to Jade's house. When Dylana got back inside the house she saw that Jade was on the couch asleep, and when Dylana went back to room, she woke up in and went to sleep.

Chapter Sixteen

Summoning

The next morning, Dylana got up, and she went to find Jade to talk to her about seeing Damien yesterday. She took a while to find Jade, but she finally found her outside sitting on a tree stump, looking through a big book. As Jade saw Dylana coming out of the house, she put the book down and she asked, "So, what did your bloodsucking boyfriend have to say to you?"

"Please don't call him that. He just wanted to know what happened after I got out the woods. And I think he wanted to make sure I was all right." Dylana said.

"Oh, is that all?" Jade asked her.

"No, Niculus asked him to ask me to summon my mother. He wants to ask her something and honestly I'd love to talk to her myself." Dylana said.

"I see, so do you need some help with that?" Jade asked her.

"Yes, I could use help, since I don't know how to summon the dead." Dylana said.

"Do you want to summon your mother now?" Jade asked her, and Dylana said sure.

"Okay, I just have to get a few things we need for the spell," Jade said to Dylana, as she headed inside the house. After a few minutes, Jade came back out of the house with a bag full of stuff.

"Come on, we have to find the stop in the woods to do the spell, it has to surrounded by the elements. Could you grab that book that's on the ground for me, we need that to?" Jade told Dylana, and she grabbed the book off the ground she followed Jade into the woods.

"So, what's in the bag?" Dylana asked Jade, as they were walking.

"In the bag I have seven white candles and seven purple candles. We need them to form a circle." Jade told her, as they came to a circle-shaped clearing that had a spring by it.

"This should work nicely, Dylana you can put the book anywhere. I need you to help me with the candles." Jade told her, so Dylana put the book down. She walked over to where Jade was, and she helped Jade put the candles in a circle around the edges of the clearing. As Jade was putting the last candle. They heard someone coming from behind them.

"Who's there?" Jade asked. There was no answer, but they could still hear someone walking around in the woods behind them.

"Come out and show yourself before I attack you." Jade said, as she pulled out two knifes, one from each of her boots. Just as Jade was about to attack whoever was behind us, Trinity came out of the woods.

"Are you really going to hurt me with those knives if yours, little cousin?" Trinity asked as she looked at us with a devilish smile on her face.

"Only if I must, so why are you here Trinity?" Jade said, as she put her knives back away in her boots.

"Oh, Dylana forget to tell you that I was going to help you two summon Debathena. Also, since Niculus can't be here himself, I will ask her the things that Niculus wants to know about," Trinity said.

"Right sorry I did forget to tell you that Jade. So, Trinity what does Niculus want to ask my mother?" Dylana asked Trinity.

"Your mother knows about something that Niculus want to know about," Trinity said.

"Like what?" Dylana asked Trinity.

"Niculus wants to know something that has to do with the treaty." Trinity said.

"Are you talking about the treaty that the witches and the Vampires made with each other?" Jade asked Trinity.

"Yes, my dear little cousin, that treaty." Trinity said, and Jade was getting mad at Trinity.

"Okay, fine but if you will be here. I don't want to hear you say anything until we've summoned Dylana's mother. Okay?" Jade asked Trinity.

"That's fine, but are you forgetting it takes three Witches to summon the dead?" Trinity said to Jade.

"Yes, but Dylana has the Redfire." Jade told Trinity.

"It doesn't matter that Dylana has the Redfire or not; It still takes three to summon the dead. So, that means you will need my help, and like I said, I'm here to help the two of you summon Debathena." Trinity said, and Jade looked even madder when Trinity said that.

"Okay, fine, Trinity, I guess that we have no choice, but to let you help us." As Jade said that, Dylana could hear her teeth grinding.

"Jade," Trinity said.

"What is it now, Trinity?" Jade asked Trinity, with irritation in her voice.

"I just thought I would tell you you're setting up the circle wrong." Trinity said.

"What are you talking about?" Jade asked Trinity, after she said that Dylana wanted to laugh at them so badly, because the two of them sounded like two bickering little kids.

"Well, you forgot the two candles that have to be in the middle of the circle." Trinity said.

"No, I didn't forget that, I just didn't put them in the circle yet." Jade said, and Dylana did not understand what the two of them were talking about with the candles. So, she just stayed out of the conversation, and for about a half an hour, Dylana watched as Jade and Trinity kept on moving the candles one way, and then another way. It was entertaining for her watch them doing this. When the candles were in the proper place, Jade opened the spell book she had Dylana carry out here, and Dylana watched her look in the book until she got to the right page. Dylana couldn't read what the page said, but she thought it looked like Latin, so she asked Jade what it said. Jade told her that in English it says,

Summon a Dead Witch

to the moon we pray

to the ground where we stay

with the wind we sway

to the sun we come from

to fire that ignites all flames

to water that surrounds us all

we pray to the mother

from the earth where we all slumber

to bring back another

Jade also told Dylana that it says that you need three to do this incantation, and Dylana thought so, Trinity was right. Jade also said that we had to say the incantation three times and to think of the Witch we wanted to bring back.

"Okay let's get this over with," Jade said, as she was glaring at Trinity.

"Are you sure we're ready?" Trinity asked Jade.

"Yes, why, what is it now?" Jade asked her.

"I was just making sure, that's all." Trinity said.

"Okay then, let's get this over with. Okay everyone in the circle." Jade said to them. Jade was the first one in the circle, and then Dylana sat in the circle next to Jade, and Trinity sat next to Dylana. They all took hands, and then they chanted to the goddess, the sun, and then to the ground, and as they were chanting the candles started to light themselves one by one. After the third time they said the incantation, a bright light appeared in front of us. The other two looked at this like it was normal to them. Dylana however was staring at the light with her mouth opened wide, and she was drooling. The light slowly started to turn into her mother.

"Well, what took you so long to summon me, my darling?" Her mother looked right at her, as she said that.

Chapter Seventeen

Answers

Dylana didn't know what to say to her mother, when she first saw Debathena appear in front of her. Dylana was in shock that the spell had worked, and that she was looking at her mother again. It amazed Dylana by how her mother looked. Dylana thought Debathena looked like an angel, in a glowing white dress. Jade noticed that Dylana was just staring, so she hit Dylana with her elbow, to get Dylana to say something.

"I didn't know how to summon you, Mother. That's why I didn't do it sooner." Dylana blurted out.

"Dylana, you read none of the books are in my trunk, did you, my darling?" Dylana's mother asked her, and Dylana told her no, not really.

"Oh, well if you did, you would have found a spell I've made up so you could have summoned me by yourself." Dylana's mother told her, and then Debathena said, "Well, I'm just so happy to see you again, my darling."

"I'm so happy to see you too, Mother. I've missed you so much." Dylana told her mother, as she fought back some tears.

"Well, are you going to introduce me to your new friends, who I figure are Witches too, and they are your cousins too, am I right?" Debathena asked Dylana.

"Yes, Mother. This is Jade," Dylana said, as she pointed to Jade, and she said, "And that's Trinity." As she pointed to Trinity.

"Jade, Trinity, it is very nice to meet you girls. I have to ask you girls, who are your mothers?" Debathena asked them, but before they could answer her question, Debathena added, "Wait girls let me guess. Well, Trinity, I can feel from you you've had a lot of pain in your life. But you've overcome a lot, and you're on the right path now, and you will achieve all your life goals. Your mother must be Serena, am I right?"

"Yes, Serena was my mother. She's dead now to." Trinity said, with pain in her eyes.

"I'm so sorry about your mother. When we were kids, we did almost everything together. Did she ever talk to you about me?" Debathena asked her, and Trinity said that she had.

"How and when did your mother die?" Debathena asked her.

"My mother die about three hundred years ago, and someone that the both of us had trusted killed her." As Trinity said this, she had tears in her eyes because it was still painful for Trinity to talk about it.

"I see, well no wonder I didn't know. I don't think I'd talked to her for about that long," Debathena said, as she put a hand on Trinity's shoulder.

"Jade, I feel that you have not found your right path yet, and that you're still a very young Witch. Your mother must be Misty am I, right?" Debathena said to her, and Jade said yes.

"My mother is always telling me that both of you never liked each other, why is that?" Jade asked Debathena.

"That's true, the two of us never really liked each other. The reason for it is a long story, maybe I'll explain that to you girls later, but for now let's get to why the three of you have summoned me." Debathena said to them.

"Well, Mother I have a lot of questions for you." Dylana told her mother.

"I bet you do, so ask away." Debathena said to her, and Dylana didn't know what to ask her mother first, so she just asked the first thing that came to her mind.

"Why didn't you tell me I was a Witch when you were still alive? Why did you take away my memories when Damien told me the truth about being a Witch, and why did you lie to me every time something magical happened?" Dylana asked her.

"Well, I had a feeling that you would ask me those questions first. I was trying to protect you, and I wanted you to have a normal life. I was planning to tell you you were a Witch, when you came of age and got your full powers. Which is when a Witch turns twenty-three, but when I saw my death, I knew that I had to leave you a letter to explain it all to you." Debathena told her?

"Mother, I know that you think you were protecting me, but you left me unprepared for what was out there. If it wasn't for the Redfire, I'd be dead. When Damien told me the truth, why didn't you tell me the truth about everything you were keeping from me?

Another thing if a Witch gets their powers at twenty-three, why do I have my full powers now?" Dylana asked to her mother.

"I can't say how sorry I am for leaving you unprepared, but I know that Damien would keep you safe. Dylana, you got your full powers early because if a Witch's mother dies before they come of age. They get their powers the moment that their mother dies. I wish that I could have told you all of this myself and not in that letter." Debathena told her.

"Oh, but Mother the day before you died, I got the feeling I would lose you." Dylana said, and Debathena told her it was her hidden powers warning her of her mother's death. Debathena also told her that Dylana had a lot of power in her even before she got her full powers.

"Well, that would explain why I got mine early." Trinity said.

"Did your mother tell you what you were before she died?" Debathena asked her, and Trinity said yes, and then Debathena asked Jade and Trinity to take a walk, so that and she and Dylana could talk alone.

"So, Mother, how can the Redfire work by itself, without me doing anything?" Dylana asked her.

"Well, sweetie, the Redfire can work by itself if it has to protect you, and it can sense when you're in trouble. Why? Did something happen?" She asked Dylana.

"Niculus and Trinity were trying to hurt me, and I think the Redfire threw them away from me, and into some trees. When they came back, I put up my hands and then fire came out of them, and I didn't know how that happened." Dylana said to her.

"Dylana, you can channel the elements through the Redfire, and fire is one element that can channel through your body. I think when they came back towards you, you must have been thinking about fire. The Redfire will do whatever you will it to do." Debathena said, and Dylana told her she understood what her mother was saying. Dylana didn't tell her mother about freezing her father in ice, but Dylana had a feeling that her mother already knew about that.

"Mother," Dylana said a little nervously.

"Yes, what is it, darling?" Debathena asked her.

"Can you tell me about Viterlea?" Dylana asked her.

"Okay, sure, where do you want me to begin?" Debathena asked her, and Dylana told her to start at the beginning.

"Okay," Debathena said, and then she cleared her throat, and she said, "Well, in the beginning there were these two gods named Eleanor and William. They were so powerful that the two of them created Viterlea, and they also created the Vampires and the Witches. The Witches seemed to be from the sun itself. I think the Vampires came from a black hole or something. Dylana I'm sorry, but I don't know what the first two Vampires names are. The first Witches names are Dena and Dolo." After she said that, Dylana asked her why she didn't know what the Vampires names were.

"I don't know because my mother never talked about the Vampires." Debathena told her.

"What happened to the first Vampires and Witches?" Dylana asked her.

"They died a long time ago now." She told Dylana.

"How did they die?" Dylana asked her.

"I don't know for sure. The story that my mother told us was that her parents died were poison from a of the Vampire's arrows. To be honest with you, I don't think it was the Vampires that killed them. I think my mother killed them and blamed the Vampires. I don't know what happened to the first Vampires. Maybe you could ask Damien." Debathena told her, and Dylana told her she would.

"Well, back to what I was telling you, I'm sure you know that the King and the Queen of the Witches had two daughters." Her mother said to her. Dylana told her, "Yes, Jane and Lilith."

"Yes, and my sisters, and my brother, and I are Lilith's children." Her mother said.

"Where is your brother? Is he on Earth too?" Dylana asked her.

"No, he still lives on Viterlea, so I haven't seen him in a long time, when I left Viterlea, to come here, and I never went back there." Debathena told her, and Dylana asked her if she missed her brother.

"Yes, I miss him so very much." Her mother said, with tears in her eyes. Dylana was a little surprised that a spirit or angel could cry.

"So, Dylana the first thing you should know about Jane and Lilith is that the two of them never saw eye to eye on anything, and they were always fighting. When they both came of age, it was Jane that got the Redfire. This made Lilith mad, and when Jane fell in love with a Vampire, Lilith came up with a plan to get rid of her sister. Dylana, in my mother's mind it was not acceptable for Jane to marry a Vampire and she wanted to make Jane pay for going with a Vampire, and not her own kind." Debathena told her.

"She sounds evil, for planning to kill her sister." Dylana said a little scared.

"Oh, you don't know the half of the things she's done. Dylana, I really hope you never meet her." She told Dylana, with a serious look on her face.

"After Lilith made her plans, she started a war with the Vampires, just to rid herself of Jane. Jane, unlike Lilith, hated bloodshed like her mother. So, she thought she could get Lilith to stop the fighting, and she went to talk to Lilith to see if they could come up with a compromise. I don't know what they said, but you can always ask Damien that, he was there with his mother, but whatever they said didn't make Lilith happy at all, so she killed Jane." Debathena told her.

"So, that really happened?" Dylana asked her, and her mother told me yes.

"How did Lilith kill her?" Dylana asked her mother.

"I didn't see my mother kill her, but there was a scream, and then I saw Lilith dragging Jane's head outside, and she put her head on a spike in front of Jane's Vampire lover, Dmitry, and their children. She did it in front of my sisters and my brother too." Her mother said.

"Mother, how did you get the Redfire?" Dylana asked her.

"When Lilith killed Jane, the Redfire went to its new owner, which was me," she said.

"Why did the Redfire go to you? Why didn't it go to one of Jane's children?" Dylana asked her.

"The Redfire went to me because it has to go to a person with pure Witch blood. And it had to go to the oldest after Jane and Lilith, because their time to have it was over. It's now your time to have it, because it had to go to someone in the next generation." She said.

"If the Redfire goes to the oldest Witch in the next generation, why didn't it go to Trinity or Jade?" Dylana asked.

"It went to you instead of them, because you're the only one out of the three of you, that is a pure Witch. I sensed that Trinity has Vampire blood in her, and I don't know what Jade is." Debathena told her and Dylana said, "Oh, I didn't know that. So, what does Viterlea look like?"

"It's a wonderful place to see my darling. There are flowers everywhere, and I used to love to run through them with my sisters, and we'd pick flowers and put them in our hair." As Debathena was talking, Dylana could see that she was getting lost in her memories.

"Mother," Dylana said.

"Yes, dear?" she said, and Dylana asked her if she was okay.

"Yes, I'm fine. I was just thinking, with this war, the flowers must all be dead now." She said, and after she said that, Dylana thought she should change the subject.

"Mother, if you knew Damien was a Vampire why did you let me date him?" Dylana asked her.

"I let him date you because he's your soul mate and I couldn't keep away from you even if I wanted to. He made me a promise he would protect you, and that he would never stop protecting you." She told Dylana.

"Well, Mother he's kept his promise. I love him so much and I know that he'll protect me no matter what, even if that meant dying for me." Dylana said.

"I'm glad to hear that, and darling, I know that he loves you more than anything." Debathena told her.

"What should I do about Niculus? He wants me to do something for him." Dylana told her mother.

"Do you know what he wants you to do, Dylana?" She asked her, and Dylana told her she didn't know yet.

"Then my darling, don't say yes or no until you find out what it is. Also, be careful around Niculus." Debathena told her, and she told her mother okay.

"Dylana is there anything else you want to talk about?" Debathena asked.

"Yes, I have a few more questions. Why didn't you want me to tell my father anything?" Dylana asked her.

"I had a feeling that you'd ask me that. There are some things you don't know about your father. He's also from Viterlea, and he's a Witch too. He's not a powerful Witch though, but he can do some magic. When I first met him, we fell in love quickly, and we got married on Viterlea. When we got here, we got separated, and it took years to find each other again. We were still in love and I trusted him so much. After you were born though, I started to get suspicious of him, and one-night Niculus came to our house. It wasn't uncommon for Niculus to stop by back then, when you were little, from time to time. We were friends back then." She told me.

"Wait, Mother, are you telling me I knew Niculus when I was little? Why don't I remember that? And why were you a friend to him?" Dylana asked.

"Yes, you knew him when you were little. You just don't remember because I took those memories away from you. I was friends with him back then because he's one of our cousins and it was nice to have family around. Do you want those memories back? I can give them back to you with one word, but it might change how you feel about him." She said to her, and after Debathena said that, Dylana first thought was, I'm dating my cousin.

"Did I know the rest of them when I was little? If Niculus is my cousin, that means that Damien's my cousin, and that's so freaking weird I'm dating my cousin." Dylana said.

"No, the only one that knew you was Niculus. I know that it must be weird dating your cousin, but you never know who your soul mate will be, and he was waiting a long time for you, just don't think about it. With Beings from Viterlea, it's not uncommon for us to date our cousins, just look at Trinity and Niculus." She said.

"Okay, good point, and how did you know that they were together?" Dylana asked her.

"It was just a feeling, and she smells like him." She said.

190

"Mother, I want my memories back." Dylana said to her.

"You're sure?" She asked her, and Dylana told her yes.

"Okay, close your eyes and think of the person you used to call Nicky." She said, and as she said the name Nicky, Dylana remembered Niculus.

"He's Nicky?" Dylana asked her.

"Yes, are you okay?" She asked her.

"You're right it changes things. I loved him, and I loved it when he came over to babysit me when you and Dad went out for dinner. He would play with me until I fell asleep in his arms, and I remember that he always called me little one. If we had a past like this, why did he try to hurt me?" Dylana asked her.

"I don't know, but I'll say something to him about that, but now back to what I was saying about your father. So, one night, as Niculus was playing with you, your father was acting weird. I questioned him about it, and I found out he was under Niculus's control, and that he was telling Niculus things I didn't want him to know. After I found out what Niculus was doing, I tried to kill him, but Christopher showed up and he told me that Niculus was the Vampire King, and that if I killed him, the Vampires would seek revenge on me, and anyone I care about. As they left, I told Niculus that he just made an enemy. That's why I said to be careful around your father." She said.

"Why didn't you break the control that Niculus had over my dad?" Dylana asked her.

"I was mad at your father, and if he couldn't stop Niculus from controlling him, then he deserved his fate. I left him there and took you and ran," Debathena told her.

"I see, so why was Niculus at our house in Rome? What was with that tiger?" Dylana asked her.

"I see that your memories of that day came back to you too. I knew that those memories would come back to you, and I knew that you'd ask that too. I know that you knew that I was lying to you. He came there to give me a message. That something would happen to you. That's why the tiger went for you." She told Dylana, and she could say, "Oh.".

"Mother, I have one more question. Do you know who killed you?" Dylana asked her.

"Well, Dylana, I don't know who killed me. If I could guess, I'd say it was a Witch that killed me. At the party, I knew was the main target. Whoever killed me wanted me dead." Her mother said, and all Dylana could say was oh again.

"Mother, do you know who wanted you to use the Redfire?" Dylana asked her.

"In the past, my mother has tried to get me to use the Redfire for plans of hers, and I've always told her no. Also, Niculus has tried to do the same thing, and I have always said no to him too. Now you have the Redfire, and you have no children for it to pass to, so you will have to choose a side, the Vampires or the Witches." She told Dylana.

"Can't I just stay out of it all?" Dylana asked her.

"No, my darling, Niculus and Lilith will make you choose a side in the war." She said, and what she said made Dylana worry.

"Is there anything else?" Her mother asked her, and Dylana told her no.

"Okay, why don't we have your friends come back then?" She said, as Jade and Trinity came back.

"How did you guys know that we are finish talking?" Dylana asked them.

"I saw it." Jade said, and Dylana told Jade oh, and she thought to herself, that she keeps forgetting that Jade can see things.

"Jade, you have a powerful gift of seeing, don't you?" Debathena said to Jade, and Jade said yes.

"Do you think you could tell us why you and my mother don't like each other?" Jade asked Debathena.

"Okay," Debathena said, and then she paused for a second, and then she continued talking by saying, "Well, I guess it must do with the fact that Lilith put it in Misty's mind that all Vampires are evil, and that they all must die. I let's say that I was the rebel of the family; I have always believed that Vampires aren't all evil. I also believed that if the Vampires weren't here to stop us, we would have done more horrible things we haven't done yet, and that we were the bad ones. I know that it's not our fault we're like this, if it's anyone's fault it's Lilith's. That means that if the Vampires didn't keep us in our place, the humans would have no hope at all, and most of them would be dead by now. So, I thank the suns they are here to stop us."

"Mother, if that's true, are the Vampires the good guys?" Dylana asked her mother, and she told them they still should be careful around Vampires because they can be just as bad as Witches when they want to be, which I know that you've experienced firsthand. After she said that Dylana thought about Niculus, and that she must be careful around him.

"Is that true, that my mother really thinks like that?" Jade asked Debathena, disbelieving.

"Yes, but like I said, Jade, it's not your mother's fault for thinking like that, and to be honest with you girls, Lilith also messed up her mind to make her believe that, and to make her do some horrible things that were wrong." Debathena said to them.

"Like what, what horrible things has my mother done?" Jade asked.

"I can't tell you, it's too terrible to say out loud." Debathena said, and then Jade asked really, and Debathena told her yes.

"Why didn't Lilith make all of her children like my mother?" Jade asked her.

"Like I said, I was the rebel of the family, and I wouldn't let her get her hands on me. Serena was a lot wiser than our mother, and we left the same day that Lilith killed Jane. Misty had no way to find us. If we'd stayed there, she would have done the same thing to us. Girls, I hope that you never see the things I've seen in my long life. I also hope that this war between Vampires and Witches ends peacefully and not with any more bloodshed. And Jade, I want you to know that your mother was a great person when she was a little girl. If I'd known the things I know now, I would have protected her from Lilith." Debathena said to Jade, as a tear fell from her eye.

"Is there any way I can help her now?" Jade asked her.

"No, it's too late, she's too far gone. The only thing that could help her now is to kill her and let her soul be at peace." Debathena said.

"Are you sure that's the only way?" Jade asked, and Debathena told her yes.

"How do you know that's the only way?" Jade questioned her, and Jade said that with anger in her voice.

"I know that when a Witch dies one of two things happens. If they've had a good life, and they found the right path for themselves, like me, they become angels to watch over their descendants and to help guide them to their right path. If they've had a troubled life like Misty did, who never found her right path in life, but had someone else controlling it. They would go back up to the suns to be reborn, and it would give them the power to overcome what had made them lose their way." Debathena said.

"Okay, but what has she done to deserve to die?" Jade asked, but it wasn't Debathena, who answered Jade, it was Trinity, and she said murder.

"What are you talking about?" Jade asked Trinity.

"Do you remember when I told you that someone, we trusted killed my mother?" Trinity asked her.

"Yes, and your point would be?" Jade asked her.

"Well, it was your mother who we trusted, and I walked in on her as she was killing my mother, and she also gave me this." Trinity said, as she unbuttoned her top and showed them a scar that went from shoulder to shoulder.

"If it weren't for Niculus coming to my house at the right moment, I would have died too." Trinity said.

"Why would she do that?" Jade asked, with tears pooling in her eyes. But Trinity said that she didn't know why.

"Do you know why Misty killed my mother?" Trinity asked Debathena.

"I think Serena had a spell book that Lilith wanted, and that Lilith made Misty kill Serena to get the book." She said to them.

"I can't believe this," Jade said.

"Believe it or not, I'm sure that's what happened." Debathena told her.

197

"You're sure that if she dies, she'll be at peace?" Jade asked, and Debathena told Jade yes.

"If you think your mother should die and be at peace, I'll do it." Trinity said, with a smile on her face.

"Okay, but please don't make her suffer." Jade told Trinity, and as Jade said that, Dylana couldn't believe that Jade would let Trinity kill her mother. Dylana was so shocked, she didn't know what to say. She thought what Jade wanted Trinity to do was wrong.

Chapter Eighteen

Prophecy

"Okay, I'll be right back then." Trinity said, and then she left and Dylana held Jade in her arms, as Jade started to cry. Trinity walked over to Misty's house, but as she got close. She saw that Misty lying on the ground by a tree, with thirteen knife wounds in her back. Trinity walked over to her to see if she was still alive. Even though she knew that Misty was already dead. Trinity closed her eyes, as she was wondering who could have done this and why they cause Misty so much suffering. As left Trinity Misty's house and walked to where Niculus and his brothers were waiting, Trinity started to feel sorry for Misty.

"Hey, boys, there is no spell over Misty's land now, if you want to follow me, you can talk to Debathena yourselves." Trinity said.

"How, what did you do?" Niculus asked her, as he was reading her thoughts.

"I was planning on killing Misty and give her soul peace, but when I got there someone had already killed her horribly. I hated her, but she didn't deserve to die like that." Trinity said, as started to walk away from them, and they started to followed Trinity to where Dylana and Jade were.

Dylana and Jade knew that Misty was dead when Trinity came back through the woods Niculus, Christopher, and Damien behind her. They came over to where Dylana, Jade, and Debathena were, and the three boys looked at Debathena, and Niculus said, "Hello, cousin."

My mother looked at Niculus, Damien, and Christopher, and with a smile on her face she said, "Well, hello Niculus, Damien, Christopher. It's been a while since I've seen the three of you all together."

"Yes, it had been a while, since all three of us have been together, and it's nice to see again Debathena." Niculus smiled at

Debathena, and Damien thought the last time she saw the three of them together was on Viterlea.

"So, Niculus what is it that the three of you want to ask me? I assume that's why you're here, am I right?" Debathena asked Niculus.

"Yes, Debathena, you're right as always and boy do, I have a few questions for you. You still know me so well, my dear cousin." Niculus said, and Dylana thought it was weird the way he was talking to her mother, it sounded like he was flirting with her, and it was a little creepy.

"I think I going to head back home." Jade said, as she was wiping away more tears from her eyes.

"Why so soon? I haven't got to know you yet," Niculus said this, as he was taunting her a little.

"Niculus, leave her alone, you hear me?" Debathena said to him threateningly.

"Fine, I'll leave her alone. For now," Niculus said.

"Goodbye, Jade, take good care of yourself, and I'm sorry." Debathena said to her.

"Bye, Dylana, I'll call you later." Jade said.

"Okay, I'll talk to you later than." Dylana said, as Jade started to walk out of the woods. Then the three guys took seats on the ground, with Trinity and Dylana.

"Niculus, if I answer your questions, do something for me." Debathena told him.

"Name it, anything you want. I'll do it." Niculus told her.

"I want you to release Russ and his new wife from your control, so that my daughter will feel safe staying there. I don't want you to go near them again." Debathena said to him. He agreed.

"I want your word on this, Niculus." She said to him, and Dylana didn't get why she wanted his word. Damien heard Niculus cursing in his head. Damien knew that Niculus hated giving his word, because he couldn't take it back. It was a surprised Damien when Niculus looked Debathena straight in the eyes, and with a serious look on his face said, "You have my word, I will take all my mind spells off them, and I will leave them alone from now on."

"One more thing, I don't want you threatening my daughter ever again, or I will make you pay for it, you understand me, Niculus?" Debathena said threatening him. He looked her in the eyes again, and he told her he wouldn't do it again.

"Dylana, I'm sorry for the other night I tried to hurt you. I was mistaken, and I think something was wrong with me that day. When I thought you were trying to run away from me, something else took over. Later that night, Damien and I talked, and he told me you were just trying to get back over to him right, little one?" Niculus asked her, as he looked in her direction, and in his eyes, she saw the Nicky that she remembered, maybe he was right about something being wrong with him that night. Damien was smiling as Niculus was talking, because he knew that there was someone else in the woods that night. Who was making Niculus react like that, and he thought he'd going to thank whoever was in the woods?

"Yes, you're right. I was just trying to get back to Damien," Dylana told Niculus.

"What is it you want me to do, anyway? You never said." Dylana asked Niculus, wondering what he wanted her to do for him.

"I'll tell you that later, little one." He told her, and she told him he'd better.

"So Debathena, I have heard that you were the last person who had the Vampire and Witch treaty that has a prophecy in it. I'm referring to the prophecy that Eleanor and William made. So, is it true? Do you still have it?" Niculus asked, with a very serious look on his face.

"Yes, that's true, I had it," she answered him.

"What do you mean you had it? Where is it now? What did you do with it?" Niculus asked.

"It's gone, Niculus." She told him.

"What do you mean it's fucking gone? Did you fucking lose it or something?" Niculus screamed this at Debathena with anger, and Damien could feel his anger as if it were his own.

"Niculus, do not scream or curse at me. I mean it's gone, because I burned it about three years ago," she told him calmly.

"You fucking did what to it?" He yelled her, as he went for her throat, but Christopher held him back.

"Why did you burn it?" Christopher asked, calmer than Niculus.

"I burned the treaty, because our grandparents made it to keep us at peace forever, but we're at war again, or we will be soon. So why do we need treaty if we're at war all the time?" She said.

"Why did you burn the prophecy too?" Niculus asked, as Christopher let him go.

"I burned the prophecy so that Lilith couldn't get her hands on that part," Debathena told him.

"What do you mean by that part of it?" Christopher asked her.

"Are you telling me you don't know that the prophecy's in three parts?" She asked them, and they all had dumfounded looks on their faces, but Dylana noticed that Damien's face showed that he knew about the prophecy being in three parts. This made me wonder how he knew about it.

"I'm also guessing you don't know that Lilith has two of the three parts of the prophecy. I couldn't let her get her hands on the part I had, so I burned it. The part I burned was the most important part of the prophecy." She told them.

"Why's that?" Christopher asked her.

"One part that Lilith has talks about herself and Jane. The other part she has talks about the two great Witches. I don't know what those two parts say exactly, though." She said.

"Do you still know what the part you had said?" Niculus asked her, and she said that she still knows what it says.

"So, tell me what it says then." Niculus said, with a lot of impatience in his voice, and a lot of anger, because Debathena seemed to play with him, and Dylana could tell that he didn't like it.

"Okay, Niculus, why don't you calm down and I'll tell you. The prophecy talks about a girl and of you too, Niculus, but it also talks about the two great Witches. It says that when the two great Witches are dead. This girl will be born of Vampire, Witch, and Ancient blood. She will be powerful, and the Redfire cannot hurt her, and it will have little to no effect on her. When the Vampire and Witch war is at its peak, the Witches will bring back one of the great Witches, and with her help, she will bring the Witches closer to victory. This Witch will put the girl of all three blood types into a deep sleep before she gets her full powers. So, she can't do anything to stop what's coming. It also says she won't wake until the Witches have taken control of the Earth." Debathena told him.

"What's an Ancient and is that all it says or is there more to it than that? How does it talk about me?" Niculus asked her, as he was calming down.

"I think Eleanor's is an Ancient, and I think she made this girl with her own blood mixed with Vampire and Witch blood. And that's not all it says, it also says she will be the Vampires' and the Humans' last hope against the Witches, and that she is the one who can kill Lilith. It also says she is the soul mate to the Vampire King

206

Niculus." Debathena told Niculus, and Damien thought about how pissed Lilith will be when, he tells her that this girl will one day kill her.

"Wait, she my soulmate? Is this what you mean about this prophecy having me in it?" Niculus asked.

"Yes, I know that, but that's what it says, this girl will be your soul mate." Debathena said, and he looked like he didn't know what to say after she said that to him. Dylana looked at Trinity and she saw that Trinity had a look of jealousy on her face, because she wasn't Niculus' soul mate, and one day this girl will take him from her.

"Does it mention who the two great Witches are?" Dylana heard Damien ask her mother, and she told him she doesn't know who they are.

"Does it say anything else?" Niculus asked Debathena.

"This part also talks about a ritual that has to do with the girl." She said.

"What kind of ritual?" He asked her.

"It's a ritual that will give this girl her full powers. Niculus, the only way for her to get her full powers is to have her drink a little of your blood, to activate her powers. Your blood will, however, start to kill her, so you must drink from her to the point of death and then have her drink from you to complete the connection between the two of you. Niculus, remember everything I'm telling you, okay." Debathena said to him, and he told her he would.

"There are a few more things after she drinks from you. She will go through seven stages. The first stage is Fire, the second stage is Air, the third stage is Earth, the fourth stage is Water, and the fifth stage is Spirit. When she goes through the first five stages, it will be very painful for her, and she will change her shape. The sixth stage is the power of the dragon, and in this stage, it will give her some power from William himself. The seventh stage is the power of the sun, and in this stage, it will give her some power from Eleanor herself." She told Niculus.

"What does she get in the first five stages?" Niculus asked her, and Debathena told him she'll get the power to turn into the elements. Christopher asked his brothers, "Niculus, Damien do you guys feel that?"

Chapter Nineteen

Lilith

"Yes," Niculus and Damien said to Christopher.

"Okay, it's time for us to go. It's been nice talking to you as always." He said that to Debathena with a smile.

"Damien, what's going on now? Why do we need to go?" Dylana asked him, but Damien wasn't the one who answered her, it was Niculus, and he said, "Lilith's coming, we can feel her presence."

"She is?" Dylana asked Niculus, and he told her yes.

"Dylana, help me blow the candles out." Trinity said to her, but it was too late for that, because Lilith was already facing them. She appeared out of nowhere, and Dylana saw that her skin was bronze, and it also seemed to glow purple. Her hair looked like golden silk, and her eyes were an icy purple.

"What do we have here?" Lilith asked in a cold, high-pitched voice, and she was very scary, Niculus just looked at her and said that it's no concern of hers.

"My daughter, who has summoned you from the dead? And why?" Lilith asked Debathena, completely ignoring Niculus as if he hadn't spoken at all. No one said anything until Lilith asked, "Well?" Dylana just stared into her cold, icy purple eyes as Lilith looked at her, and she said to Lilith in the calmest voice she could muster, "I summoned her. I did it because I wanted to see my mother again."

"Oh, I see, and what's your name?" Lilith asked her, as she took a step toward Dylana.

"Dylana," she said to Lilith. She was shaking now, because as Lilith came closer to her, she looked even scarier. She was still exquisite to look at.

"Well, Dylana, why are they here?" Lilith asked me, as she pointed at the Vampires like they were vermin. Dylana didn't know what to say to her, but she didn't have to say anything, because someone answered for her.

"We're here because I had to ask Debathena something, and Dylana here so kindly summoned her for us." Niculus said to Lilith, and then he added, "And she's on our side, so why don't you just go the fuck away, and leave us alone."

"Niculus, why don't you try to make me leave. If you didn't know, you're on my daughter's land, and I have a right to be here. How did you get through Misty's wards?" Lilith asked him.

"Oh, Lilith, you don't know Misty's dead." Niculus said, with a smile on his face.

"What?" Lilith said, in a high screech, and then she took off onto the woods to Misty's house. Trinity and Dylana sent Debathena back to where she came from. Damien grabbed her hand, and they ran out of the woods. The whole time they were running, Dylana kept thinking, why did we have to leave so fast, after Lilith left? She also kept on trying to ask Damien why we had to run. He didn't answer her though, he just put his finger to his lips, and after that he put his hand over her mouth, to keep her quiet. That pissed her off and as they got back to Jade's house, Damien let her go and he told her to get in Trinity's car. She did as he said as she glared at him.

As Dylana was sitting in the car, she watched as they looked around the house, and she knew that they were checking to see if Lilith left Earth. After they were sure she wasn't there anymore, Damien got into the car with her and Trinity followed and Niculus and Christopher drove another car and we followed them. Dylana noticed that they were driving toward her house. The whole car ride was silent, and when Damien looked back at her, Dylana stared at him with rage. When we got to my house, we all got out of the cars and Dylana didn't say a word to anyone, she stared at them all and when she looked at Damien, all she could feel was anger. She thought about who she could talk to and who would answer her back, instead of telling her to be quiet. She finally turned toward Niculus.

"Nicky, why did we have to leave the woods in a hurry after Lilith left?" Dylana asked him. Damien thought it wasn't a surprise when she asked Niculus and not him, but he shocked that she called him Nicky. Damien was wondering what was up with that, and he saw that Niculus seemed surprised that she was asking him, but Niculus smiled when he heard her called him Nicky.

"Dylana, why did you call him Nicky?" Damien asked her, but she just ignored him, because she didn't want to talk to him right now.

"Damien, it's a long story, short version is that I knew Dylana, when she was little, and Nicky was the name I told her to call me, because when she was little, she couldn't say my full name. I guess that her mother finally gave her memories back to her." Niculus said.

"What?" She heard Damien ask, as he just looked at his brother, confused.

"Damien, just drop it for now." Niculus said, and then he looked back at Dylana.

"Well, Dylana, why don't you ask your boyfriend Damien over there why we had to leave in a hurry?" Niculus asked her, and she now looked at him with anger.

"Because I'm asking you, Nicky, and, to be honest, when I tried to ask him, he put his hand over my mouth." She said to him, and she saw Damien put his head down and he tried to walk over to her. As he got close to her. She looked at him, and he could feel her anger rising and she didn't want to hear anything from him. He got the message, because he backed away from her.

("**Niculus, tell her what she wants to know?**") Damien told Niculus with his mind.

("**I'll only tell her what needs to know and nothing more.**") Niculus replied.

"Well, Dylana, before I tell you anything you really know how to shut my brother up, and I have to say I've never seen a girl do that before. You aren't the same little girl I remember, are you? So, please don't call me Nicky anymore." Niculus said with a chuckle. Damien started to roll his eyes at what Niculus said, but deep down he knew that Niculus was right. And Dylana was good at keeping him quiet, but he could never keep her quiet, but he thought soon things will change.

("**Christopher, Trinity, you can go. I think Damien and handle her.**") Niculus said.

("**Why do you have to say it like that, brother? She just wants you to answer a few questions.**") Damien said.

("**Because I can Damien and she can't hear me. Brother, she has the Redfire and we don't know what side she's on yet, and that makes her a threat to all if us.**") Niculus said. Damien stated to get the feeling that Niculus cared about her, and he thought that could be a problem for him, that is until he tells Dylana that

Niculus had a hand in her mother's death. As Damien and Niculus were talking, Trinity and Christopher left in Trinity's car, and Dylana looked like she had missed something.

"Where are they going?" She asked Niculus, and he told her he told them they could go home.

"When did you say that, I didn't hear you say anything to them?" She asked.

"Dylana, Vampires can communicate with their minds, that's why you didn't hear me say anything to them." He told her.

"That's interesting that you can communicate like that. Damien told me that Vampires could do that." She replied.

"So, you have some questions for me, sweetie?" Niculus asked her, with a smile on his face.

"Well, first things first, don't call me sweetie, and secondly why did we have to get out of the woods so fast, after Lilith left?" Dylana asked him.

"Well, we had to get out of the woods in a hurry because if we'd stayed there, Lilith would have tried to kill us. Another thing is that if we stayed in the woods, we'd risk the chance of Lilith trying to take you with her, and she would have done to you what she did

215

to Misty." Niculus paused for a second, and then he added, "You can believe what I'm trying to tell you or not, but we couldn't let that happen to you." After Niculus said that, Damien almost laughed because he knew that Lilith wouldn't have tried to kill them. He knew that she was waiting for Niculus to break the truce.

"Okay, I see, and why couldn't you let that happen to me?" She questioned him.

"We couldn't let that happen to you because like I said before, I need your help. Also, if that happened to you, I know in my heart it would destroy my brother, and it would send him on a killing spree. If that happened, I fear that I would never see my brother ever again, and I love my little brother. I know that you love him very much, because he even tried threatening me, that if I tried to hurt you, he'd killed me, and trust me, my dear, that's a serious threat coming from him. You should know that Damien would die for you if he had to, and he would also kill for you if he needed to." Niculus said to her, and she looked at him in shock and she thought about how to respond. After a few moments, she looked at Damien and she said, "Damien, I understand now why you wanted me to be quiet, I'm sorry I didn't listen to you."

"It's fine love, I know how curious you are." Damien said, and he walked over to her, and he pulled her into his arms, and he whispered into her ear he loves her, and then Dylana kissed him on

216

the lips. While she was in Damien's arms, she turned to face Niculus and asked him what he wanted her to do. Damien and Dylana watched as Niculus looked up at the sky.

"I know that the Witches are planning something big, and I wanted you to block out the suns on our planet, and then the one here on Earth. So, we could give the Humans a fighting chance at beating the Witches." He said. Dylana looked back at Damien, and she told Niculus that she'd think about it. After that, she started to kiss Damien again. When they stopped kissing, they saw that Niculus had left, and then she asked Damien about the treaty that her mother was talking about.

"I hoped that you wouldn't ask me that." He said.

"Why's that?" She asked him, and he connected to her mind and he said, (**"I'll tell you later, I don't want Niculus to hear us. He doesn't know that I'm a traitor to the Vampires."**)

"Did I hear you in my head? What do you mean you're a..." she asked, but before she could finish saying the last word, Damien said, "I'll tell you everything when we'll alone, okay?"

"Okay, but we will talk about it." She said.

"Yes, we will. So, about the Treaty I know that was made to keep the peace, but it also made for us to learn from each other.

When we were all kids, I mean my brothers and sister and I, we did learn a lot from the Witches. We learned most of the stuff from your mother and Serena and their brother Fantos. We were close to them when we were young." He said to her.

"What happened to the peace then? How did the war start?" She asked him.

"The main thing that happened was the Witch King's disappearance after someone killed his Witch Queen, and then Jane got the power that Lilith wanted. That's the main reason she wanted to kill Jane." He told her. She looked at him with shock on her face.

"Did she kill your mother? My mom told me you were there when it happened." She asked him, and he looked at her, with a smile, but before she could ask him why he was smiling, Niculus came out of the house.

"Yes, I was then, and after Jane was dead, Lilith dragged her head out of the castle, and she put it on a spike." Niculus said.

"What did you guys do after seeing that?" She asked Niculus.

"We did what the rest of our kind did. We killed and killed, until our father killed Lilith's husband." Niculus said, and then he told us he took the spells off her parents and that she could trust them now. Dylana asked him if her parents were okay. He told me they were just fine, and so was her sister. Niculus walked over to they, and he kissed Dylana on the forehead, and then he left. Damien and Dylana went into the house, and her parents were nowhere, so they snuck up to her room.

Chapter Twenty

Past

"So, it's later, care to explain how you're a traitor?" She asked him.

"It's a long story." He said.

"I've got time," she said.

"Well, to start, I go by two names. The Vampires call me Damien, but the Witches call me Michael, and also two different people. I was born, with part of Niculus's soul inside me, and because of that Jane hated me from the first time she laid her eyes on me. She also tried to kill me seven times. My father always stopped her every time, because if I died, Niculus would die too. After a while, I figured that my father was only saving me, to save Niculus." He said.

"So, does that mean you have two souls? Do your brothers and sister know that and do they know that Jane tried to kill you seven times?" She asked him.

"No, my father kept it from them, and only a few know that I have two souls." He told her.

"If you have two souls, who am I really talking to?" Dylana, asked, as she figured out that Damien must not really be Damien.

"You're smart like your mother, and since I can't lie to you. Damien here, he's not in control in the moment. I'm Michael, and honestly, I care about you and love you just like he does. You're safe with me love." He told her.

"You make it sound like I'm dating two people." She said.

"Well love in a way you are." He told her, as he kissed her cheek, and he said, "So, do you want to continue talking about how I'm a traiter?"

"Yes, so how Jane try to kill you?" She asked him.

"Jane tried to kill me with Witch poison, the first six times." He told her.

"What's Witch poison?" She asked him.

"It's a bunch of herbs and some other plants that are mixed with a Witches' blood, and it's very poisonous to Vampires, and if not cured, it can weaken us to where we can't move, and then all a Witch would have to do is drag the vampire into the sun." He told her.

"What did she do the last time?" She asked him.

"The last time Jane tried to kill me, she dragged me into the suns, and then she tried to undo the spell on my ring, but my father stopped her just in time. After that day I tried to stay away from Jane as much as possible, and one day I went to see Lilith and from that day she protected me from Jane." He said.

"Okay, I understand why turned away from your family, but why did you trust Lilith?" She asked him.

"Well, when I went to see Lilith, she told me that Jane wasn't my real mother, and that she was really my mother, and you're probably wondering how that could be. Well you see love, Lilith cast a spell on Jane to steal one of her children. I was the child that

Lilith stole from Jane. So, Jane may have given birth to me, but I'm really Lilith's son." He told her.

"Okay, that's a lot to take in. So, back to the traitor part?" She asked him again.

"I'm a traitor, because I turned my back on the Vampires. And, after everything that happened with Jane trying to kill me. I found out that Lilith wanted the Redfire on her side. So, the two of us planned to get rid of Jane for good. So, the plan was to have the Witches attack the Vampires, and by doing this the truce between the Witches and the Vampires would end. One night the Vampires were talking about what they could do about the Witches. Niculus thought maybe Jane could convince Lilith to stop the fighting, but Jane didn't want to go alone, so I said that I'd go with her. My father and the other Vampires agreed that I could go with her. Jane had no choice but to have me go with her." He said.

"So, you brought Jane to Lilith, and she killed her own sister?" Dylana asked him.

"No, Lilith didn't kill her, like your mother says, that's just what we wanted people to believe. I killed Jane, and then Fantos knocked me to the ground to make it look like he overpowered me. Lilith then dragged Jane's head outside, so that the Vampires could see that she was dead. Lilith then hung Jane's head on a spike, and then the war broke out between us again, and then the Redfire went to your mother. After that, your mother and Selena left for Earth. Dylana, you now know all my darkest secrets, and these are the things I kept from my dragon. Does knowing all of this change how you feel about me?" He told her.

"Michael, I don't know what to say." She said, using his other name.

"Do you want me to go?" He asked her, smiling, because he like her calling him his real name.

"I don't know, are you only here, because of Lilith. Does she have plans for me, just like Niculus?" She asked him.

"Like I said before I can't lie, she wants me to get you on her side, but I can't force you to join her, but that's not the only reason for me being here, I was telling you the true I do love you, and if you join the Vampires. I'm respect that, and I will still try to you to keep you safe, and I will never stop loving you, but we will be on different sides in this upcoming war, because I will never go back to the Vampire's side." He told her.

"Do I really have to choose? Can't it just be you and me against them all?" She asked him.

"I wish, but our world's not like that." He said.

"I see, and you don't have to go. I still the safest when you're with me, and I love that you can't lie to me." She said, and they got into her bed and she fell right asleep in his arms.

Chapter Twenty-One

Fire

Hours Ago, at Christopher's House

When Niculus got home after leaving Dylana and Damien, the only thing he could think about was what Debathena said about the prophecy. He walked into his study and sat down. He got lost in his own thoughts. He thought for him to be with his soul mate, that he'd have to lose Trinity. And if he lost Trinity, it would hurt him so much. He didn't know if he'd be able to let another girl into his heart. He didn't think this girl would understand him how Trinity knew everything about him and how she would do anything for him. As he was thinking about how Trinity would do anything for him, he remembered that he had her check out if what Damien told him was true or not, and if she could find out what Damien was doing before, he met Dylana. Just as he thought this, Trinity walked in and she asked him, "Are you okay, lover? What's on that mind of yours?"

"I was just thinking about what Debathena said about this girl from the prophecy, and I know that prophecies always come true. I just don't want to lose you." He said, as he pulled her toward him.

"Niculus, don't worry. I'm not going anywhere. Besides, we can always fight fate, right?" She asked him, and he paused when she said that, and she noticed that he paused, as he thought she wasn't his soul mate went through his head, and he knew that she listening to his thoughts. Niculus loved Trinity, but he never had the spark of true love with her, and he knew that they never would, because she gave her heart away to someone else a long time ago, but when they first got together, they started off hot and heavy, but lately it felt like they're just friends that like to kill and get down and dirty, when they were in the mood.

"Trinity, you know that I love you, and that I would do anything for you, but I have a feeling that this girl is my one and only soul mate." He said.

"Niculus, how can you say that to me?" She questioned him, with jealousy in her eyes.

"I just never felt a spark between us that's all, and I think you never felt it either. Am I right?" He asked her.

"No, I never did, and I love you too, but I guess that James was my soul mate. So, where do we go from here then love? Are we breaking up?" She asked him, and he wasn't expecting her to be this understanding. He thought if he ever told her this, she'd throw something at his head or stab him with something.

"No, I still want to stay with you until the end of time, just like I told you I would when we got married, my Queen. And I promise you I'll fight fate with you. If you'll still have me?" He said to her, as he pulled her into her lap, and he kissed her, and for the first time, they felt a spark that made a flame that got them feeling a fire that burned all night long,

He woke up the next morning with Trinity cuddling against him, and for a second, he felt lost because when he looked around. he saw that they were lying on the ground in the woods. And then he remembered that Christopher was complaining about how loud they were being. So, Trinity said, why don't we do it in the woods? And before the word woods came out if her mouth, they were already out there. He just wished that they brought an extra pair of clothes out there with them.

"Trinity," he said to her.

"Just a few more minutes, Niculus, I was dreaming about us fucking in the woods." She said, and Niculus laughed.

"What are you laughing at?" She asked him.

"Open your eyes, it's not a dream." He told her, and she opened her eyes, and saw where they were, and she laughed too.

"I guess not. That was some spark. I guess we just had to be honest with each other to get it. So, where are our clothes, or did we come out here naked?" She asked him, and Niculus suddenly looked up and he found their clothes, hanging from the tree above them.

"Trinity, look up they're up in the tree above us." He told her, and then he got their clothes down, and he knew that she was just staring at him the whole time.

"Here are your clothes, we should get dressed and head back. There is something I wanted to talk to you about last night, but that didn't seem to happen." He said, as he handed her clothes to her, which were just a black bra and black jeans that looked like something tore them to shreds, but they still covered most of her.

The only clothes of his he found were his jeans, and they were in the same state as hers. As they were walking back.

"So, what did you want to talk to me about, sexy?" She asked him, as she smacked his ass, and he smiled at her.

"Wow, who knew that us being honest with each other would bring us back to how we were at the beginning of our marriage." He said.

"Maybe we should have tried it sooner, and thanks for that hot, fiery sex last night, love." She said, and he grinned at her.

"Sorry, I'm getting off track. What do you want to talk about?" She asked him.

"Did you find out if Damien was telling the truth or not?" He asked her.

"No, I have found nothing yet, but what he said doesn't add up, and it makes little sense. I mean our people had seen him on Viterlea about seven months ago, but no one knows what he was doing there." She said, as they got back to the house, Christopher was sitting in the kitchen like he was waiting for them.

"Did you two have fun last night?" He asked them.

"Yes, *Dad,* we had fun last night. Now I'm going to shower and change and then head out to see what I can found out Misty's death." She said, joking with Christopher and then she kissed Niculus before she went upstairs.

"Well, she's in a good mood. So, how are things with you, Niculus?" Christopher asked him.

"I'm good, better than I've felt in a long time." Niculus said as he grabbed a bottle of blood and sat down at the table next to his brother.

"So, when do you think Damien will be here?" Christopher asked Niculus.

"I think he'll be here soon." Niculus said, as Trinity came back down and threw Niculus a pair of not ripped pants.

"Thanks, love." He said, and then she kissed him goodbye, and then she left. After she left, Niculus and Christopher sensed that Damien was outside, and Christopher said, "Guess who's here."

"I know, I feel him too. Why is he just standing outside? Does he want an invitation to come in?" Niculus said, and they laughed.

Chapter Twenty-Two

Ceremony

Half an hour ago at Dylana's house

The next morning, Dylana woke to her father opening the door to her room, heard him said, "Dylana, it's time to get up."

"Daddy, do I really have to get up?" She asked.

"Yes, Dylana, you must get up. You must go to school, silly goose." Her father said.

"Okay, I'm getting up." She said to her father as she sat up in bed, and he told Jan was downstairs making breakfast for her. She thought it was odd that her father mentioned nothing about the last few days. When her father left the room, she just went back to lying down on her bed. She closed her eyes as she was wondering where Michael had gone. Maybe he was hiding in her closet. She then felt someone kiss her forehead, and she opened her eyes and saw Michael.

"Where were you, Michael?" She asked him, and he told her he was just outside, and that he didn't think her father would be happy to see him in bed with his daughter.

"You're right. My dad would have been mad if he saw you in bed with me. So, Michael, do I have to go to school? I could just ditch and spend the day with you. I've missed spending time with you. What do you think?" She asked him.

"Well, if you ditch school, your father will be mad at you, and we can hang out when you get back." He said to her, and then he kissed her on the lips, but then he suddenly pulled away, because he felt his fangs extend. He bit the inside of his own lip, to fight the blood lust he was feeling, to stop himself from biting her and draining her dry. The thought of that made him want to do it even more. He would have drained her of all her delicious Witch blood, and he thought she smelled so good to him, and he knew that she would taste even better. She smelled just like lilacs and sunshine to him. Dylana didn't seem to notice why he was pulling away, or that he was biting his bottom lip, or that he was thinking about draining her of her blood. She thought he finished kissing her.

"Fine, you win, Michael. I'll go to school." She said to him, and he told her she should get in the shower and get ready for school.

"Yes, sir," she said, smiling at him.

"I have to go love, but I'll be back later." He told her. She tried to kiss him goodbye, but he told her, "No, love, that's not a good idea, I really need blood, and I don't want to risk attacking you. It's been awhile since I've had blood."

"Okay, I understand, see you later." She said, as she grabbed her robe, put it on, and headed to the bathroom. When she was out of the room, Michael left though the window. After Dylana showered and got dressed, she headed downstairs. Her father was downstairs in the kitchen waiting for her.

"Oh, there you are, sweetie, have a seat and eat up, we don't want you to be late for school." Her father said, and she took a seat and ate. While she was eating, she was thinking of asking her father about him being a Witch, and what he was doing for Niculus, and a few other things were on her mind.

"Hey, daddy, there are a few things I wanted to ask you." She said to him.

"Okay, like what, sweetie?" He asked her.

"Well, I don't really know how to start this conversation with you, but I found out a lot of things in the past month." She said, and then she stopped talking, and sat there thinking if what to say next.

"Dylana, it's okay. I think I know what you're trying to ask me. I know that this will be a long conversation, and I guess you're not going to school today, since we have a lot to talk about. Why don't you finish eating, and then go change your clothes, and we'll take a walk and talk, sound good?" He said. Dylana didn't know how to respond. It shocked her, when he said that, because she thought he would say that he would tell her later. So, she nodded her head and finished eating, and then I changed my clothes and followed him outside.

"So, what question do you have first?" He asked her.

"Did you know that I was coming here before I called you?" She asked him.

"I'm kind of surprised that you didn't ask me if I was a Witch, or if I knew that you were one too. Or if I remembered you turning me and Jan to ice, and to answer your question, yes, I knew that you would come here. Your mother called me a few days before and she told me she knew that something bad would happen to her, and that, most likely, you'd be coming to live with me. I painted your room that day, and I just knew that you'd love the black and red." He answered.

"I kind of found out about you being a Witch from Jade and Damien mentioned it to before, and I'm sorry about the whole freezing you in ice, and, yes, you're right I love the black and red together." She said.

"Is Jade the friend you mentioned that her mother was crazy? It's okay about the ice. The Redfire was protecting you." He said.

"Yes, Jade is the friend with the crazy mother. I've been at her house the last few days." She asked.

"So, the crazy mother was Misty, but Dylana, Misty wasn't always crazy, when she was young, she was a sweet girl. I hate that Lilith made her crazy and turned her into a murder. Why was Jade at your school?" he asked.

"She knew that I was coming to Maine. She was there looking for me. She helped the other night, and we went to her house, because Niculus couldn't get me there. She also helped me summoned Mom, and she answered a lot of my questions. And dad there's something you should know about Misty, she's dead." She told him.

"I'm glad that Jade found you and helped you when I couldn't, and about Misty, I hope that she has a better next life. Before Niculus left late night, he told me, that your mother made he reverse the spells he had over my mind and Jan's, was that truth or did you make him?" He asked her.

"No, Mother did that even though she's dead, I think Niculus is afraid of her." She said.

"He should be, because I know that as a spirit, your mother still has a lot of power." He told her.

"So, how did that guy you knew in Rome sent my stuff here?" She asked him.

"The guy I knew in Rome wasn't really the one who sent your stuff. It was his wife, who's a Witch like us, and she did it by magic." He said to her, as they started to enter the woods, and they headed down the same path that Damien had her take the other day.

"How many Witches are on Earth?" She asked him.

"There aren't that many, Lilith doesn't like her kind on Earth, so there are about a hundred at the most." He said.

"Why's that?" Dylana asked.

"She doesn't like Witches to mix with Humans. Most of the Witches Lilith sent here are to spy on the Humans." He told her.

"I see. So, Dad, where are we walking to?" She asked him.

"We're going to a sacred place in these woods, that your mother created with the Redfire, so we would have a place on Earth to perform a coming of age ceremony. This ceremony usually performed when a young Witch turns twenty-three, but since you got your powers early, we have to this now." He said.

"What does this ceremony do?" She asked him.

"It's basically a blessing over your soul, and it will give you knowledge of everything." After he said that, the path ended and then there were only trees in front of us.

"Dad, did we take a wrong turn?" She asked him.

"No, we didn't take a wrong turn. We have to keep going straight." He said.

"Okay, but what about the trees in front of us?" She asked him.

"We have to walk through them." He said, and she asked him how. He grabbed her hand, and they walked straight at the trees, and they passed right through them.

"Wow, that's so cool!" She said, and then she saw that her mother was on the other side, and she was standing on a stone altar.

"Mom, how are you here? I thought someone had to summon you?" Dylana said, as she stuttered a little, because she felt a little lost. She watched her father walk over to Debathena and she said to him, "Thank you for bringing her, Russ."

"Anything for you, my soul mate," he said, and then Dylana felt lost.

"What's going on?" She asked them. He told her, "Your mother came to me in a dream last night, and she told me everything that was going on, and that I had to bring you here sometime today. I was going to bring you here when you got out of school, but when you started to ask me questions, I figured it would be better if I brought you here this morning. Oh, and I'm sorry I forgot to tell you that your mother would be here for this too. Both parents must be here for this ceremony, even if they're dead. And they're forced to appear for this."

"Okay, I understand that, but what's up with the two of you flirting like that? I thought you guys didn't love each other anymore?" She asked.

"We never stopped loving each other, but with Niculus controlling your father, it pushed down his real feelings, and he couldn't feel anything for me anymore." Debathena said.

"So how does this ceremony work?" She asked them.

"All you have to do is stand right here, in the middle of the altar, while your father and I chant," Debathena said, as she pointed to the white altar. Dylana stepped onto the altar and her father and mother joined hands and made a circle around her. They started to chant in a language that Dylana couldn't understand, but it sounded like they were singing. When they stopped chanting Dylana saw a white light formed around her, and it covered her whole body, and then it went inside her. The White light filled Dylana with warmth, and then she fell to the ground, because it felt like my head was getting overloaded with information, and it was just too much for her, and she passed out.

Chapter Twenty-Three

Damien's Story

A few hours ago

When Michael was heading to Christopher's house, he knew that Niculus and Christopher would be there waiting for him. He had to remind myself not to let Niculus intimidate him.

He arrived at Christopher's house in about seven minutes. Michael could smell Niculus and Christopher inside, waiting for him. Michael stayed outside, thinking up a good story to tell them. He thought maybe he should tell the truth of where Damien was when they couldn't get a hold of him, because Michael had a feeling, they didn't buy what he told them the other day. When he walked inside, his brothers were in the kitchen.

"Come, have a seat at the table with us, brother." Niculus said to him. Instead of following orders, Michael went to the fridge to get some blood. He could feel their eyes on his back. He drank faster than he should have and started to cough up the blood. He heard his brothers laugh at him from behind.

"So, if you're done with your drink, or should I say, coughing up your drink. Brother, I will ask you to have a seat one last time, or I'll make you." Niculus threatened. Michael knew that Niculus's threat was real. He took a seat at the table.

"So, what's up, brothers?" He asked them, and Niculus noticed that Damien sounded a little too cheerful, and he thought something was up with Damien.

"It's not what's up with us. It's what's up with you, brother?" Christopher asked him.

"What do you mean, Christopher?" Michael asked him.

"Why were you on Viterlea seven months ago?" Christopher asked.

"I've told you already," Michael replied.

"Well, brother, I had Trinity checkup on your story, and she told me that some of it doesn't add up. Brother, you tell us you've been on Earth, with Dylana the whole time, but the fact is, I know that's not true. A Vampire saw you on Viterlea about seven months ago, and when I visited Debathena before she died, she told me you and Dylana have only been together for three months. So, do you mind telling us what you were up to before you met Dylana? And why couldn't I get in touch with you? No more lies." Niculus said. Michael knew he had to tell him the truth. It was the only way that he would fool Niculus into thinking he was still on the Vampire's side.

"Shit, I had a feeling that you guys didn't buy what I told you before. I just afraid and I didn't know how to tell you guys the truth." He said.

"What is it, that would make you afraid brother? No more lies just tell us the truth." Niculus said.

"Well, I knew that the prophecy was in three parts. I found the other two parts of the prophecy about seven months ago, and I was on my way to Viterlea to bring them to Marcus, but Lilith and seven of her witches got to me before I had the chance to get to you. She must have known I had them. She kept me in a cage and tortured me until I finally agreed to translate what the parts said, and then she let me go." He told them.

"Are you kidding me, Damien?   If that's what really happened, why did she just let you go? Why didn't she just keep you locked up?" He asked him.

"I don't know why she let me go. Maybe it's because she got what she wanted and didn't need me anymore and if she killed me, she would have killed you, and she would have broken the truce." He said. Niculus stared at him for a few moments. Then he asked, "Do you remember what they said?"

"No, I don't. Before she let me go, she made me forget what I told her," he said.

"Damien, I'll make Lilith pay for what she did to you, but how did she tortured you without me feeling it?" Niculus asked.

"She had me inside a magical cage that disrupted our bond so you couldn't feel what she was doing to me," Michael said, as he was remembered how scared Damien was and how much Damien's fear effected him, and in that moment Michael feared what Lilith would do to him if he ever went against her.

"Is there anything else you have to tell us?" Niculus asked him.

"I don't think so, but I'm still wondering why was Dylana was calling you Nicky? You never told me you knew her." Michael asked him.

"I knew that I had to tell you this sometime. When Dylana was little, and before her mother knew that I put spells on Russ. I got close to Debathena. Back then she trusted me, even though I was using her. I would go over to their house a lot, and I would watch Dylana when they would go out." He said.

"So, you babysit her when she was little?" Michael asked him and started to laugh. Niculus told him to shut up about it, and he told him that Dylana's not like the little girl he remembered.

"What do you mean?" Michael asked him.

"When she was little, she feared everything, but now she seems like she's fearless." Niculus said.

"Hey, before I go, did you find out who killed Misty?" Michael asked.

"No, but Trinity's looking into Misty's death to find out who did it, but I'll say this, it looks like the Witches may have another enemy besides us. Damien, would you stop by later for a family dinner?" Niculus told him.

"Sure," but as Michael that he thought right a family dinner, that sounded like a joke to him. He thought there was no way he would come to dinner with them, and Michael figured that Niculus was trying to get him back there so Trinity to interrogate him. Michael left Christopher's house, and he walked into the woods to meet up with an old friend of his.

Chapter Twenty-Four

Fury

When he was far into the woods, he called his dragon, Fury. Michael closed his eyes and called her name with his mind. Fury came to him in a split second. As he opened his eyes, she was standing right in front of him. She is beautiful. She is fiery red, and her scales glow in the sunlight. As she flies, her scales look like they fire. She knows most of his secrets, or at least the ones he told her about, and when he hears her talk in his mind, it sounds like she's singing to him. He touched her head with his hand.

(**"Hello, Fury, my dear."**) He said to her.

("Why haven't you called me in a while, Damien?") She asked him.

("I know that I haven't called you in a while, it's because I know what you will say to me, and I don't want to hear it Fury.") He told her.

("Well, you will hear it anyway, Damien. What you're doing is stupid, as usual. You will get yourself killed one of these days.") She yelled at him.

("That's only if Niculus finds out what I've done, and what I will do, but I know that he won't find out what I'm up to, or at least not until I want him to know. I doubt that it will get me killed because, if I die, so will Niculus. The worst thing he could do to me is lock me up somewhere. And you know I'm a hard person to lockup, since I can get out of anything, and I can crack any lock.") He told her.

("You'd better hope he doesn't find out, Damien.") She told me.

("He won't find out, so stop all this worrying.") He said, as he patted the scales on her back.

("Now we have that settled, take me to Viterlea.") He said to her, and he climbed onto her back. She took off from the ground though the blue sky above. Michael loves flying through the sky on her back. It always makes him feel free. The only thing he doesn't like about flying was that it was always a short ride when he wanted to go to Viterlea, because of how fast she had to go to make to hole through space to get to our planet. After she soared through the swirling hole in space, Viterlea came into view. As she was about to land on the Vampire side, he told her to land on the Witch side of the planet. because the person he was here to see is Lilith.

When they landed, Michael saw that Lilith wasn't here yet, but he saw Fantos was, waiting for him. Fantos was Lilith's only living child left. When he got off Fury's back, he told her to go and that he'd call her when he was really to leave.

"You're late, Michael," Fantos said as Michael walked over to him.

"I'm sorry, Fantos, Fury, and I had another argument." Michael told him.

"I see, so she thinks you will get yourself killed, or something like that, again?" Fantos said.

"Something like that," Michael replied.

"So, tell me, Michael, are your brothers still buying the stories you have been telling them?" He asked.

"They believed what I told them today, but it was half true. Although Niculus is always going be suspicious of what I tell him and I'm sure that Trinity will be a problem." Michael told him, and Fantos smiled.

"Don't worry about her, as long as you have him fooled for now at least. Just so you know, Lilith's not thrilled with you right now." He said.

"I know. So where is our mother?" I asked him.

"She'll be here soon." He said.

"How soon," Michael asked, as Lilith appeared.

"Hello, mother," Michael said to Lilith as he bowed his head to her.

"Michael, how could you let Trinity kill Misty?" she asked him coldly.

"Who told you it was Trinity?" Michael asked.

"Jade told me that Trinity killed Misty, when I went to Misty's house to see if she was dead. Why Jade lying to me?" Lilith questioned Michael.

"Mother, as much as I would want to blame Trinity for Misty's death. She didn't kill Misty, and Jade probably told you it was Trinity, because Jade asked Trinity to kill her mother, so she'd be free from you. I apologize for her loss mother, and how angry it has made you." He said to her.

"Thank you, for saying that Michael. If it wasn't Trinity, then who did killed Misty?" She asked.

"I don't know who killed her. Trinity said that she would try to find out who killed Misty. Mother, I think whoever did it wanted to make you suffer." He told her.

"I guess that means I have another enemy to worry about. Let me know what Trinity finds out. I will miss my Misty, but at least I have her daughter to take her place." She said.

"Yes, I guess so, and as soon as Trinity knows something, I'll let you know. So, Jade is here on Viterlea then?" He asked her.

"Yes, she is. She has a lot to learn about magic though. Misty didn't teach her the right way at all, but with my help, she'll be powerful one day, but then again, if she is not, then I must get rid of her. Well, now to you, Michael, what news do you have for me?" She asked me.

"Well, Dylana summoned her mother to ask her about how the Witches came to be and to ask her mother about the Redfire." Michael said to Lilith, and she started to smile, a scary smile.

"So, I did see the Redfire around that girl's neck. I had a feeling that Debathena's daughter would get the Redfire, when her mother died, that's why I sent you to her. How are you doing on completing the soul mate connection? Do you think you can get her on our side?" she asked him.

"Sure, that's not a problem. She's in love with me, and I must admit I'm fond of her as well and there's no way I'm going to let her join the Vampires. I'll just have to explain to her who really killed her mother. If that doesn't do it, I could always do a soulmate bond with her." Michael told Lilith. She looked at him, puzzled.

"Who really killed my other daughter?" She asked him.

"Trinity and Niculus are to blame for Debathena's death." He told her.

"Well, I'm not shocked that the two of them are to blame. I hate Niculus and Trinity. I wish that I could kill him, but then I'd lose you too, and I can't lose you, my sweet boy, but at least I can kill her. She will pay for Debathena's death, and when I find out who killed Misty, they'll die too. Also, Michael I want you to do the soulmate bond with her, even if she agrees to join us, so we'll have control over her if she tries to turn against us. So, tell me, what did Niculus want from my daughter in the woods, anyway?" She demanded.

"He wanted to know what the prophecy says." Michael told her.

"Why did he want to know about that? What did my daughter tell him?" She asked him.

"I don't know why he wanted to know about it. He never told me. She told us that the part she had talked about a girl. A girl who will be born with Vampire, Witch, and Ancient blood. She also told us that the girl will be born when the two great Witches are dead." Him told her.

"Well, in the parts you gave to me, didn't one of them say who the two great Witches were?" She asked him.

"Yes, it said that two of your daughters would give birth to the great Witches. One of the great Witches will have the power of the Redfire, so that's Dylana. The other one will be more than a Witch. She's also part Vampire, so that's Trinity." He told Lilith.

"I see. What else did my daughter tell you?" She asked him.

"She also said that this girl will be the soul mate of Niculus, and that she is the only one who can kill you." He, as he backed away a little, because he wasn't sure how she would react to that.

"What? How can this girl kill me? I did a spell to ensure my immortality." She yelled.

"Well, mother that's what she said, this girl is going to kill you, it's her destiny." As he finished talking, he backed away a little more.

"Then, Michael, there's only one solution. I must get rid of this girl when she's a baby or even better before she's even born." She said, with a wicked smile on her angelic face.

"Yes, that's a good plan, but we don't know who this girl will descend form." He said to her.

"If the two great Witches are Dylana and Trinity, like you say, then this girl must descend from one of them, right?" She asked me with curiosity.

"If she is to descend from one of the great Witches, then she will descend from Trinity's line." He told Lilith.

"Why does it have to be from her line?" Lilith shrieked.

"It has to be from her line, because she has a daughter, and Dylana has no children." He said.

"Do you think you can find her daughter and kill her?" She asked him.

"I can find her easily but killing her will be hard. Trinity's daughter has a lot of other children and they'll do anything to protect her." He said.

"If that's the case, just kill all of Trinity's line." She told him.

"Oh, I see, so just kill them all. Okay, and how would I explain that to my brothers and sister, or to Trinity?" He asked her.

"Tell them someone bewitched you to do it." She told him.

"They wouldn't believe that, they're not that stupid, mother." He told her, and she smiles like a shark.

"Oh, yes they will, because I will put a spell on you that will force you to do what I say." She said to him.

"You mean you'll use the Bewitching Spell on me? Mother, I thought that spell was forbidden to use?" He asked as he smiled.

"You're right is it forbidden to use, but not for me, my sweet boy." She said, with the same scary look on her face. She told him to kneel before her. He knew that her doing the spell would help him fool his brother. He did as she said.

"Mother, one more thing, what about Dylana, she will be really worried if she doesn't hear from me?" Michael said to her, and she told him she'll take care, and then she told Fantos to hold Michael in place. He felt Fantos's hands on his shoulders pushing him down and holding him still.

Lilith grabbed his head with her hands, and he could hear her voice in his head saying the Bewitching Spell. She was saying the spell in the old language, of our planet, which most of the Witches and Vampires no longer spoke. As soon as she finished saying the spell, he started to feel his free will slipping away from him. He then felt like nothing, and the only thing he thought about was making his Queen and master happy. She took her hands off him, and then she told him the stand up and to come closer to her, and he did. Then she told him to go to Dylana, and to tell her you had to go somewhere to do something for Niculus, and that you'd back in a week.

"You got that?" She asked him, and he nodded, and then she told him to kill all of Trinity's line.

"When do I start, my queen?" He asked her. Lilith told him to start now. Michael called Fury with his mind, and she landed a little away from them. Michael turned and walked toward her, and got on her back, but she refused to move. So, he got off her back and told her to take him to Earth, or he would make her do it.

("No, Damien, I'm not taking you anywhere with those icy purple eyes. She put you under a spell, and nothing good can come from that.") Fury said to him, and he started to smile at her.

("I'm so sorry that this had to happen, if only you'd listened to me when I told you to take me to Earth.") He said to her, and he felt Damien take control and he tried to stop Michael from attacking Fury, but all he really did was make the spell cause them feel a surge of pain, and even Damien couldn't fight the power of the spell, so he had no choice but to give in. The spell made Damien kick Fury hard in her side. He could hear her inside his head screaming in pain. She started to beg for him to stop. As Michael got control back, he kicked her more.

"I won't stop until you say you'll take me to Earth," he said. The whole time that Michael was hurting Damien's dragon, he was feeling all the pain he was causing her. Hurting his dragon felt like he was hurting Damien too, and Michael could feel his pain, and he felt Damien trying again to fight the spell as hard as he could to stop

Michael from hurting her anymore. Damien was so weak, and he was no match against Lilith's spell.

Fury finally said that she'd take him to Earth. So, he got on her back, and then she took to the sky to go back to Earth, to Dylana. It didn't take that long. When they landed, he climbed off Fury's back; he climbed up a tree was by Dylana's window, and he about the knock on the window when he felt that Russ was in her room with her and he waited for him to leave,

Dylana woke up in her bed, and she saw that Russ was sitting in a chair in her room, and she thought he'd fallen asleep waiting for her to wake up. She sat up in bed. "Dad?" He woke up and opened his eyes, and she saw relief in his eyes.

"Hey, sweetie, how are you feeling?" He asked her.

"I feel okay, I guess. My head's not bothering me anymore, sorry for passing out on you. How long was I out for?" She asked him.

"You were out for three days, and your head's not bothering you because of the Redfire. If you had it on before, you wouldn't have passed out. When some Witches get their full powers early and undergo this ceremony, their minds can't handle it, and they pass out and die. I got back just here in time to put the Redfire around your neck." He said, and she didn't know what to say to him, she was so shocked that she almost died, and that she was out for three days, but somehow, she thanked him.

"Anything sweetie, why don't you go back to sleep and I'll be back to check on you later." He said, and then he left the room. Before she went back to sleep, she was wondering if Damien stopped by or if he called her. So, she checked her phone, but there were no missed calls or messages on it. As she was wondering where he was, she heard a tapping on her window. So, she got up and shut her bedroom door, and then she went to the window, and she smiled when she saw Michael. She opened the window to let him in, and he climbed though.

"Where have you been, Michael?" She asked him.

"I was talking to my brothers, and I had to report to Lilith." He told her.

"You were there all this time?" She asked him.

"Yes, I'm sorry that I've been away for three days. I know that I must have worried you, but I was on Viterlea and time works differently there. Three hours there is three days here, and a day there is like a year on Earth." He told her.

"What did you talk to your brothers about? Also, what did you tell Lilith?" She asked him.

"They wanted to know what I was up to, but I don't think they believe what I told them, and I think Niculus has Trinity spying on me. And I reported to Lilith to tell her want your mother told Niculus. So, what have you been up to?" He said.

"Nothing much, my parents perform this ceremony over my soul, and I passed for three days. I just woke up." She told him, and he pulled her into his arms and said, "I'm so glad you're okay, that ceremony has killed others."

"My dad say it almost did, but he got the Redfire on me just in time." She told him.

"And why didn't you have it in the first place?" He questioned her.

"I don't enjoy showering with it on, and I forgot to put it back on." She explained.

"Hey, Michael, what's up with your eyes?" She asked him when she noticed that his eyes were purple instead of black.

"What are you talking about?" He asked her.

"Why are your eyes purple and not black? Is that a Vampire thing? Can you change them?" She asked him.

"No, I can't change the color of my eyes. Lilith has a spell on me, and it made my eyes purple." He told her.

"What kind of spell?" She asked him.

"I can't say." He said, as he felt a wave of pain from the spell.

"Are you okay, Michael?" She asked him, as he started breathing heavy, and from the look on his face she could see that he was in pain.

"No, Dylana, I'm sorry, but I will be away for about a week." He said to her.

"Why are you going away for a week?" She asked him, and he told her he had to do something for Niculus, and he felt more pain as spell forced him to lie to her, and then he left.

After he left her house, he ran through the woods to find a spring so he could do a spell. After a few minutes of running, he came across a clearing that had one by it. He took a seat on the ground by the water. I started a locator spell to find Trinity's family. He put his hands into the water, and he chanted, "Waters show me

261

whom I seek." The water in front of him started to change and showed him all the people in Trinity's line. There were twenty people in all. He put his hands in the water again and I chanted, "Waters lead me to those I seek."

The waters showed him one location: Amethyst, which was a tiny island in the middle of the Indian Ocean. After discovering where they were, he thought to himself that it would be easy killing them, since all of Trinity's family was in one spot. He put his hands into the water for the final time and chanted, "Waters show me how to get to those I seek." A map appeared in the water. It showed him how to get to Amethyst, and as he was touching the water map appeared in his mind. He got up and started to make his way to Amethyst. Suddenly, Fury crushed through the trees and pushed Michael back down onto the ground with one of her back legs.

("Damien, I was watching you. You don't have to do this. Fight the spell that Lilith has put on you. I know that you don't want to kill Trinity's line.") She said, as she held Michael down to the ground.

("How do you know what I want to do, Fury? You may know a lot of about me, but there are some things that even you don't know. You think you know, but you're wrong. There are things I never told you. I let Lilith put this spell on me, and even if I didn't have this spell on me, I would still do whatever Lilith

told me to do, without questioning her. I hate Trinity, and I love causing pain and tormenting others just for fun. And, Fury, if I ever get the chance, I will kill her.") He said, laughing at her

("What? Why would you do that, Damien, are you that stupid or are you just crazy? Why are you're on Lilith's side in the first place? I mean, she killed your mother. Why are you betraying your family for her? What is she to you? And I don't get why you would want to hurt Trinity like this. What did she ever do to you?") She asked.

("Do you really want to know the truth, because I really don't think you'll be able to handle what I have to say to you?") He said, threatening her, and he could feel that she was afraid of him. But she must not have been as scared of him as he thought, because she started to push down on him harder.

("Tell me what you're hiding. What things have you not told me, Damien?") Fury asked him.

("Okay, Fury, I'll tell you. First, I'm not Damien, my name's Michael. As for your first question, why I'm doing this, well, I'm not stupid, and I'm not crazy. I'm on Lilith's side because she's my real mother.") He said, and she interrupted by saying that what he was telling her was not true.

("It is true, Fury, Lilith's my real mother, and she didn't kill Jane, we just wanted everyone to think she killed Jane. I killed Jane. And as for my brothers and sister, they're not my family. They're Damien's family, and if I could, I'd kill them all in a heartbeat. I'm fooling them to get information for Lilith. As for Trinity, I want to hurt and kill her, because that's the only way I hurt Niculus. And that lost will destroy him.") Michael said, with a wicked smile.

("That can't be true. The spell must make you say these things. I will take you to Niculus, and tell him what you just said, and maybe he can help get you back to normal.") She said.

("I don't think so, Fury. There's something you should know, this spell I'm under isn't making me do anything now, this is all me. So, Fury, tell me, do you like the real me?") He asked her.

("No, I don't like this part of you at all, and if this is who you really are, I will stop you, from hurting anyone else.") As she said that, she backed up and then she charged at him, and she knocked him backwards, and then she was on top of him again, and she pushed down on him with her leg. He smiled at her as he grabbed her leg with his hands, and then he threw her off him. She went crashing into the trees. It didn't take her long to recover she got back up and charged at Michael again. Just as she was about to swing her tail at him, he made his sword appear, and he cut off her tail. As she wailed in pain, Michael went up to her.

("You will not stop me from doing anything, Fury, and it'll thrilled me to get rid of you.") He swung his sword at her and killed her, as he took her head clean off. He made his sword disappear, and he left her right there on the ground, and watched as she bled out all over the ground, staining it with her black blood. Since he had just killed Fury, Michael knew that he'd have to make to Amethyst on foot. He started to run through the woods in the direction he had to go. He cast a spell to make me run faster, and he was going so fast he could run on water. The trip only took him about three days.

Chapter Twenty-Five

Amethyst

When Michael got to Amethyst, he quickly checked the place out first before he killed Trinity's line. He saw that there were only seventeen people in the whole village. He sensed that only one of them had any real powers, so he saved her for last. He knew that Trinity would feel each kill. So, he knew that he'd have to work quick to kill them all, before she figures out what he's doing to her family, and before she tries to stop him.

Michael waited out of sight for the moon to rise before going near any of the houses that Trinity's family lived in. He walked up to the first house and sensed that there were only five people inside, and that all of them were sleeping. He made his sword appear again in his hand, and he quietly opened the door, and went to where they were sleeping, and swung his sword at them, slaughtering four in their beds. They didn't even scream or fight back. It happened so fast; they didn't have time to wake up, and now they never will again. He heard a girl screaming from the corner of the room. Michael looked out the window and saw that all the lights were on in the other houses now.

"You won't get away with this, murderous bastard." A little girl said, as he walked closer to her.

"You want to bet?" Michael smiled as he walked closer to her, and she screamed, and he cut her head off. Her head fell to the floor before her body hit the floor. As he was heading to the door to kill the rest of Trinity's family, a man stepped right in front of him, and he trembled with fear, when he saw the dead girl's body on the floor inside the house.

"Why are you doing this, Witch? How are you able to be here? No Witch can be here?" The man said to Michael, as the man was stuttering a little.

"Well, I'm not a Witch. I'm a Vampire." Michael said, to muck him. He looked shocked, and he asked Michael why he was killing his family. Michael told him that his mother told me to. After

Michael said that, he cut the man completely in two. As Michael walked outside of the house. He stepped over the dead man's body. There were three more men outside waiting for him to come out. They had swords, but Michael could tell that they were not as skilled as he was with a blade.

One of them told Michael to drop his sword and surrender, and Michael just laughed at him. Michael didn't drop his sword. Instead, he moved closer to them, and they backed away from him, but they stayed ready to fight. Michael got bored with the cat and mouse, so he quickly moved behind them, and he killed all three with one swing of his sword. He smiled as he did that, and thought seven more to go, and then he'll get to kill the one who has power.

He took two more days to track down the other seven of them because they were hiding in the woods, but they were the easiest to kill. And now there was just the one he sensed when he first got here, the one who has real power. He took three more days to find out where she was staying. He had to focus his magic to find her house, because it was cloaked with magic. It was in the woods little away from the other houses.

When he walked in, she was sitting in a chair, waiting for him, because she knew that he would come there to try killing her. She looked at him closely as he walked up to her. As he got close to her though, he could hear two heartbeats, and instantly he knew that she was the one who would have the girl, from the prophecy. He had to kill her, so she didn't kill Lilith.

"Hello, Damien, you killed my family, didn't you?" She asked him.

"Yes, I killed them all, and I will kill you too, and your child." He said threatening her, as he moved closer to her with his sword. She put up her hand, and Michael went flying into a wall.

"Well, you will be a challenge. This will be fun. I love challenges." He said, and every time he got close to her, and swung his sword at her, it would just miss her by an inch. Michael could tell someone well trained her, and that she really had some of Niculus's blood running in her veins, because no Witch could move that fast. Things were looking up though, because Michael finally got her cornered, and she had no way to get away from him.

"Why are you doing this, Damien?" She asked me.

"To prevent the girl, you're carrying from being born, so she can't grow up to kill Lilith. Plus, I like to cause Niculus pain by making your mother suffer. I will enjoy killing you, and your baby." He told her, and he heard a faint "don't," as he started to cut her with his sword, but he didn't know who said it. He threw that thought out of his head, as he wondered if Trinity was feeling every inch of her daughter's pain.

I cut Trinity's daughter thirteen times with my sword. He could smell her blood and her daughter's blood. The smell of their blood in the air was so intoxicating that he felt his fangs extend, and just as he was about to bite into her bloody throat, and deliver the killing blow, someone else appeared, and slammed Michael into a wall. He looked around to see who attacked him. It was his grandfather, Dolo. As he was about to kill him too, Michael felt like someone was calling me. He tried to fight it, but the people who were doing the spell were too strong for him to fight. He closed his eyes as he felt his body being pulled through a vortex.

Chapter Twenty-Six

Missing

Seven days ago

Damien didn't show up for dinner. It wasn't a shock to Niculus, but then again, he felt like there was something wrong with Damien. Niculus was also having trouble getting ahold of him. Damien wasn't answering his phone or answering Niculus when he called to Damien with his mind. Niculus told Selene and Christopher about this, and the two of them thought Niculus was right, because they couldn't contact him either, or that meant that something was wrong. Niculus wanted to go look for him, because he had a feeling like these seven months, when he couldn't find him, and it turned out that Lilith's had him. Christopher told him to relax, and to wait for Trinity to get home and get her advice so that Niculus does nothing stupid. So, they sat there at the kitchen table, not talking as they were waiting for Trinity to get home.

Trinity got home at about eleven o'clock Saturday night, because she spent three days at Misty's house checking to see if there were clues to help her figure out who kill Misty. She didn't find much, and whoever killed Misty knew how to cover their tracks. She was disappointed that she couldn't find out anything, but she would not give up. She walked into Christopher's house, and as she entered the kitchen, she saw Niculus, Selene, and Christopher sitting at the kitchen table waiting for her. They all had anxious looks on their faces, and it made her wonder what she'd missed. she walked over to Niculus and sat down on his lap.

"Niculus, what's wrong, love? Why do the three of you look so worried?" She asked him.

"We can't get ahold of Damien. He's not answering his cell phone, and he's not answering me telepathically either. I know that you must think maybe he's just ignoring me. But he said that he'd be here for dinner three night ago, and he never showed up. I just have a feeling that something happened to him and so do Selene and Christopher." He sounded concerned for his little brother.

"Don't you think maybe he's just with Dylana, and to be honest Niculus this isn't the first time you couldn't get ahold of him," she said. and then Christopher put his hand on Niculus shoulder.

"She's got a point there, Niculus. Maybe he's just mad at us for questioning him a few days ago." Christopher said.

"Maybe you're right, and I'm overreacting. I just can't help thinking about what he told us," Niculus said.

"What did he tell you?" Trinity asked Niculus, and he said, "Damien told us that Lilith had he as a captive, and that she was torturing him for information, about two parts of the prophecy that him had. He said she attacked him when he was bringing them to me."

"When was that?" Trinity asked.

"Seven months ago, around the time we couldn't get ahold of him before." Christopher said.

"Niculus, do you think Lilith captured him again to find out what Debathena told us?" she asked.

"Yes, but I don't know for sure. I just don't want to lose him." Niculus said, as he looked at Trinity, and she took his hand in hers.

"So how long before look for Damien?" Selene asked Trinity, and Niculus looked at her, as she asked.

"I say give him a week to come back he'll need blood, eventually." Trinity said, and Niculus agreed. Selene said that Trinity had a point.

"So, are we going to have dinner then?" Christopher asked us. Selene said yes, as she got up to get us all a bottle of blood out of the fridge. Niculus put a plate of vegetarian casserole on front of us. We ate our food in silence, but Trinity noticed that Niculus seemed to play with his bottle of blood, instead of drinking it, she was happy that he at least ate his food. As Niculus continued to play with his blood, Trinity started to remember the last time that Niculus couldn't get ahold of Damien, and Niculus went out of his mind with worry, he stopped drinking blood like he should, and Niculus attacked Christopher and he almost killed him. The only way she could get him to stop was to chain him up, and she had to keep him like that until they could feed him enough blood to get him thinking straight. As they finished their meal, Selene went to work at one of the nightclubs at Niculus owed. Christopher went to bed. Niculus asked Trinity if she found out who killed Misty.

"I couldn't find out anything. There wasn't even a magical trail I could find." She said to him.

"Do you think this person is a threat to us?" he asked her.

"I think they are a threat to us, just like the Witches. I don't know then they'll attack us, but when they do, we won't see it coming," Trinity said.

"That's not good, but right now we have to focus on the Witches. This other threat will have to wait, but we'll be ready for their attack." He said.

"Niculus, if Lilith held him captive and tortured him, why weren't you hurt by him being tortured?" She asked, and he told her, "He said that she did a spell, so I couldn't feel him being tortured. I think there's still something he's not telling us."

"Do you want me to talk to him, when we find him? You know that no one can lie to me." She said, and he told me yes.

"Are you going to stay here tonight in your study, or are you going to go home with me?" Trinity asked him.

"I will stay here. Can you stay here with me?" He said.

"Sure," she said, as he picked her up into his arms, and carried her to his study he had in Christopher's house. He sat her on a couch, and she watched him as he walked over to his desk to look over his plans for the eclipse, but there wasn't much that he had to do though, because the plan was simple.

"Niculus," she said, and he turned around to look at her.

"Yes, lover, what is it?" He asked.

"I saw that you were playing with your bottle of blood tonight, and I was just wondering, when you drank blood last? I don't want what happened the last time you weren't drinking blood to happen again." She said to him with concern.

"Relax, lover, it's only been a few days." He said.

"Niculus, what will happen when a few days turns into a week or a month? We have a battle coming up soon, and you need to be strong. If you don't want to drink the bottled blood, that's from Viterlea, then drink from me, to put my mind at ease. My blood should put your mind at ease love." She said, as she walked over to him and sat on his lap.

"No, Trinity, if I drink from you, then you'll be weak." He said, making her mad.

"Niculus, I don't care if I'm weak, at least you'll be strong." She told him.

"I'm not going win this fight, am I?" He asked me, and she told him no.

"Okay then, lover." He said to her, and he extended his fangs and flashed her a smile, and then she felt his sharp fangs go into the right side of my neck. As he was still drinking from her, he picked her up and he put her back on the couch. And he laid on top of her, and he was full. He pulled his fangs out of her neck. And he thought she was right about her blood putting his mind at ease, and he fell asleep on top of her. As Trinity was sleeping, she hoped that Damien would come back soon, so she could question him about what he was up to. She thought Damien may able to lie his brother, and not have the truth come out, but Trinity knew that she could get him to tell her everything he's lying about.

Chapter Twenty-Seven

One Week Later

The whole week that Damien was missing, it felt like it went by fast. Trinity had a feeling something bad was happening, but she wasn't sure what it was. And the pass few days she would get this painful sorrow feeling though my whole body, but Trinity wasn't sure what this feeling was. When Trinity got home early Saturday morning, she had the worst feeling she'd had all this week. Trinity still had this feeling when she climbed into her bed, and just as the pain was going away, and she was about to fall asleep, she heard a cell phone ringing. She grabbed her phone to discover that it wasn't hers that was ringing at all; It was a phone underneath her bed. Trinity answered it.

"Hello?" She said to whoever was calling.

"Fuck, now you answer your phone, where have you been, and why didn't you answer your phone before? I've been so worried about you all this week! Do I have to keep yelling at you? Answer me already!" As Trinity listened to Dylana yell into her ear. She thought, Niculus was right something happened to Damien, that would explain why Dylana was so mad.

"Dylana, please stop yelling," Trinity said as calmly as she could.

"Who's this, and I'm sorry for yelling at you?" Dylana asked me, in a calmer voice. Trinity was glad, because if she had yelled at her one more time, Trinity would have yelled back at her.

"It's Trinity," she told her.

"Trinity, I didn't know that it was you that would answer Damien's phone. I'm sorry again for yelling at you. I thought you were Damien. I've been calling his phone every day this week, and I've been so worried about him. Can you put him on the phone for me, please?" Dylana asked her, as she remembered to said Damien and not Michael, because she Trinity to answer her about who she was talking about.

"I'm sorry to tell you this, Dylana, but he's not here." Trinity told her, and she heard Dylana clear her throat.

"Why do you have his phone, if he's not there?" She asked Trinity.

"I guess that he must have left it here, last time he was here." Trinity told her.

"Why would he do that? He goes nowhere without his phone?" Dylana asked.

"Maybe he just left it somewhere to keep people from contacting him." Trinity said to her, and she thought if this is the case it would explain why Niculus hasn't been able to contact him, and this is the first day this week that Trinity's been at home.

"Why wouldn't he want people contacting him?" Dylana asked, and Trinity told her she thinks maybe he's in trouble. Or maybe something bad happened to him.

"Like what?" Dylana asked her.

"Like maybe Lilith did something to him." Trinity told her, and then stopped talking for a second, and she asked, "Dylana, when was the last time you talked to Damien on the phone, or saw him?"

"He came to my house a week ago. He told me he'd going for a week, and that he said that he had something he had to do." Dylana stopped talking for a second, as she was thinking about telling Trinity that Michael told her that Lilith put a spell on him, but she decided against it and said, "He didn't seem like himself. I think there was something else that he wanted to tell me, but it was like he couldn't. There's one more thing I noticed: his eyes were purple." As Trinity heard that his eyes were purple, she knew that he was in trouble, and that Lilith was the one behind it.

"I'm sad that said this, but if his eyes were purple, it means that he's in trouble and that Lilith got to him somehow. I think Lilith must have put a spell on him, to put him under her power, and that would explain the purple eyes." Trinity told her.

"Like the one that Niculus had on my father and Jan?" Dylana asked.

"Kind of like that one, but no, the spells that Lilith uses are powerful, and deadly." Trinity explained to Dylana, and she was silent for a moment.

"So, what can we do to find him?" Dylana asked.

"We will need a spell, and I think it's in of your mother's books, but I don't know which one it's in. It's been a while since I've seen the spell." Trinity told her.

"Do you know the name of the spell?" Dylana asked, and Trinity told her she doesn't remember.

"Do you remember what the spell was about? Anything that could narrow the search down a little?" Dylana asked.

"Yes, I think it has something to do with teleporting someone from one place to another, or something," Trinity answered her.

"Okay, I'll look for the spell. I'll call you if I find anything." Dylana told her.

"Dylana, you don't have to call me back. I will come over to your house so I can help you look for it." Trinity told her, and she replied with okay.

"See you in a little while then," Trinity said to her, and then they hung up their phones.

Trinity got dressed quickly and almost ran outside to get in her black car. As she was getting in her car, she pulled out her cell phone and tried calling Niculus, but he didn't answer his cell. So, she left him a message saying he was right, and that his brother was missing, and that Lilith's got something to do with it. She also told him she was heading to Dylana's house to help Dylana look for a spell to bring Damien back home.

Trinity drove to Dylana's house in about ten minutes. When she got there, she was glad that Dylana seemed to be the only one that was home. She got out of her car, walked to the door, and knocked on the door. Dylana didn't answer, so Trinity knocked again, but a little louder this time. After that, she heard Dylana coming down the stairs, and she opened the door.

"Hey, Trinity, come on in." Dylana said.

"How's the search going for that spell?" Trinity asked her, hoping for good news.

"No luck so far, I've been through about three of the books, and some spells in the books are in Greek or Latin and there are some books that have some symbols, and I can't read any of it, so I've been using my computer to translate most of the writing, but the ones are in symbols have no translation I can find." She said.

"Dylana, lead the way to the books, so I can help you, and I can help you read the spells you can't translate." Trinity told her.

"Trinity, do you know why the books are in four different languages?" Dylana asked before they headed upstairs.

"The symbols language is the oldest, and the first language every spoken or written on Viterlea, and that Eleanor and William created the language for the Vampires and Witches, so we could communicate with each other." Trinity said.

"Who were Eleanor and William again?" Dylana asked, and Trinity told her they created Viterlea, and they created the first two Vampires and the first two Witches.

"That's cool, are they still around?" She asked.

"I don't know where they are now, or if they're still alive. The legends say they just seemed to disappear. The language that Eleanor and William created is 'Way' and in English it means Spirit." Trinity said, and then she explained that as we learned to travel to Earth, we learned Greek, Latin, and English, and now on Viterlea, we use those three languages to communicate. After that, Dylana turned away from Trinity, as she led the way up the stairs and into her room. Trinity walked into the room behind her, and Trinity saw books all over the floor.

"Wow, your mother sure did have a lot of books." Trinity said.

"I know. Do you think we'll be able to find the right spell?" Dylana asked.

"Well, what ones did you go through already?" Trinity asked her, and Dylana told her that the ones she went through already were the ones on her desk. Trinity walked over to the desk and looked through them one more time to double check, as Dylana started to go through more of the other books. Trinity discovered that the books were on Dylana's desk were about plants and herbs. Trinity told Dylana that she was right and that they were useless to them right now. The girls must have looked through thirteen more books each, when Trinity noticed that Dylana was looking at her.

"Trinity, how did you and Niculus meet?" She asked, and Trinity looked up from the book she was reading.

"Well, that's a long and short story depending on how you look at it, but I guess we have some time. I was living in London with my mother, and the year was 1727." When Trinity said the year, Dylana's eyes went wide.

"Yes, Dylana, I'm that old, but to Niculus I'm only a child." Trinity said.

"I wonder what Damien must think of me then." Dylana said, and Trinity started to smile and told Dylana that's an easy question, you're a baby. they both laughed at that.

"So, I was living in London, and I was living with my mother. Niculus was always coming to our house to see us, and that's how we got to know each other. Back then he was always looking out for me, like a big brother I didn't have, or wanted." Trinity said to her.

"So, was that the start of your relationship with him?" Dylana asked.

"No, it wasn't. Before I was with Niculus like we are now, I was with this guy named James." Trinity told her.

"So, who's James?" She asked, with a smile.

"James was the first love of my life. We got together when I was thirteen, and we married when I turned seventeen." Trinity told her, and then she asked what James was like.

"James was the nicest and the most honest man I've ever known. He worked as a sailor, and he loved the sea just as much as he loved me. He always had a tan, and he had tattoos all over his body. And what a body that man had, and I loved his long black hair." Suddenly Trinity stopped talking about him, because talking

286

about James was making her tear up. As she started to cry, she had loved him so much, and she had lost him so tragically. Dylana looked at Trinity with concern, and she put a hand on her shoulder.

"Did something bad happen to James?" She asked.

"Yes, James die at sea. Some pirates attacked the ship he was on." Trinity told her, and Dylana told her she was sorry to hear that.

"Thanks, I thought I was over his death." Trinity wiped her tears and said, "I guess it still gets to me when I talk about him, but at least one good thing came out of our love."

"What was that?" Dylana asked.

"Well, when he died, I was already seven months pregnant. I moved back in with my mother, Misty was living there too, and my mother and I got close to her." Trinity said, starting to shake with anger, "After about three weeks of Misty living with us, I went out for something one night, I don't remember what it was now. But when I got home that night, I walked into the house, and I watched as Misty took a knife out of my mother's stomach. And then she looked at me, and then she started to come at me with the knife. I was so scared that she would kill me and my unborn baby I couldn't move. I just froze as she came toward me with the knife. She took the knife in her hand, and she cut me with it from one shoulder blade to the other. I then fell backwards, but I didn't hit the floor instead I fell against Niculus. He caught me as I was falling, I didn't know where he came from though, but at that moment I was just glad he was there, and he scared Misty out of the house. I watched him cut himself and he told me to drink from him, and as I was drinking his blood, I started to go into labor. I gave birth to my baby girl right there on the floor." As Trinity said that, she wondered what she was up to these days. Trinity started to wonder if she did the right thing by giving her daughter to a friend of hers to raise. Trinity knew that couldn't raise her, with her being a new Vampire. Trinity didn't want to risk hurting her. Dylana then took Trinity's hand as if she could tell what Trinity was thinking about.

"So, where's your daughter now?" Dylana asked.

"I don't know where she is. I gave her to a friend of mine to raise her. I only hope she's safe, wherever she is." Trinity told Dylana.

"What's your daughter's name?" Dylana asked.

"I named my daughter, Lily, after my favorite flower on Earth," Trinity said.

"And from that night, Niculus and I have been together, and I think the two of us will be together until one of us dies." Trinity told her.

"I think that's beautiful and tragic how the two of you got together." Dylana said.

"Thanks, Dylana, so how did you and Damien meet?" Trinity asked her.

"Well, when I was living in New York City, I was on my way home one day. I took a wrong turn or something, and some guys from my new school followed me and they attacked me. Damien saved me, and he scared them off. We've been together ever since, and if I had to move, he would always follow me to wherever I was moving to." Dylana said and Trinity thought to herself, so Damien can be sweet, if the right girl to bring it out of him.

"That's sounds nice. He must really care about you, so why don't we get back to looking for the spell, so we can get lover boy back to you?" Trinity told her. They kept on looking through more of the books until there were only two books left to go through. Trinity looked through a book as Dylana looked through the other one. The book that was Trinity looking in was the wrong book to find the teleport spell but had the forbidden spells in it. And it says how to reverse them. Dylana suddenly looked up from the book she was looking at.

"Is this the spell?" She asked, and Trinity took the book from her and smiled, and Trinity told her that this was the spell they needed. Dylana asked what it says in English, because it was in Greek, and Trinity told her it translates into Teleport a lost love.

Chapter Twenty-Eight

Spell

Once they found the spell, Trinity cell phone rang loudly in her pocket. Trinity answered the phone right away because she knew that it had to be Niculus calling, and he asked her, "Trinity, I just got your message. So, I was right, wasn't I? He is missing, and no one knows where he is?" After he said that, Trinity didn't want to answer him back because she knew that he was right.

"Trinity, when will you learn that I'm always right, when I can't get ahold of my brother that something is wrong?" Niculus said to her, as she rolled her eyes.

"I don't know, lover, maybe never." Trinity said to him, as she was messing with him a little, and she thought Niculus wasn't always right, he can't even tell when Damien's lying to him.

"You're so stubborn, lover." He said to her, with a little chuckle.

"Yes, I am, that's why you love me." As Trinity said this, she saw that Dylana had a lost and confused look on her face. Trinity told Niculus to give her a second, and she told Dylana that Niculus bragged that he was right about Damien missing. Dylana told Trinity to fill him in about what she said earlier, and that we found the spell we were looking for. After that, Dylana got up and left the room to get some water from the kitchen.

"So, what are you at Dylana's house for, lover?" He asked, and she didn't answer him.

"I mean if he's not there, and he's missing? Why didn't you come here and wake me up, instead of leaving me a message on my cell phone?" He asked.

"I wanted to find out if he told her anything before, he disappeared. She told me he told her he would be away for a week, and that he said that he had to do something." Trinity told Niculus. After she said that Niculus ran as fast as he could to Dylana's house.

Just as he would go through the front door, something stopped him and then he banged on a force field that was blocking his way. Trinity heard someone banging on the door downstairs.

"Niculus are you here?" Trinity asked him, but she already knew that answer because she could feel him.

"Yes lover, but I can't get in." He told her. Trinity told him she was coming to the door and hung up the phone. As she made her way down the stairs, she started to smell blood in the kitchen. Trinity walked in there, and she saw Dylana on the floor, and there was a lot of blood on the floor. She rushed over to her and put her hand on the cut on Dylana's head, and she started to chant a healing spell. She had to say this spell three times before the wound on her head closed, and she waved her hand and made the blood on the disappear. It relived Trinity when Dylana opened her eyes, and asked, "Dylana are you okay? What happened to you? How did you fall?"

"I was on my way back upstairs to my room, when I heard someone smash into the door loudly. It must have scared me so much that I dropped the glass of water on the floor, and I must have slipped on a piece of glass." She said to Trinity, a little dizzy from the fall still.

"Oh, sorry about that it's just Niculus. He banged into the door, because your house wouldn't let him inside." Trinity told her.

"I guess that's why my father was walking around the house as he was chanting something before, he left." She said.

"Yes, I think he was probably doing a protection spell to keep Niculus out." Trinity said.

"So, how's he going to get in then?" Dylana asked.

"He doesn't have to come in. We have what we need and now we can all go back to Christopher's house, and on the way there I can fill Niculus in with what we will do to get Damien back. Dylana, could you get those two last books we went through?" Trinity told her.

"Two, but I thought we only needed one book." Dylana said.

"No, we need both. The spell will help us find him, but we need the other book to tell us how to take the spell off him." Trinity told her. As Dylana went back upstairs to get the books, Trinity went outside to see Niculus. She opened the door, and Niculus was standing by her car with a worried look on his face.

"Is Dylana okay? Why do we need two books, lover? What do you think happened to Damien? Didn't you mention that it has something to do with Lilith?" he asked, as he was reading what was on her mind.

"She's fine, you terrified her though. She fell on some glass, and I had to heal a cut on her head. I told you in the message, I think Lilith did something to him. I think maybe she put a spell on him to make him do whatever she wants him to do, and that would explain why the last time Dylana saw him, he had purple eyes. Niculus, I didn't tell you this, but the pass few days I've been feeling like something bad was happening. I've been feeling a lot of pain and sorrow, and I'm thinking now that maybe she sent him to do something to my family." Trinity told him.

"Lover, if you're right about Lilith putting a spell on my brother. Then the question I have for you is how did she get ahold of my brother, and what spell did she use on him? Why would she put a spell on him to just hurt your family?" Niculus asked her.

"I don't know how she got a hold of him, but I think Jade told her I killed Misty. I think she used the bewitching spell on him." Trinity told him.

"That's possible and would explain why his eyes were purple." He said. Dylana finally came out of the house, carrying two books in her arms. As they all got in Trinity's car, Niculus told Dylana that he was sorry for frightening her. Trinity drove to

Christopher's house, and it was a silent car ride, but they got to there in no time at all.

"Let's get this over with so we can find out what really happened to Damien," Niculus said.

"Niculus, before we do the spell to get Damien back, we have to make a potion to undo the spell I think he's under." Trinity told him, as they all got out of the car.

"Christopher can make the potion while we do the spell." Niculus said.

"That'll work," Trinity said, and Dylana looked at her confused, because she didn't know what Trinity was talking about.

"Trinity, which book has the potion in it?" Niculus asked, and Trinity handed Niculus the right book, and she told him what page the potion was on, so he could tell Christopher.

"So how do we get him back then?" Trinity heard Christopher asked Niculus, as they walked into the house.

"Glad you asked that, brother. I need you to make a potion to undo the spell he's under." Niculus said.

"Okay, so what potion do I need to make?" Christopher asked, and Niculus put the book on the table, and showed Christopher the page I told the potion was on. Christopher looked at the potion we needed. "I can have it ready in about a half an hour." He said, then left the room, to get started on the potion.

While Christopher was downstairs, Trinity was explaining the spell to the others, when she got a shot of pain in her heart, and she knew right at this moment that Lilith didn't send Damien to just hurt her family. Trinity knew that she sent Damien to kill her daughter. Trinity felt every wound that Damien caused with his sword. Trinity started to fall to the floor from feeling her daughter's pain, but Niculus grabbed her just as she almost hit the floor, and Trinity screamed.

"What's happening to you, love?" Niculus asked Trinity.

"Lilith sent that son of a bitch to kill off my whole line." Trinity screamed through the pain, said, "I can feel him killing my daughter. Get his ass here now, so he can't kill her." Trinity screamed more when she said that. Niculus set her on the floor, and he told Dylana how to say the spell in English. She heard Dylana say the spell in English as Niculus and Selene said it in Greek, and Trinity heard them saying,

bring my lost love to me

through time and space

teleport my lost love to me

They kept on saying the spell until Michael appeared in the room, and when he opened his eyes, it infuriated him to see that he was at Christopher's house. Michael watched as Niculus and Selene then started to chain him to a chair they forced him to sit in.

The pain that Trinity was feeling went right away, and that told her that Lily was still alive. If she wasn't, the pain would have been worse. Trinity got up and walked up to Michael, and she knew that she was right about the spell he was under, because his eyes were purple, like Dylana said they were. Trinity could also feel Lilith's magic on him.

As Michael sat there, he was screaming, and shaking from the pain the spell causing. He started to fight to get out the chains and finish what Lilith told him to do. He was trying to get away, because the longer he was chained up, he could feel the pain from the spell getting so intense that he couldn't move, and he felt like he was going to pass out. Christopher then came back into the room with the potion, but instead of going to Michael with the potion, he went over to where Dylana was, and he told her that the potion needed some of her blood.

"Why does it need my blood?" Dylana asked him.

"The potion won't work without your blood." He said, and Dylana let Christopher pricked her finger, and put a few drops of her blood into the potion. He then shook it up and told the others it was ready. Michael saw Christopher was coming toward him with something in his hand, and he knew that he could not finish what Lilith wanted him to do. Niculus grabbed Michael by the jaw, and he held Michael's mouth open as Christopher forced the potion down his throat.

It took about a minute or two for the potion to work. They knew that it had worked, because his eyes went back to being black. When the spell was reversed, the only thought on Michael's mind was blood, because the spell left him weak. Michael looked around the room, and when he saw Dylana, he saw that she was bleeding from a small cut on her finger. The smell of her blood made his fangs came out, and he licked his lips, because he wanted her blood so badly. He started to break the chains to get to her. Niculus told Dylana to get out of the room until he's fed. Niculus and Trinity held Michael down as Christopher forced blood down his throat. After about three bottles of blood, Michael started to know who they were, and he calmed down, and his blood lust passed. Niculus asked him, "What happened to you, Damien?"

"I really don't know what happened, one-minute I was talking to Fury, and the next moment Fantos came up from behind me and he hit me with something that knocked me out cold." Michael told them.

"Then what happened?" Niculus questioned him.

"I woke up on Viterlea and Fantos was forcing me to my knees, and then Lilith had her hands on my head. She made me tell her about what Debathena told us. She then let me remember the other two parts of the prophecy, so I figured out who the two great Witches were." Damien told them.

"Who are the two great Witches?" Trinity asked him.

"The two great Witches are you and Dylana." He said, and as he said that he looked at Trinity. He then stopped talking for a second and then he said, "She also asked me who I thought the girl from the prophecy would descend from, and I told her it had to be from your line Trinity. She then made me kill anyone from your line. Trinity, I'm sorry. I tried to fight the spell for as long as I could stand the pain that the spell was causing me. The spell made me hurt Fury too, where is she, is she okay?"

"We don't know. We only brought you here," Niculus said to Michael.

"I have to find her." Michael said, as he was trying to get out of the chains.

"Brother, I'll have Night find her for you okay, plus we still have some things to talk to you about." Niculus said, as he left to call his dragon, Midnight, to find Fury.

Chapter Twenty-Nine

Searching

Niculus walked to the back of the house, because it's a better place for Night to land. He used his mind to call Night to him. he didn't have to wait long for her to come to him, and then she landed right next to him.

(**"Hello Night."**) He said to her.

(**"Niculus, what's wrong?"**) She asked him.

(**"Damien was under a spell, and he thinks he hurt Fury really badly. I need you to help me find her."**) He told her.

("Poor, Fury, climb on my back, and we're find her. I hope that she's okay.") She said.

("I hope that she's okay too.") He said, as he climbed on her back. It only took them a few minutes to find Fury, because was so close by. They found her in a small clearing, and she was lying on the ground. Night and I hoped that she was still alive, until we saw that someone detached her head from her body. There was nothing we could do for her, because her was dead.

After they found Fury, Niculus had Night use her fire to burn Fury's body to ash, so that no humans would come across a dead dragon in the woods. And then he had Night bring him back to the house. As they were flying, he heard Night crying about Fury being dead, because they were sisters, and he was feeling her lost too, because he felt a tear go down his face. After she dropped him off, she headed back to Viterlea to tell the other dragons about Fury's death. As he headed back inside the house, he heard Trinity and Damien yelling at each other.

Chapter Thirty

Questioning

While Niculus was Gone

Trinity then told Christopher to make sure that Dylana stayed out of the room until she had finished talking to Damien. He nodded to her, and he left the room with Selene.

"So, Damien, I know that you've been lying about some things in that story you told Niculus. So why are you lying?" Trinity asked Damien.

"What are you talking about, Trinity, I'm not lying about anything, but why don't you tell me what you think I've been lying about?" He said to her, with a wicked smile on his face.

"It's not that I think you're lying, but I have a feeling that you're not telling us everything." Trinity said. Michael said nothing for a while, and he was thinking about what to say to Trinity.

"Okay, Trinity, you have me. There are things I don't tell you or Niculus. I'm entitled to my own secrets, just like you." He said bitterly to her.

"I don't care. Just tell me what you're hiding?" Trinity said.

"Well, Trinity I have to say that's none of your concern. But you'll all find out soon what I've been doing, but it won't be today." Michael said to her, and Trinity didn't know what he meant by that.

"Night found Fury," Niculus said, as he came back into the house.

"How is she? Is she okay?" Michael asked, with concern, but Trinity could tell that he didn't mean it at all. Trinity could also tell that he already knew what happened to her, and that he seemed like he was happy about it.

"Damien, I'm sorry to tell you this, but she's dead." Niculus said, he and Trinity watched as Michael started to cry fake tears, and then Dylana came back into the room, and she started to hug Michael. Niculus knew that the conversion was over, but he heard Trinity tell Damien, (**"I'll find out what you're up to."**)

(**"Good luck and, Trinity, I really enjoyed killing your family and causing you pain."**) He replied to her, and before Trinity could say anything back, he was out of the chains with no problem at all, and then he and Dylana left in his Jeep to go back to her house.

306

Chapter Thirty-One

Lily

"So, Trinity, what did I miss? Did you get anything out of him?" Niculus asked her.

"I told Damien that I knew that he wasn't telling us everything. And he told me it was none of my concern. Niculus, he sounded like a different person and he told me he enjoyed killing my family. He's hiding something big from us, and I have a feeling that it has something to do with Lilith," Trinity told him.

"I see, was there anything else?" he asked me.

"No, that was all I got out of him. Sorry I couldn't get anymore." Trinity said to him.

"That's fine. At least now we know that we can't trust him. How are you doing? lover? Do you know if Lily's okay?" He asked me, as he pulled me into his arms.

"The pain went away when we brought him back here. If he had killed her, it would have intensified to pain I was in, and it would have been too much for me to endure, it would have killed me too." Trinity told him.

"I know that you haven't seen Lily since she was born, but do you want to go see her, to make sure she's okay?" He asked, Trinity just looked at him, thinking how she would love to see her Lily, but she didn't know where she was.

"Niculus, you know that I would love to see her, but even if I could just see her. I don't know where she is, or even if she'll want to see me after I gave her away." Trinity said to him.

"Trinity, there is something I never told you. when you asked me to bring Lily to your friend Jennifer, I told her the dangers that could happen if she raised Lily, like about Lilith, and that one day, Lilith would see Lily as a threat. Also, that Lilith would want to kill Lily, and anyone was with her. Your friend is so brave, because she told me she didn't care about the dangers. Unlike her, I cared about the dangers, so I told Jennifer that I wanted to give her and Lily my protection. She said okay, and I made them a safe place, called Amethyst to live so that the Witches couldn't get to them," he told her.

"Why didn't you ever tell me this before, Niculus?" Trinity asked him, but she was so grateful to him for making sure my little girl was safe, and the felt so much love for him right then.

"I'm sorry that I didn't tell you this sooner, lover, abut I'll ask you again, do you want to go see Lily?" He asked.

"Yes," Trinity said, thrilled that she'll Lily after all these years.

"Okay, come with me then, lover." He said, as he grabbed her hand, and they walked outside. He called Midnight she landed before them, and he asked her to take them to see Lily. They got on her back, and she took to the sky. It didn't take her long to get to where Lily was living. When she landed on the Amethyst Island, Trinity saw dead bodies covering the ground, and there was so much blood on the ground, that from above all she saw was red.

"So, Damien did all this?" Trinity asked Niculus, as they got off Midnight.

"I believe so, Trinity. Night, please stay here, and wait for us to come back. Come on, Trinity, Lily's house is back this way." He said to her.

"How do you know that?" Trinity asked him.

"I check in on her every few years." He told her, and she just looked at him, thinking about how much she loves him for taking care of her daughter, like she was his own. Trinity followed him to this small house that was a little way away from the village, and he knocked on the door. When no one answered, he knocked again, and then Lily answered the door.

"Hello, Niculus, what are you doing here?" Lily asked him, and Trinity waited for Niculus to answer her, because she last for words.

"We came here to see if you were all right. We know that Damien attack you and almost killed you, and we wanted to make sure you were okay." He said.

"Who's behind you?" Lily asked him. He moved aside so that Lily could see Trinity. As she saw Lily for the first time since she was a baby. Trinity started to cry from joy. Trinity saw that Lily's purple eyes were watering to, and then Lily ran at her and she gave Trinity a big hug, and Trinity didn't want to let go of her.

"Mother, I'm so happy to see you. Niculus told me so much about you. I always knew that I'd get to see you again." Lily said, and Trinity didn't know what to say to her. She was just so happy to see her

"Mother, are you okay?" Lily asked.

"Yes, I'm fine. I'm just so happy to see you too. I want you to know that I love you, and I wish that I could have raised you. Oh, Lily, you grew up so beautifully, and you look just like your father." Trinity said through more tears.

"I love you too, Mother, and I understand why you gave me up. You just wanted me to be safe." She said.

"Yes, what have you been up to these long years? Did you enjoy being raised by Jennifer?" Trinity asked her.

"Yes, Mother, Jennifer was wonderful at bringing me up, and when I got my full powers, I did a spell to make her live forever. She lives in Greece now with a Vampire that Niculus set her up with. She still comes and sees me now and then. I have been up to little stuff lately. I got married to a guy I love, and we have a daughter and we're expecting a child right now." She said.

"I'm so glad about Jennifer. She always wanted to see Greece, and I'm glad she found someone to make her happy. So, who's this guy you married?" Trinity asked her.

"I think you know him already. He's over there talking to Niculus, but it may be a shock since most people think he's dead." She said.

"You married Dolo?" Trinity said as she saw Dolo come out of the house and walked up to Niculus and Lily and Trinity continued talking as Dolo said to Niculus, "Hello Niculus, it's been awhile." And Niculus looked at who was talking, and he saw that it was his mother's dead father, Dolo, or at least he thought he was dead.

"Grandfather Dolo, but how are you here? I thought you were dead." He said with shock.

"I'm not dead. I just left Viterlea after Lilith killed my love. So, how is my murderous daughter these days?" Dolo asked him, and Niculus told him she's the same as always, and she wants me and my kind dead.

"So, what happened here?" Niculus asked him.

"I don't know what happened, but my guess is that your brother came here, and he started to kill everyone that was living on this island. I came here when I felt him hurting my Lily," he said.

"What do you mean by your lily? What do you mean you felt him hurting her? I thought Witches could only feel the pain of their children?" Niculus asked him.

"She never told you we're married, for a least seven hundred years, and she's pregnant. I felt Lily's and the baby's pain. If I didn't get here when I did and healed them, they would be dead now." Dolo told him, and Niculus thought if it weren't for Dolo healing them, he would have lost Trinity too.

"I have a question for you, Grandfather Dolo." Niculus said to him.

"Okay, what is it?" Dolo asked him.

"Are you guys going to have a girl?" Niculus asked him, and after he asked that he heard

"Yes why," Dolo asked him.

"Trinity, Lily, could you two come over here?" Niculus asked them, and they went over to where the boys were.

"Niculus, what's wrong?" Trinity asked him, as she noticed that he looked worried about something.

"Lily, Grandfather Dolo, do you two know anything about the prophecy?" He asked them, and they said no.

"Niculus, are you thinking what I think you're thinking about?" Trinity asked him.

"Yes, lover, I think I am," he told her, as he read her mind.

"What are you two talking about?" Lily asked them.

"Well, Lily, Grandfather Dolo, there's a prophecy about a girl that will be born with Witch, Vampire, and Ancient blood. I think maybe the prophecy is about your daughter. When is she supposed to be born?" He asked them.

"We thought Lily would have had the baby a long time ago. What does that have to do with anything? And what are you talking about?" Dolo asked.

"She hasn't been born yet, because it's not time for her to be born, and she'll only be born when the two Witches are dead." He told them.

"That sounds like something I've heard before. Doesn't it also say that this girl will kill Lilith?" Dolo asked Niculus.

"Yes," Niculus said.

"Do you know when the two great Witches will die?" Dolo asked Niculus, and Niculus told him he didn't know, Trinity was getting upset, because they were talking about her death.

"Dolo, would you do me a favor?" Niculus asked him.

"Sure, what is it, Niculus?" Dolo asked him, and Niculus told Dolo he thought the two great Witches will die soon, and that he didn't want Dolo to leave Lily's side and they should somewhere else for safety, so Lilith can't find them. He also told him that when the child is born, Lilith will come after her and try to kill her. Dolo agreed to what Niculus told him, and then Niculus and Trinity went home.

Chapter Thirty-Two

Joining a Side

One Hour Ago

When Micahel and Dylana got back to her house, there was no one else home. They went upstairs to her room, and she asked him, "Michael, why were you crying? Did Trinity do something to you?" She asked him.

"No, Trinity wouldn't even think about touching me, and if she ever did, I'd kill her," Michael told her, with a wicked smile on his face.

"Do you really hate Trinity that much that you'd kill her if she touched you?" She asked him.

"Well love, it's not that I hate Trinity. I hate Niculus and if I hurt her, it hurts him. Plus, it makes me mad that, she blames me for her mother's death." Michaeltold her.

"Why would she blame you for her mother's death? She told me it was Misty who killed her mother." She asked.

"Love, there's one thing that Trinity didn't tell you. I was the one who told Misty where to find them." Michael said to her.

"Why did you do that?" She asked him.

"I told Misty where they were because she wanted to see her sister. I didn't know that Lilith had ordered Misty to kill them. So, love before you asked me why I was crying. I was crying, because I just lost my dragon Fury, she's dead. I had her since I was little; she was my oldest friend. I loved her, but I'm glad she's gone because she was always nagging at me. Dylana, when I was born, I got to pick a dragon, because I have royal blood, and no one without royal blood can have a dragon." Michael told her, and she asked me if his brother and sister had dragons too, and he told her yes.

"What happened to your dragon, Damien? How did she die?" She asked him.

317

"Well, love, I killed her. She was trying to stop me from killing Trinity's family, and she wouldn't do what I wanted her to." Michael explained to her.

"You really don't care that she's gone?" Dylana asked him.

"I guess that I'll miss her a little. We did have a lot of good times together. Before the war, we used to fly all over the planet, and I could talk to her about anything, but there were only a few things I hid from her." Michael said.

"What do you mean by that?" She asked him, and he told her that Fury could read his mind, and he could read hers, but there were some things he kept from his thoughts so she couldn't get them out of his mind.

"What did she look like?" She asked him.

"Well, love, Fury's scales were red, and they glowed in the sun, and she could breathe fire. Her wings had a lot of yellow and orange colors on them, and when she flew, it looked like her wings were on fire." Michael told her.

"She sounds beautiful. I wish I could have seen her fly." Dylana said.

"I think you would have loved it," Damien told her, and then she replied by saying, just like you love me.

"Yes, love, just like I love you. Hey are your parents going to be home soon?" He asked her, as he changed the subject, because Michael didn't want to talk about Fury anymore, because talking about her was making Damien sad, and Michael couldn't stand Damien's feelings anymore. Michael then thought Fury in the past now, and he could be on the Witches' side without having to hear her complaining, and without her trying to stop him.

"Well, Michael, they will be away for the next three days." She told him, and he asked her why they were away. She told him they were away visiting Jan's family. He then put a devilish smile on his face.

"What's with that smile of yours?" She asked him.

"Nothing, I'm just happy that we're alone? So, what else do you want to talk about?" He told her.

"Can you tell me more about the Vampires, like what's a myth and what's true. Also, who were the first two Vampires?" She asked him.

"Well, a god named William created the first Vampires. The first two Vampires were my grandparents, but I never got to meet

319

them. they died before I was born. My father told me that their names were Deva and Fontos." He told her.

"I'm sorry that you never got to meet them." She said to him, with a sad look on her face.

"So, you also wanted to know more about the Vampires? Well, one thing is that the things in movies and TV, or in books, are just all myths, and none of that stuff is true. We are very strong, which you already saw firsthand. We can also control another person's mind." He told her, and she said oh really.

"Yes, love, we can, but I don't really use it. I know that you already know about us communicating with our minds, and you already know about the rings that let us go into the sunlight. If we didn't have these rings, though the sun on Earth still wouldn't hurt us, because it isn't as strong as the three suns on Viterlea. If I didn't have my ring on Viterlea, the suns would burn me from the inside out, and then I'd be a rotten corpse on the ground. We don't turn to dust or burst into flames. Is there anything else that you want to know about Vampires?" He asked her.

"That sounds like a horrible way to die?" She asked him.

"Yes, it is." He said.

"So, do you know what happened to Jade? I've tried calling her, but she doesn't answer the phone." Dylana asked him, as she changed the subject.

"All I know about is that Jade's on Viterlea, she's Lilith's side." Him said to her, and then he stopped talking for a second, and then said, "Lilith is probably training Jane to be a more powerful Witch, and how to fight. She also told me that Misty didn't train her well at all, but then again, it may have to do with the fact that Jade's part Human."

"Why is Lilith teaching her how to fight?" She asked him.

"Lilith's training Jade for a war that will happen soon." He said to her.

"What war will happen soon? I mean, is Lilith just training her to fight Vampires, or is there something else that the Witches have to fight?" She asked him.

"Well, lover, if I tell you that, you must join Lilith's side too. We can't have my family finding out about Lilith's plans. Would you be willing to join Lilith's side? She's not as bad as your mother says she is. She's nice to the people are on her side. Lover, she can teach you how to use the Redfire better than anyone else." He told her.

"But my mother told me terrible things about Lilith and that she's a terrible person." She said.

"Your mother told you that because your mother only saw that side of her, and that's because your mother rebelled against Lilith. If your mother didn't leave Viterlea, she may have seen a different side of Lilith." He told her.

"I don't know what to do." She told him.

"There is something I have to tell you, but first tell me what you think of Niculus?" he asked.

"I think he's a good guy." She said.

"I hate to tell you this, but he's not a good guy," he said.

"Why do you say that?" She asked him.

"Well, Niculus may not have killed your mother, that's not like him, and if he killed a Witch, it would have started a war he's trying to avoid, but he knows it's coming. Also, he doesn't enjoy killing family, but he planned the whole thing." He told her.

"So, you're telling me that Niculus is the main reason that my mother's dead?" She asked him, with anger.

"Yes, lover," he said a little scared of her anger, because him didn't want her to set him on fire.

"That fucking bastard, I will kill him." She yelled.

"Love, you can't kill him without killing me, remember." Him told her.

"Right, I forgot you said that if one of you dies, you both die. So how do I get revenge for my mother's death?" She asked him.

"We'll take someone he loves away from him, like the person who ended your mother's life." He told her.

"If it wasn't Niculus, who killed my mother?" She asked him.

"Trinity," he told her.

"Are you sure it was Trinity?" She asked him.

"Yes, as I was leaving to get help, I watched her attack your mother." He told her.

"Why didn't you tell me this sooner?" She questioned him.

"I didn't know how to tell you, and I wanted to give you time to mourn your mother." He explained to her.

"Thank you, for that Michael, and I guess I'll join Lilith's side." She said.

"I'm so glad to hear that, there's only one thing left to do." He told her.

"What's that?" She asked him.

"Lilith told me that if you agreed to join her, that I would have to form a special bond with you." He told her.

Chapter Thirty-Three

Bond

"What kind of bond?" She asked him.

"It's a bond that will bound you to me, and it'll give me power over you." He said.

"What, you can't be serious." She said, as she backed away from him.

"Dylana, you know that I can't lie to you. And love, there's one more thing you should know. I may love, but at the same time if would give me great pleasure to hurt you as well." He said, as he walked over to her and pinned her against a wall.

"Let go of me, Michael, you're scaring me?" She said, as she was trembling.

"Dylana, you should be scared, and I really don't need your permission to do this bond, but I need to take this off first." Michael said, as he lifted the Redfire off if her.

("Stop this, Michael, let her go, you're hurting her.") Damien screamed at Michael.

("You want me to let her go, then talk her into doing the bond, because if I do this bond by force, it will damage her mind. Do you want that?") Michael asked to Damien.

("No,") Damien said.

("That's what I thought. You have ten minutes to convince her, or I do if by force.") Michael said.

("Fine,") Damien said, and then Michael let Damien come to the surface to talk to Dylana.

"Dylana, are you all right?" Damien asked her, as he let her go and he backed away.

326

"What just happened?" She asked.

"Michael, let me come the surface so I could talk to you," Damien told her.

"So, you're really Damien? Don't tell me, that he let you come to the surface so you could talk me into doing this bond thing?" She asked him.

"You will not like to answer to that question." Damien said to her.

"You've got to be kidding me. Why don't you fight him and take back your body?" She questioned him.

"He's stronger than me, and Niculus couldn't even bet him in a fight. Dylana, if you don't do what he wants, he'll force you and if he does that, it'll leave your mind damage and after a few years that damage will kill you. I can't bear the thought of you dying." He said, as he kissed her on the cheek.

(**"Times up, Damien,"**) Michael said, as he took control over before Damien could say anything.

"So, Dylana, now that Damien's back there he belongs, are you going to give me any problems with doing this bond?" Michael asked her.

"No, what do I need to do?" She asked him, because she didn't want her mind damage and she didn't want to die.

"I'm glad you asked love. First you will give me permission." He said.

"Permission to do what?" She asked him.

"To drink your blood and keep in mind, I would love to take your blood by force." He threatened her.

"I give you permission." She said, and then he protracted his fangs and he smiled at her as he pushed her against a wall again and he bit into the left side of neck. As he was drinking deeply from her, he thought her blood tasted better than he thought would and he never tasted blood that was this sweet and powerful before. When he had almost drained her of all her blood, he retracted his fangs and he whispered into her ear, "I give you permission." Michael then cut himself with a knife on the wrist and brought his bloody wrist to her mouth. As the first drop touch her tongue, she immediately started to drink from him and part of her try to stop, but she was unable and the more she drank from him, she started to feel different, and she thought the other thing that matter was what Michael wanted her to do. When Michael pulled his wrist away from her, he could feel the bond was complete and that she was his now.

Chapter Thirty-Four

Jade

"How do you feel love?" Michael asked her.

"I'm fine. I just feel a little different, and I don't think it changed me that much." She said.

"It changed more than you realize." He said to her, as he looked at her arm and he smiled then he saw that she had a red rose on the forearm, just like his.

"So, now you're on Lilith's side, do you want to know what Lilith's plan is?" He asked her, and she told me yes, I want to know.

"Lilith's plan is to finish the war with the Vampires once and for all, and then she wants to start a war with the Humans on Earth." He told her.

"Why does she want to start a war with Earth?" She asked.

"She wants to expand her kingdom on Earth. She wants to rule over the Humans, and there is nothing they can do to stop us from conquering them." He told her.

"Why's that?" She asked him.

"Well, the Human's weapons are no match against magic, and they can't fight the armies that Lilith is building." He told her, and before she could ask about Lilith's army, there was a knock on the door.

"I wonder who that could be?" Dylana asked.

"It's Jade," he said, as he grabbed her hand and they walked downstairs together to greet Jade. When they got to the door, Michael opened it and asked, "Hello, Jade, did Lilith send you?"

"Yes, Lilith wants to see you. and Dylana, it's been a while since I've seen you, how have you been?" Jade asked.

"I'm good, I'm so happy to see you Jade. I've just missed you. How have you been?" Dylana asked her, as Michael left them at the door to grab the Redfire from upstairs.

"I've been very busy lately." Jade told Dylana.

"What have you been doing?" Dylana asked her, thinking about what Michael said to her.

"Can we talk inside? I want no one to hear us taking." She said, and then Jade stepped inside and they walked into the kitchen.

"Is anyone else here?" Jade asked as she looked around.

"No, it's just Michael and me here." Dylana told her.

"That's fine, I know that he's on our side. I was just wondering if your father or step-mother were here, because of the power that Niculus has over them." She said.

"Niculus has no power over them anymore." Dylana told her.

"What, why not?" Jade asked.

"My mother made him undo the spells he had on them, and my father put a spell around the house so that Niculus can't get in here, and he's already tried, and it didn't end well." Dylana said, and Jade said well that's good.

"So, are you joining Lilith's side too?" Jade asked.

"Yes, Damien told me who killed my mother, and I want to make that person pay for what they did." Dylana said.

"So, who killed your mother?" She asked.

"Damien told me it was Trinity. He also told me that Niculus planned to have my mother killed." Dylana told her, and Jade said really.

"Don't worry; they'll pay for what they did." Jade said.

"I don't get that. You told her to kill your mother." Jade said.

"Yes, I did, but I told her to not let my mother suffer. As I was walking out of the woods to go back to my house, I knew that it was the right thing to let Trinity kill my mother. I wanted her to be at peace, but as I was walking to the house, I started to cry, because even though It was the right thing to do, I still felt her loss, I started to come in view of my mother and I saw how Trinity killed her. It looked like she made my mother suffer. I saw fear on my mother's face. Trinity had stabbed her at least thirteen times, and there was a lot of blood all over the place, and there was blood still gushing out of some wounds." Jade said, and it shocked Dylana.

"Trinity hurt my mother so much, and I want her to pay for it." She said.

"Oh, my god, I'm so sorry Jade. So how did you meet Lilith?" Dylana asked her.

"Just as I would move the body, Lilith came out of the woods. Even though she didn't say a word, I saw that she was mad and sad by the death of my mother. After a few minutes, she asked me, who did this, which one of these Vampires did this to my sweet girl. I told her it was Trinity," Jade said.

"After I told Lilith that it was Trinity who killed my mother, she said another Witch did this, and then she said that means she's a traitor and we kill traitors. She then asked me if I was Misty's daughter. I told her yes, and then Lilith asked me how I let Trinity kill my mother." Jade said, and then she added, "Lilith was mad, so I told her I didn't let her do anything. Lilith then told me not to bury my mother here, and that they should bury my mother on Viterlea, so she told me to grab the body, and she brought us to Viterlea." After she said that, Dylana just nodded her.

"Have you been there all this time?" Dylana asked her, and Jade told her yes.

"What have you been doing there?" Dylana asked her.

"Well, Lilith's been teaching me how to fight the Vampires, and she showed me how to use my powers better. I'm a lot more powerful than I was before, and I can see the future better now, too." She said, and then Dylana said cool.

"So, Dylana, I don't know if you're wondering this, but Lilith sent me here to bring you and Michael to her. She wanted to get to know you better, and she has some questions for Michael," Jade said. After she said that, Dylana realized that she wasn't wondering why Jade was here at all, Dylana was just happy to see that she was all right.

"What kind of questions does she have for him?" Dylana asked Jade.

"Lilith needs to talk to Michael, and ask he if he killed the people, she wanted dead. When she sent me here was, she was mad about something, so I think Michael in trouble." Jade said, as Michael came into the kitchen.

"Why is he in trouble?" Dylana asked her, but Jade didn't answer her.

"She's probably mad at me, because she knows that I failed her, and I think I blew my cover with Niculus." After he said that, Dylana asked him what he meant by that.

"Well, since I came to Maine, I've been playing them and lying to them well, but when I came out of the spell that Lilith put on me, I let myself slip, and Trinity was already suspicious of me. She saw right though me, and by now Niculus knows that I follow Lilith or something like that." Michael said.

"How do you know that they know that you're on Lilith's side?" Dylana asked him.

"Well, I know them well enough that, they'll most likely come here and ask me if it's true first. I know that they wouldn't see through my lies anymore, and then they'll try to take you and they'll try to lock me up somewhere. And, lover, I don't want you to take the Redfire off." He said to Dylana, as he handed the Redfire to her.

"Thanks for getting it for me, Michael." Dylana told him.

"Lover, I want nothing to happen to you." He said, as he pulled me into his arms.

"So, does Lilith want to see us right away?" He asked Jade.

335

"Yes, now would be best. You know that she doesn't enjoy waiting." Jade told they, and then Jade pulled out a spell book, and it had a lot of weird symbols on it.

"How can you read this?" Dylana asked her.

"It wasn't easy when Lilith first taught me it, but after a while I got it down. I can teach you how to read it too if you'd like." She said, and then Jade told us to hold hands as she started to chant in a language that sounded like nonsense.

Chapter Thirty-Five

Viterlea

The spell that Jade was chanting worked, and when Dylana opened her eyes, she saw that they were on Viterlea. As Dylana looked around she saw how beautiful it was there, and it was so much more wonderful than what her mother told her. Dylana watched as Jade and Michael headed toward this castle was ahead of them. Dylana thought that must be where Lilith lives, and she thought the castle looked enchanting. Instead of following them she turned to look at everything around her. Dylana wanted to take in everything around her. Michael noticed Dylana wasn't behind him and he looked back and saw she was walking toward one tree, Dylana thought the trees were pretty. The trees she saw had leaves on it that looked like they would have on Earth, if it was autumn. The colors of the tree's leaves were orange, red, and yellow, but there were some that were blue, white, and purple. These trees also had these weird berries growing on them. Dylana was just about to grab a berry when the tree spoke to her.

"Let me get that for you, my dear." The tree said in a sweet voice, as it handed her a berry. Dylana felt Michael put his arms around her, as she took the berry from the tree.

"Try the berry, they're fantastic and sweet." He said, and she tried the berry, and she thought he was so right. I thought this berry was the sweetest thing she ever tasted.

They then heard Jade calling to them, and they followed her to the castle. As Dylana looked at the castle, she saw that it big, and it shined so wonderfully in the sunlight. Dylana saw that there were Witches all around the castle. As they got closer, they stepped out their way to let them pass. When they walked inside, there was a guy, that Dylana didn't know, standing there waiting for them. Dylana watched as Jade went up to him, and she hugged him.

"It's good to see you, Uncle Fantos," Jade said to the guy.

"Yes, it's good to see you too Jade." The guy named Fantos said to Jade, and then they walked over to Dylana and Michael.

"Dylana, this is our Uncle Fantos." Jade, and Dylana said hello to him.

"Hello there Dylana, it's nice to meet you. Well now, that you're all here, Lilith's waiting for you two. So, if you'll just follow me." Fantos said. As they were following him to Lilith. Dylana was looking at everything was inside the castle. The walls looked like something made them of hand-carved stone with crystals, and the floors looked like gold. They stopped at a wood door and had a painting of an exquisite woman on it. Dylana thought this woman in the painting must be someone of importance, and she wished she knew who the woman was, "Hey Fantos, who's that in the painting?" He told her that the painting was of Eleanor, and she thought Eleanor was very enchanting with the blue scepter in her hand and her blue wings.

Fantos then opened the door, and he showed them inside. When Dylana walked in the room, the first thing she saw was Lilith. Lilith was sitting on a gold throne that had crystals all around it. Lilith wasn't paying any attention to them as they walked in, until Fantos said, "Mother, your guests are here."

"Dylana, Michael, please have a seat you two." Lilith. They did as she said, and then Jade left, and then Fantos shut the door, and left.

"Well, it's nice to have the two of you on my side." She said to them, and Dylana was wondering how Lilith knew that she joined her side. "How do you know I joined your side?"

"I know a lot of things my child. I can see into the future." Lilith said.

"Did you see that my mother would die?" Dylana asked her.

"No, I missed that, and I'm so sorry she taken from you." Lilith to Dylana, and then she looked at Michael, "Michael could you please put on fresh clothes?" Lilith asked him, and he mumbled a spell, and he replaced his bloody clothes with clean ones.

"How did you do that?" Dylana asked him, and he told her magic.

"So, Michael, did you kill of Trinity's line?" Lilith asked him.

"No, Mother I didn't get the chance to kill them all. As I was trying to kill Trinity's daughter, I got attacked by someone from behind. Also, Trinity must have known what I was doing, and they summoned me to them." Michael told Lilith.

"What, I knew that you failed me. She was your main target and only a few beings can sneak up on a Vampire. Who attacked you?" She demanded.

"Dolo attacked me, and I think he was protecting Lily. There's something else that I to tell you." He told her.

"Well, I think it's about time I kill Dolo to stop him from interfering with my plans. What else do you have to said?" Lilith asked him.

"I didn't notice it at first, but I think I heard two heartbeats, and that could mean that Lily and Dolo are the prophecy girl's parents." He said.

"If that's true, maybe I don't have to kill her, and that I could use her when the time is right. In the meantime, I could just put her someplace for safekeeping. So, this girl in my little sister, how sweet." Lilith said laughing.

"How do you plan to get a hold of her?" Michael asked her.

"Don't you worry about that. So, Michael, how could they summon you? I didn't think their magic was strong enough for that kind of spell." She asked him.

"I helped them summon Michael, I was worried about him." Dylana said.

"I see, so Michael do you think you can still fool Niculus?" Lilith asked him.

"No, Mother, when I came out of the spell, I could not control my thoughts. I let myself to Trinity, and she knows that been keeping things from them, and I'm sure she'll already told Niculus." He said.

"Michael, I never thought you'd be a disappointment to me like my daughters. If you can't fool Niculus, then you ruined my plans. I thought I trained you better than this." She yelled at him.

"Mother, I know that I messed up, and I'm sorry for disappointing you. I think I know a way to still fool Niculus." He said.

"What's your idea?" Lilith asked him.

"Maybe Dylana, could go to them and pick up where I left off." He said.

"How would I do that?" Dylana asked him, and he said, "I want you to tell them everything I've told you about myself. After you tell them all my secrets, I'm sure they're trust you."

"And then what do I do?" She asked him.

"After that, get as close as you can to Trinity. And when if they trust you, they'll bring you back to Viterlea on the day of the eclipse, and take your revenge on Niculus, and kill Trinity." He told me.

"Michael, I don't know if I can really kill someone," Dylana told him.

"Even after what she did to your mother?" He asked her, and she told them she knew that. Dylana didn't know if she could kill someone and take their life away.

"I can help you with that lover." Michael.

"And I can help you too, Dylana. I can give you a knife that will do all the killing for you. All you have to do is stab her with it." Lilith said.

"If it's that easy, why do I have to wait then?" She asked them.

"Well, that's because of me. Niculus probably knows that I'm not on his side, and he'll be suspecting something like this to happen. Also, you must wait for the eclipse to start before you kill her." He said, and she told him okay, but saying okay made her worry she wouldn't be able to pull this off. She was happy that Michael and Lilith would help her through this. As she was in thinking, Lilith got off her throne and she told them to follow her to the weapons room.

They followed her out of the throne room and down a narrow hallway that seemed to go on forever. The door to the weapons room was at the end of the hallway. When they got there, she opened the door. Dylana looked around the room and she saw that every wall in the room was full of weapons of all kinds. Dylana saw that there were people in there too, and they were training with swords. Lilith told them to wait at the door as she walked to the other side of the room. Michael and Dylana just stayed there in the doorway, waiting for her to come back. Lilith came back a few minutes, and Dylana saw she had a purple knife in her hands and Lilith handed it to her.

"Dylana, I made this blade of a special metal that has poison mixed into it. This blade can kill anyone that has Vampire blood in their system." Lilith said.

"Can it kill Niculus?" Dylana asked them.

"Sadly, no, but it would make him weak." Lilith said.

"Well, Dylana, good luck with what you have to do. I most likely won't see you for a long time." She said.

"Why's that?" Dylana asked.

"Well, you see my dear, after you kill Trinity, Niculus will most likely kill you." Lilith said, and then Dylana looked at Michael.

"Don't worry love. If he kills you, I have the power to bring you back from the dead. So, you won't be dead for long." After he said that, Lilith just left them standing there, without another word.

Chapter Thirty-Six

Dark Plan

They looked at each other as Lilith walked away. Michael then grabbed my hand, and he said, "Lover, come with me, we have to find Jade to take us back to Earth." They didn't have to go far to find Jade, because after he said that she walked toward them.

"Ready to go back to Earth you two?" Jade asked, and Michael told her yes. She opened the book as she did before, and she said the spell again, and they were back at Dylana house once again, but Dylana noticed that Jade wasn't there with them. Dylana thought maybe the spell she just said just sent Michael and her back, while Jade stayed on Viterlea. Dylana walked inside the house with

Michael on her heels. Dylana was so happy that her parents weren't home she didn't think she could have dealt with them with all the other stuff that was going on. She walked into the kitchen and she told Michael to have a seat. She didn't say much of anything else to him; she just kept on pacing back and forth. Finally, she said, "How am I going to do this, Michael? How am I going to make him believe me? What will they do if they figure out the true, that I'm just playing them, and that I'm planning to kill Trinity?" She asked him, and Michael didn't answer her at first.

"Lover, after you start this, the two of us can't be near each other, or they'll smell my scent on you. All you have to do is go over there and see them, and you must make sure you went there for their help." He told her.

"Why do I have to do that, and why would I have to?" She asked him.

"Well, the thing about my brother is that he has a soft spot for people are in trouble, and he'd love to have you on his side. There is one more thing I must tell you about him. When he finds out I hit you, he'll give you some of his blood to heal you. After he does this, you must be very careful about what you say to him. He'll know better if you're lying to him." He told her.

"What why would you hit me?" She asked him.

"That's the only why he'll believe our lie, is if I hurt you, and then you will get in your car, and drive there, and then I'll try to follow you. When you get there, run inside and tell them I hurt you. Tell them I told you stuff, you couldn't believe, and then we got into fight and then I hit you and that you had to get to a safe place and that you had to get away from me, so I couldn't hurt you anymore." He said.

"You think that will work?" She asked him.

"Yes, and when you get him alone, I want you to tell him everything I told you." He told her.

"Why," she asked him.

"So, that he'll know that I'm a lost cause. If you tell him those things, he will stop trying to help me." He told her.

"Okay, Michael, so when do we start, I mean should we do this now?" She asked him, and he walked over to her.

"Lover, the sooner the better, but remember you can't come and see me, and you will most likely not see me again until I bring you back from the dead." He said.

"How will I keep in touch with you?" She asked him.

"Lover, you won't be able to. If we have any contact, Niculus will know something up." He said.

"Okay, so how do I hide this blade?" She asked him. He told her to hold the Redfire in her hands and wish for it to disappear. She did what he said to do, and it disappeared.

"How do I get it back?" she asked him.

"You just have to wish for it to appear. Okay, so here we go. First you should take the Redfire off, because it won't let me hurt you, but don't forget to take it with you when you leave. Then I will hit you in the face. I will hit you as hard as I can, and it will hurt a lot." He said, and she told him okay, and she took off the Redfire, and put it on the table by her cell phone and keys. She watched as he made a fist, and just as he was about to hit her, he heard Damien said, (*"Don't you hurt her, you monster."*)

(**"Really Damien, if I'm such a monster, why don't you try to stop me. Oh wait, you can't because I have more power than you do, and you couldn't even stop me from making Dylana mine. And honestly you haven't had complete control over your body since your mother tried to kill you the seventh time, so why don't just shut up."**) Michael said.

("I will not shut up, not this time. Michael, she's my soul mate, and I will not let you hit her. She's not aware of how much control you have over her, but I will do everything in my power to keep you from physically hurting her,") Damien said.

("Well, good luck with that little brother.") After Michael said that, Damien didn't say another word, Michael hit Dylana square in the jaw, and she seemed surprised, and thanks to Damien taking control for a brief second, Michael couldn't hit Dylana as hard as he wanted to, but he could tell that it still hurt her a lot, and she started to cry.

"Are you okay, Lover?" He asked her.

"Yes, let's keep going." She said.

"Grab your stuff off the table, and then try to run away from me." Michael said, and she turned and grabbed her things off the table. She then took a step away from him, and he used his super speed and then he was right in front of her. He grabbed her arm, and he told her to knee him in the groin and then to run away from him. She did as he said, and he let go of her, and she ran outside and got into her car. As she was driving, she saw in the rear-view mirror that Michael was running behind her car. She noticed that Michael was getting closer to her car, so she drove faster.

The whole time she was driving, she was trying to make herself cry, which was hard for her to do, so she thought about her mother dying in her arms. After she thought about that, she couldn't stop crying as she pulled into Christopher's driveway. She stopped the car, got out and ran to the door. She banged on the door. She heard someone inside saying I'm coming. I'm coming. The one that was talking opened the door. She saw that it was Niculus himself, and she ran into his arms.

"Nicky, I told Damien that I was through with him, because he's working for Lilith, and then he started to beat me up. I think he was following me here." She told Niculus, though her tears. He looked at her with a shocked look on his face. He put his arms around her, and he pulled her all the way inside the house, and then he locked the door.

"Dylana, come with me to my study. We can talk about what happened in there." Niculus said to her.

"What about Damien? He can't get in here, right?" She asked him.

"No, he can't get in here. Trinity put a spell around the house that won't let him in. It's just like the one that your father put on your house to keep me out." He said, and she asked him if anyone else was here.

"Yes, but they're all sleeping right now." He told her. As they entered his study, he told her to have a seat on the red couch was in there. As she sat down, she looked around the room and there was a dark wooden desk full of papers and some books. She didn't see much of the walls because there seem to be bookcases against every wall and they were all full, and there were still more books in a pile on the floor. She didn't even know how many there were.

"So, tell me what happened to you?" He asked her with concern, as she thought this room was more like a library than a study.

"Damien was telling me stuff he said was true, but I just couldn't believe the stuff he was telling me and then he hit me in the jaw, and then I tried to run away from him, and then he was right in front of me, and he grabbed my arm." She said, as she showed Niculus her arm, but he didn't know what he had hit her with. He saw that her face didn't look that bad, but he thought he should heal her face and arm tomorrow after she's got some sleep.

"I kicked him in the groin, and he let me go and I drove here, there was nowhere else for me to go." After she said that, she started to shake a little.

"Okay, calm down, Dylana. You're safe here. So, tell me what he told you?" he asked her.

"Well, I think he was just telling me lies about you, and they made none since, because of what my mother told me about Vampires." She said.

"What did he say?" He asked her.

"He told me you planned my mother's death, but that's a lie right. You had nothing to do with my mother's death, right?" She asked him through tears.

"No, Dylana that's not true. I think your mother's death was an accident." He said.

"I have a weird question for you." She said, and then he said that she could ask him anything, but he didn't know if he could be truthful with her though.

"Why were you at my house in Rome? I saw you outside my window?" She asked him.

"I had a feeling that you'd ask me that. I was there to play a prank on your mother, because that's something we did when we were kids. Did I scare you?" He said with a playful smile.

"Yes, you did, and why did your tiger come after me?" She asked him.

"I told him to scare your mother. He didn't tell him to go after you." He told her.

"If that's true, it would explain why she didn't freak out about the whole thing." She said to him.

"Well, now we have that straightened out. What else did Damien told you, my dear?" He said, as if he was flirting with me, and it was creeping her out.

"I think this was true, because I saw in his eyes it was. He said that Lilith didn't kill your mother." She told him, and he asked threateningly, "If not that bitch that killed my mother, then who killed my mother?"

"Damien said that he killed her." She said scared, because she didn't know how Niculus would react.

"What, he killed her?" He shouted. He threw stuff as he yelled. It surprised her that no one woke up and walked into the room and asked what was going on, because he was making quite a ruckus.

"Did he tell you why he did it?" He asked, as he was trying to calm down.

"He said it was because of the fact she tried to kill him when he was little." She said, as she was shaking, because Niculus was scaring her a little.

"I'm sorry if I'm scaring you, Dylana. I'm just mad. My mother was always telling me not to trust him, and I guess she was right, and I should have trusted her more and I should have not let her go to see Lilith with him. Did he say how long he's been on Lilith's side?" he asked her.

"I think since he was born." She said this, as she back away from Niculus.

"Fuck, well that explains a lot, that little fuck. I only wish I could kill him. Do you have the Redfire on you, my dear?" He asked, and she told him yes.

"Why can't you kill him?" She asked him.

"The two of us are two halves of a whole. If one of us dies, we both die." He told me.

"It is how we were born, my mother told me that Damien should have black eyes and a black rose, but as I was being born my head came out as his arm came out at the same time. We get marks when our skin gets exposed to light for the first time." He said.

355

"Well, Dylana can I count on you to help us?" He asked, and she told him yes.

"Good, I'll show you to where you can sleep, and tomorrow we can heal your wounds and we can talk more. And Trinity can teach you how to do the spell." He said, and she told him okay, and he showed her, to one of the spare bedrooms, which was bare except for a bed. He told her to have a good night and then he left the room. As she was trying to sleep, she heard Michael tell her to brew a truth potion to get the truth out of Trinity, and to tell them she was brewing it for him.

After Niculus showed her to the spare room, he went to his room to join Trinity to tell her about Dylana being here.

"Trinity wake up, love. I have something to tell you." He said, as he woke her up.

"What is it, Niculus?" She asked him.

"Dylana's here. I guess that she had a fight with Damien, and she came here to get away from him," he told her.

"What? Is that why I heard you talking to someone in your study?" She asked him, and just as he was about to answer her. He stopped, and then he said, "Do you think maybe her being here is an act? Do you think Damien sent her here?"

"Do you think he would hurt her, to fool us?" She asked him.

"I don't know love, but it wouldn't shock me. We'll just have to keep a close eye on her and hope he doesn't have power over her." Niculus said.

"I agree that we should keep a watchful eye on her, but for now let's just sleep." She said, and he climbed in bed with her. After they were sleeping for a few hours, Dylana woke them by screaming in pain.

"Is that Dylana screaming?" Trinity asked.

"Yes, I think so, maybe she in pain from her face being hurt?" He said.

"I'll be right back, Niculus." Trinity said to him, as she got out of bed.

"Where are you going?" He asked her.

"I will give her something to help with the pain, and to help her sleep, and then maybe we can get some sleep too." She told him, and she left their room to give Dylana something to help her sleep. While Trinity was away, it amazed Niculus that Dylana only woke up Trinity and him. I thought Christopher and Selene can sleep through anything. When Trinity came back into the room, all the screaming stopped.

"That stuff you gave her works fast." He said, and then they fell back to sleep.

Chapter Thirty-Seven

Healing

The next morning, Niculus woke up, and he saw that Trinity wasn't there. So, he went down to the kitchen to see if she there. As he walked in, she was there eating toast with Jam, and he said morning to her as he sat down next to her.

"Morning lover, do you want anything to eat?" She asked him.

"No, but I'll take some blood." He said, and then she handed him some blood, and he asked her, "Where are Christopher and Selene?"

"Selene said that she was going back to Viterlea today, she didn't tell me why she was going back there early though, and Christopher went out for a run, but he said that he'd be back soon." She told him.

"I will go check on Dylana and see how she's doing. I want you to drink all of that blood before I come back down here, you hear me." She said to him.

"All right, look, I'm drinking it." He said to her.

As Trinity went to see Dylana. Dylana was just waking from a restless sleep, because she was sleeping in a house full of Vampires, that if they knew what she was planning, they'd kill her. Dylana didn't sleep well, because she had nightmares about them killing her and some of them were of Niculus killing Michael. As she sat up in bed, there was a knock on the door, and she said come in. Trinity opened the door and walked into the room.

"Hey," she said, and Dylana said hey back to her.

"Niculus told us what happened between you and Damien last night." She then just stopped talking, as she looked Dylana's face, and Dylana saw the look of horror in Trinity's eyes.

"Wow, your face looks terrible. And it looks a lot worse than what Niculus thought it was. What did Damien hit you with?" Trinity asked, with worry.

"He hit me with his fist, why do you ask?" Dylana asked.

"Niculus," she yelled for him. Dylana heard Niculus running up the stairs to where they were, and Dylana asked her what was wrong?

"I asked you that because the whole side of your face is black and blue, and it looks like it's really swollen." Trinity said.

"If my face is that bad, why doesn't it hurt?" Dylana asked her, as was freaking out, and then Niculus walked into the room.

"Niculus and I heard you screaming in your sleep last night, and I thought it was because you were in pain from the things that Damien did to you, and we thought you were having nightmares about it. So, I gave you something to help you with the pain, and to help you sleep, and since you felt no pain. I may have given you too much." Trinity told Dylana.

"I didn't hear you in here last night." Dylana said.

"That's because of all the screaming that you were doing." She said.

"Niculus, when Damien hit her, he did it with his fist. You know what this means." She said, as she looked at him, and he ran quickly out of the room. Dylana asked her where he was going.

"He's going downstairs, and that's where we're going to. Where else did Damien hurt you?" Trinity asked her, and Dylana showed her arm to Trinity, and her arm was black and blue, and swollen just like her face.

"Okay, Niculus went downstairs to start on the potion that will make your face and arm better." Trinity said, and Dylana said okay. Dylana followed Trinity to the lab room, that was in the basement. The room was dazzling, and there were a few tables. There were plants of all kinds down here, and the cabinets had a lot of weird things in them. The room also had an odd smell to it. When they walked in, Niculus was already making the potion that Trinity had told her about.

"Is it done yet?" Trinity asked Niculus.

"Just a few more minutes, Dylana please have a seat. We just have to wait for it to cool down, before we put it on your face." He told her, and she sat in the only chair was down here.

"Niculus, we have to put it on her arm too, it looks as bad as her face." Trinity said, and he said okay.

"Niculus, why does my face look worse than it did last night?" Dylana asked him.

"To be honest with you, I don't know why it didn't look like this last night. Just be glad he didn't hit you with full force." He said.

"Why's that?" She asked him.

"If he had hit you with full force, he would have cracked your jaw, and I would have made this potion last night, because if I waited, you would have been dead before you woke up this morning." He told her.

"What's in that?" She asked him.

"It has some herbs good for healing, and it has some Vampire blood in it too." Niculus told her.

"What," she said.

"Dylana, don't worry, Vampire blood has healing properties in it, and there are only a few drops of it in this potion." Trinity explained to her.

"Whose blood is in this potion?" Dylana asked Niculus.

"It's my blood that's in this potion. It's the only thing that can heal any wounds that my brother inflicts on other people." Niculus told her, and his answer surprised her, and she wasn't sure what to say. Niculus grabbed the bowl that had the potion in it, and he walked over to her.

He then put the potion on her face where it was swelling. He also put it on her right arm where Michael had grabbed. The potion started to burn at first contact, and Dylana tried to rip the potion off her skin, but she couldn't because Trinity suddenly grabbed her arms so that Dylana couldn't move them. After a few minutes, the pain started to melt away and Niculus said that the second stage of the potion was starting.

"Dylana, in this stage there's no pain, but there is an odd sensation." He told her. When he said that, she started to feel an odd sensation he just mentioned, and she couldn't describe it at all. She thought felt like a tingly feeling, and it went all the way through her face. She could even feel it in her bones, and it was a feeling she also didn't trust. She wished that this potion didn't have Niculus' blood in it, because of what Michael told her about Niculus giving her his blood. She knew what he meant now, about Niculus knowing better if she was lying to him, because she was getting a tingly feeling on left arm, and he didn't put potion on that arm. She looked down at that arm, and she saw a faint outside of a rose.

Chapter Thirty-Eight

Michael

"Niculus, why's that on my left arm?" She asked him.

"Oh, that's just because of my blood." He said.

"Why did we have to use your blood again?" She asked him.

"Okay, dear, I'll explain it to you again. We had to use my blood because my brother hit you, and he has something in his skin that can kill people. I'm not sure what it is, but it's very poisonous to Witches. My blood with these herbs and some healing Nightspear is the only thing that can heal this kind of wound completely." He said to me.

"Oh, I didn't know it was that bad. I guess that there are still things I don't know about him." She said.

"That appears to be so, my dear. You shouldn't worry about that rose mark. It should go away in a few days, once my blood is out of your system." He said, and then Niculus suddenly looked at Trinity, and he told her, (**"So lover, do you think she's messing with us, and that this is just a trick that Damien put her up to, or do you think she's telling us the truth?"**)

(**"I think she's telling the truth, and I that she's terrified of Damien, but I also don't know it it's all an act or not. I'll try to find out."**) Trinity said to him.

(**"You don't have to do that. Doing that may push her to turn against us, and we don't want her to do that."**) He said, because he knew that she was talking about interrogating her, and Niculus didn't think that would end well.

(**"Niculus, with Damien telling her we had something to do with her mother getting killed, won't that turn her against us?"**) She asked him.

("If she doesn't know that, she should do what we want, and then I'll tell her the truth myself, and it was my fault that her mother got killed.") He told her.

("But I killed her, you know that.") She said to him.

("Yes, but it an accident. So, Trinity, for now if she asks you anything, tell her half-truths only okay. I will find Damien, and he'll answer the question if she's on our side or not.") He told her.

("Niculus, Dylana's looking at us.") Trinity told him, as Dylana was staring at them.

"Well, Dylana, it looks like you're all healed up. I'll see the two of you later." Niculus said.

"Where are you going?" Dylana asked him.

"Oh well," he said, and then he stopped talking, as he was about to tell her he would look for Damien.

"You know what, Dylana, I'll let the two of you get to know each other better, and if Trinity thinks you're on our side, and it's not just a lie, then I'll tell you deal?" He asked her, and she thought to herself shit he knows, but she tried to sound truthful when she said, "Niculus, you have a deal and I like that you're being honest with me. And for you saving my life, I'd be willing to help you do anything, to repay you." After she said that to Niculus, he started to smile. She still didn't know if he brought it or not, because she only meant half of what she said to him.

"Well then, I'm heading out, and I'll be leaving you in Trinity's hands. Trinity please tell Dylana what she has to do to help us block out the suns," he said, and then he kissed Dylana on her forehead, and then he kissed Trinity on the lips, and he left the room and headed upstairs to find Christopher. He knew that he would need Christopher's help to find Damien. When Niculus got to the kitchen, Christopher was sitting there waiting for him.

"So, how are we going to find him?" Christopher asked him, as he read his brother's mind.

"The old way," Niculus told him, and Christopher got up from his seat. They took hands and focused our combined mind powers to find Damien. It didn't take that long at all to find him; it was almost as if he wanted them to find him.

"That was easy, Niculus. He's just about a mile away. I thought he'd be miles away from us, if what Dylana says is true." Christopher said to him, and after they armed themselves for an attack, they headed out to see Damien. They found Damien in a small clearing, and he seemed to stand there waiting for them to come and find him.

"Hello, Niculus, Christopher, how have you two been doing lately, brothers?" Michael asked, as he was mocking them, because he wanted to make them mad. When Niculus looked at him, he noticed that Damien seemed like a different person.

"So, Dylana has been trying us a lot of things about you, Damien. Trinity also tells me you're hiding a lot of things from us. So, why don't you just come clean with us, and tell us the truth for once in your life." Niculus said to him as calmly as he could, without losing his temper.

"What do you want to know, Niculus? Just so you know, all the things I told Dylana are true. Even though she didn't think I was that kind of person." He said, as nasty as he could to Niculus.

"So, this is how you really are? I can see now you are just like Lilith. Pure evil. I knew that the two of you were close on Viterlea, but I never thought you would be on her side. Why are you on her side, anyway?" He asked Michael.

"Why would I tell you that? Figure it out for yourself, Niculus, you're smart." He said, and Niculus looked at Christopher and he told him to restrain Michael, and that he would get the information out of his head. Christopher quickly went behind Michael, and he pushed him to the ground, and Michael started to struggle. Suddenly michael stopped struggling, and he looked at Niculus and he laughed in his face.

"What is this about, Niculus? I thought the three of us would have a friendly conversation about my betrayal of the Vampires?" Michael said, laughing more.

"How long have you been on her side?" Niculus asked, and when Michael didn't answer him, Niculus put his hands onto Michael's head, and Niculus went into his mind, and he forced Michael to answer.

(**"Get out of my head, Niculus."**) Michael told him, as Niculus pushed into his mind more.

(**"Fine, Niculus, you win! I'll tell you! I can't take the pain you're causing me! I have been on Lilith's side since Jane tried for the seventh time to kill us. Lilith did something to me before I was born, and Jane trying to kill us that last time brought it to the surface. Lilith did a spell to steal one of Jane's children. Instead, the spell split your soul in two. The other half of your soul is inside Damien. And it's that soul that Lilith controls. So, that means I'm the other half of your soul. Hello, my mirror self, we're the same, and I control our little brother's**) body as my own. You can call me Michael from now on. Therefore, we are cursed, and that's why if one of us dies, we both die, along with our little brother. I was never Jane's child at all. I always belonged to Lilith. Jane hated me because she knew that I was always Lilith's dark child. And from the first time Jane set eyes on me, she knew that I was evil. That's why she tried to kill us seven times. Our father only stopped her, so he didn't lose you too. Oh, for another thing, Niculus, I loved killing Jane. She looked so shocked, and I just laughed as I did it.") Michael said, laughing.

("You son of a bitch, I will kill you one of these days. Do you know that you almost killed Dylana by hitting her last night?") Niculus said, as he was threatening Michael.

("Good luck trying to kill me without killing yourself. And I'll do the same. As for Dylana, I tried to kill her. But our brother Damien loves her, and he took control for a few seconds, so I wouldn't hit her at full force. Maybe I should hit her harder next time.") Michael said, and after he said that, Niculus felt something in his mind come to the surface.

("Niculus, is that you, brother?") Damien asked Niculus, and this time Niculus knew that it was Damien and not Michael.

("Damien is that you?") Niculus asked him.

("Yes, it's me Niculus, brother please protect Dylana from him.") Damien said to him.

("Damien, why didn't you stop him from killing our mother?") Niculus asked him.

("I know that you will hate me for this, but after she tried to kill me the last time, he told me he would stop her from trying to kill me again and I believed him, and I gave up on living, because this wasn't a life I wanted. I let him take full control of my body, and after a while he became so much stronger than me. I couldn't have taken back control even if I wanted to, I had nothing to fight for, and so I just let him do whatever he wanted to do. When he killed our mother, I'm glad she's gone and that she couldn't hurt me again. But ever since I met Dylana I got my will to live again. I have something I love, and I want to stop him. I want to take back my body and have control again. I want to love her the way she should be, and I have to tell that you…") Damien said. But after he said that Niculus felt Damien fade away, and he knew that Michael was back.

("Fuck, Damien, will you shut up? I don't need you telling Niculus that I don't want him to know. Sorry about that, Niculus. Just so you know, our little brother is an enormous pain in my ass. This was the first time he tried to stop me from doing something, but I have full control back now. I also don't care

about Dylana. she's not my soul mate, but she is Damien's soul mate, and I will use that love to get what I want from her. You can tell her this my mirror self. But I know that she'll still side with me., I have power over her.") Michael said, as he threw Christopher off, and he ran through the woods to get away from them.

"Well, he answered some things we wanted to know about at least, Niculus. And we know that he has power over her. We must convince her he's just using her." Christopher said, as they were on their way back to his house. Niculus said nothing back to him. He was thinking about how he would tell Dylana what Michael thought of her and he was only using her. Niculus knew that this information will put her on their side of the war with the Witches. Then Niculus thought if Michael has power over her, how is he going to convince her of the truth.

Chapter Thirty-Nine

Lab Room

A little while ago

"Well, Dylana, I hate to do this to you, but I have some things I have to do for Niculus now." She lied to her.

"Is that what Niculus was telling you with his mind?" Dylana asked her.

"Yes, but this means you have time to study with some spell books we have here. I think some of them on the shelf there have some info about the Redfire in them." She told Dylana, as she pointed out some books on a shelf.

"Okay, I'll do that," Dylana said and then she thought about the truth potion that Michael told her to make, and she said to Trinity, "Hey, wait a second Trinity." as Trinity was leaving the room.

"Yes, what is it, Dylana?" Trinity asked.

"Where would I find a truth potion?" Dylana asked her.

"What do you want that for, Dylana?" Trinity asked.

"I want to make some for Damien. I still want the truth from him." Dylana told her, and Dylana hoped that Trinity would believe her lie.

"Okay, you'll find it in that book there on the table." She said, as she pointed at a book that was right next to Dylana, and Trinity told her that everything she would need for the potion was down here. Trinity then said goodbye to Dylana, and she left.

Dylana didn't know how long Trinity would be away for, so she grabbed the book that Trinity pointed out to on the table. Dylana started to go through the book to find the right page that the potion was on. The right page was on the last page of the book. The potion was just called 'Truth'. The top of the page only said,

Truth

For those who want the truth from the liars in their lives

It said that the potion would take an hour. Dylana started to hope that Trinity would be away for that long. Dylana thought she needed this to work. She saw that she didn't need much for the potion; it said that she needed,

seven tree leaves

thirteen drops of a tiger's blood

three strands of your own hair

The ingredients sounded odd, she thought, but she thought the potion should be easy to make. She looked at the steps to see what she had to do first. She read that the first step was to crush up the seven tree leaves, and then to put them into a pot over a fire on high for seven minutes. Dylana then looked in the cabinets to find out where the tree leaves were, which were easy for her to find, because they labeled everything. She opened the jar that had leaves in it and then put seven into a bowl and she crushed them into bits. She then found a small pot on the table, and she put the now crushed up leaves in it and put the pot over a fire on high.

While the tree leaves were heating over a fire, Dylana looked at the second step, and it said to put the thirteen drops of a tiger's blood into the pot, with the burned, crushed up leaves. After that, it

376

said to let it sit on the fire on low until it bubbles. While she was waiting for the seven minutes to be up, she went looking for the tiger's blood, which was on the other table right in plain sight, and she saw that the blood was purple, and she thought that was odd. When the seven minutes were up, she dropped the thirteen drops of the tiger's blood into the pot and put the fire on low. It didn't take long for the pot to bubble, and the last step was to drop three strands of her own hair into the pot, and then she mixed it clockwise for a half an hour. The whole time she was mixing the pot, she thought her hand would fall off. She then let it cool for twenty minutes. When the cooled potion was ready to use, Trinity came back down the stairs.

"So, how's the potion making coming, Dylana?" She asked.

"Good, I think I'm all done, but I don't know if it will work or not. Would you mind if I tried it out on you?" Dylana asked her.

"I don't know about that." She said, and Dylana asked her why.

"I don't know, because I wouldn't know what I told you. That's how the potion works, and it will make me tell you the truth, but I wouldn't remember what I told you." She said.

377

"Come on, Trinity. I'll just ask you about what Niculus wanted you to tell me that's all." Dylana said.

"Okay, but I just wanted to tell you that stuff really tastes bad, you must put it in some tea." After she said that, she made two cups of tea appear, and she told Dylana to only put a little of the potion into her cup. Dylana grabbed Trinity's cup, and while Trinity wasn't looking, Dylana put the whole potion into Trinity's cup, and then she put the cup back in front of Trinity. Dylana watched as Trinity drank the potion. After Trinity drank the potion, she started to look like she was in a trance.

"What did Niculus have to do with my mother's death?" Dylana asked her.

"He planned to kidnap your mother. He wanted her to use the Redfire against Lilith." She said.

"Why did she get killed then, if that wasn't his plan?" Dylana asked her.

"The Vampires that Niculus sent with me to get your mother went rogue because someone bewitched them, and they killed everyone. I saw that one of them even knocked out Damien. By the time I got to your mother, she attacked me. I killed her by accident, defending myself." She said, and after she said this, Dylana thought if it was an accident, how could she kill Trinity?

"Why did my mother want me to be careful around Vampires?" Dylana asked her, and Trinity said, "Your mother saw us as bad as the Witches."

"What does Niculus want me to do?" Dylana asked her.

"He wants you to block out the three suns on Viterlea. And then he'll want you to help make a weapon to kill all the Witches once and for all, before they can do the same to us." Trinity said. After she said this, Dylana just stared at her, because they were planning on killing all the Witches, and Dylana didn't think all the Witches could be that bad. Dylana didn't know how much longer the potion would affect her, but as Dylana thought, Trinity started to come out of the trance, and she asked, "So did the potion work?"

"Yes, the potion worked, and I have to ask you, what kind of weapon does Niculus want me to help you guys make?" Dylana asked her.

"Oh, I see, that potion worked a little too well. We'll tell you about that later okay." She said.

"For now, the only thing we need you to do is block out the suns on Viterlea, so that our army can go to the Witch side so we can take the fight to them." She said, and Dylana told her okay, and if that's all she had to do, it sounded good to her.

"So, does this mean you're on our side and that you'll help us, because we have to do the spell in three days?" Trinity said.

"Yes, I guess so, why do I have to the spell in three days?" Dylana asked her.

"We have to do the spell then, because in three days on our planet, the moons will block the suns, and all you have to do is hold them in place." She said, and Dylana told her okay, and then Dylana told Trinity that she was going back upstairs to get some sleep. Trinity nodded to her, as Dylana left.

Chapter Forty

Truth

Dylana left Trinity in the lab room and she made her way up to the room the Niculus gave her. When she got to the room, she felt her face, and she noticed that there was no trace of the potion on it at all, and she thought maybe her skin absorbed it all. She then thought of Michael and she tried to contact him with her mind. She knew she contacted him when she heard him said, (**"How are you doing, lover, how's your face?"**) Dylana told him that her face was all right, and it was all healed up. She also told him he was wrong about his bother lying to me.

("I think it will be very hard for me to kill Trinity.") She told him.

("Why will it be hard to kill her, lover? I'm glad that your face is all healed up. I don't know what I would do if I killed you, just to trick my brother.") He said to her.

("Well, she was the one who killed my mother, but it was an accident, and she didn't want to kill her. Michael, I have to know if you were lying to me when you told me that Niculus was the one that planned her death.") Dylana questioned him.

("No lover, I didn't lie to you about that. Remember, I was there that night. The people that attacked me were Niculus's men.") He said to her, and she told him okay, because she couldn't help it, she wanted to agree with him, even though a little part of her that was telling her something was up.

("Do you know what they're planning?") He said.

("Niculus wants me to block out the suns on Viterlea and there was something about a weapon they want to create for them, but I don't anything else. Trinity said that we'll be going to Viterlea soon.") She told him.

("Okay, I'll be there on Viterlea tonight, and until you have time to kill Trinity, just do what he wants you to do. He'll

382

most likely bring you to Viterlea by tomorrow night. So, I'll see you there, lover. Oh, and Niculus and Christopher came to see me today, and this is how I know that he healed you. He questioned me harshly.") He said.

("**Are you okay?**") She asked him.

("**I'm just fine. Remember, he can't hurt me without hurting himself. He tried to imprison me, but I got away from him, and if it helps you with killing Trinity, you could always do it for Jade.**") After he said that he broke the connection.

Downstairs Thirteen minutes ago

As Niculus and Christopher walked into the house Christopher said, "Well, he answered some things we wanted to know about at least, Niculus. And we must convince her he's just using her." Niculus said nothing back at him. Niculus was thinking about how he would tell Dylana what Michael thought of her and that he was only using her. Niculus hoped that this information would put her on the Vampire's side. Then again, he thought if Michael has power over her, he didn't know if he could convince her of the truth or not. When Niculus and Christopher walked into the kitchen, Trinity was there waiting for them. Niculus saw she looked worried about something.

383

"Hey, guys, I think we may have a problem." She told them.

"What do you mean, love?" Niculus asked her.

"Dylana, wanted to do a truth potion for Damien. I thought it was harmless for her to do the potion, so I told her where the book was. But when I got back here, she asked if she could try it out on me. I think she wanted to make the potion just, so she could question me about her mother's death, and I think she knows everything we've been hiding from her." Trinity said, and Niculus just nodded his head.

"What do we do now, Niculus?" Trinity asked him.

"We tell her the truth." After he said that, Trinity grabbed his arm hard, and he started to see what Trinity was seeing at this moment. What they were seeing was terrible. They saw what the Witches were planning for Earth. And what the Witches were planning for them, and what Lilith would do to him. After Trinity let go of his arm, he quickly went to get Dylana. he had to make sure she would do what he wanted her to do, because in the vision that Trinity showed him, the suns were shining bright in the sky. Niculus walked into the room.

"Hey, Dylana can you come downstairs?" He asked her and followed him downstairs and into the kitchen. Trinity and

Christopher were already down there sitting at the table and Niculus told her to have a seat.

"So, Dylana there is something you need to know since Trinity tells me you're on our side, and I know that I can trust you now. When I left this morning, you asked me where I was going, and I went to find Damien. I just had to find out if what you told me was true or not." Niculus told her, and Trinity looked at him, and she said with her mind, (**"I never told you that, Niculus. Why are you telling her what you were doing this morning?"**)

(**"I'm telling her this because if she thinks we trust her, maybe she'll tell us the truth about things she's been doing."**) He told her, but Trinity didn't think it would work, and Niculus saw on Christopher's face he was listening to them talking and Christopher said, (**"That could work."**)

"Did you find him?" She asked him, acting like she didn't already know that Niculus confronted Michael.

"Yes, I found him. It was almost like he wanted us to find him; it was that easy. So, I had Christopher restrain Damien, as I got the truth out of his head. He really is Lilith's son, and the other things he told you were true." Niculus said to her.

"How did you get the truth out of his head?" Dylana asked him curiously.

"I used mind control on him. My mind is a lot stronger than his. Since you know that he was telling the truth to you, are you still on our side? Before you answer, Dylana, I must tell you something. When I told him he almost killed you, he didn't seem to care. He also seemed mad that he didn't kill you, and all he seemed to care about was getting back to Lilith." He said.

"Yes, I'm still on the Vampire's side. There are still things he lied to me about, and at least you haven't lied to me, right, Niculus?" She asked him.

"I will be honest with you little one. If you're on our side, there are some things I'm keeping from you. Everyone has their secrets, even you. If you do what I want you to do, I'll tell you everything, and I give you my word on that and, as you have already seen, when I give someone my word I mean it." He told her.

"Okay Niculus, and you're right about secrets, and there's something I have to be honest with you about." She said.

"Okay, what is it, Dylana?" Niculus asked her, as he thought he knew that if he was honest with her, she'd tell him what she was up to.

"I lied to Trinity, when I asked her to try the truth potion I made. I had no intention of using it on Damien. I made it so I could find out if you guys were being honest with me or not. I'm just tired of being lied to. I also asked her more than I told her I would ask. I just wanted to know what really happened to my mother that night." Dylana stopped talking as she cried. Niculus put his arm around her.

"Trinity had a feeling you asked her about that. I would tell you this later, but I think now it would be better. That day I went to your house, the real reason sent my tiger into your house was to show your mother that something bad would happen to you. The tigers on our planet mean death." He told her.

"Is that why the tiger when after me?" She asked him.

"The Tiger knew that something bad would happen to you. You don't know this, but the day your mother died, I was at your house. She did a spell on you so we could talk without you overhearing us. I wanted to talk to her about how the Tiger predicted that you would die. And that night Trinity was already at the party, before the others got there, and she saw your mother said something under her breath. Trinity then saw you go into the bathroom, just as the first one crashed through the window. Your mother saved you, because someone wanted you to die that night. Trinity tried to stop the rogue Vampires, but she couldn't fight all of them. Trinity told me that your mother was fighting well against them. When Trinity tried to get your mother out of there, your mother stabbed her, and Trinity threw her into a wall, and you know what happened." He said.

"If it was Trinity, then why didn't my mother know who killed her? And what happened to the rogue Vampires? And why didn't you stop them, before they attacked us?" She asked him.

"She didn't see my face. It happened too quickly." Trinity told her.

"I would have stopped them sooner if I knew about them, being bewitched. I only sent Trinity to get your mother, and I told my people to stay on Viterlea and that we could take care of it. Lilith must have found out what I was planning, so she bewitched thirteen of my best fighters to stop me from taking Debathena. She told them to kill everyone and to bring Debathena to her if they could. I killed them for betraying me, because I had no other choice, the spell they were under was permanent." Niculus told her.

"So, Dylana, my main plan is to block out the suns. We'll be going to Viterlea tonight. I want to be there two days before the eclipse, so that Trinity can go through the spell with you before you have to do it for real." He said.

"So, Trinity, how does the spell work?" Dylana asked her, and she told Dylana that she'll tell her that tomorrow.

"Okay, so when Trinity and I are doing the spell, what are you going to be doing Niculus?" Dylana asked him, and he started to smile at her.

"That's a good question, little one. When Trinity's showing you the spell. I'll be getting my army ready for battle, and after the suns are blocked out, we'll attack the Witches and kill them all, so they can't start a war with Earth." He told her.

"How do you know that they want to attack Earth?" Dylana asked him.

"We know because Trinity here saw it. It was terrible, Trinity saw the Witches kill almost all the Humans, and they will enslave the ones that are still alive, and Lilith will force me and all the Vampires to join her." He said, and Dylana didn't know what to say to that, and she knew at this moment she had to help stop that from happening.

"When are we leaving? tonight?" Dylana asked, and Niculus replied, "Late tonight," and he told her she should go up to her room and get some sleep. Dylana went back to the room, and she crawled into bed, and she fell right to sleep.

When Niculus heard Dylana sleeping he said, "Christopher, please go ahead to Viterlea, and tell Selene and Uncle Marcus that I'll be there tonight, and that Dylana will be with me. Have Uncle Marcus get a room ready for her and tell our people we will finish the war with the Witches. Tell them we have the Redfire on our side." And Christopher said sure, and then he left for Viterlea, and Niculus heard Christopher's dragon, Emerald, take to the skies.

"So, how are you going to get Dylana to Viterlea? You know that Midnight doesn't like strangers on her back? You remember she took a month to like me." Trinity told him.

"I know that, I thought that you could make a sleeping potion to have her sleep until we get to Viterlea." Niculus said to her, and she agreed, and then she left to make the potion. As he sat there, he thought that if everything goes how he wants it to go, and the suns get blocked out, when they can take the fight to the Witches on their side of Viterlea. He knew that this would be the start of the biggest and bloodiest battle with the Witches. The thought of so many Witches bleeding, and the smell of all that Witch blood in the air made him lick his lips. As he was thinking this, Trinity walked in and told him that the potion was ready.

"Okay, let's go home then." I said to her. We went up to Dylana's room, and he watched as Trinity gave Dylana the potion through a needle. Dylana was out cold within seconds. Niculus picked her up, and the three of us went outside.

("**Hello, Night, can you take us to Viterlea please?**") He asked her.

("**Who's she, Niculus, you know that I don't like strangers?**") She said to him, a little mad.

("**She's someone that will help us, my dear, and she's asleep and I'll hold on to her, so she doesn't touch you, okay.**") He said to her, and she said fine, and then we got on her back, and she took them home to Viterlea. When they landed on Viterlea, Christopher, Selene, Marcus, and three of Niculus' generals were waiting for them outside the castle. Niculus noticed that all of them had worried looks on their faces, and he knew that something was wrong.

Chapter Forty-One

Home

"What's happening Christopher, why do you all look so worried?" Niculus asked him, and he said, "It's the Witches. They've been trying to get on our side. We've been trying to hold them back, but it's getting harder."

"That makes little sense. Why are they doing that?" Niculus asked, and he started to think his plan would fall through if the Witches attacked first.

"Marcus, could you take Dylana inside for me, so I know that she's safe." Niculus said, and Marcus told him, "Sure, but I need to talk to you about something later."

"Okay, Marcus, we'll talk later. Trinity, would you go inside with them?" Niculus asked her, and she told him sure, as he handed Dylana over to Marcus, and then they started to walk inside the castle, and Niculus watched as Selene followed them inside.

Niculus turned to look at his brother, and he told Christopher and his generals to follow him to the border to find out what was going on with the Witches. They ran to the border, and when they got there Niculus saw the Witches were lined up against the border, and they seemed to try to get through, but his people were keeping them back. As Niculus got closer, his people noticed him, and they stood waiting for Niculus to give them the order to attack the Witches. As Niculus made his way to the front, his people moved out of his way to let him go where the Witches were standing.

"What is all this? Lilith and I have an agreement." Niculus asked the first Witch he came to, but he didn't answer someone else did.

"She knows that you're plotting against her, and we're here to stop you and your Vampire filth from attacking us first." Fantos said to him, as he walked up to the front to face Niculus.

393

"Is that so, well I know that she's doing the same thing against me, and that she's planning to enslave us. Fantos, if you didn't know, the agreement I have with your bitch of a mother, Lilith, is that she leaves me and my kind alone, and I'll do the same to her and her kind. Unless I kill a Witch or unless she kills a Vampire. As far as I know. that hasn't happened, so why don't you fucking Witches go away and stop bothering us?" Niculus yelled at them all.

"Fantos, he's right, let's go." Michael said, as he walked next to Fantos, and then the Witches followed the two of them back to the Witch side, but they stayed close by. Niculus was just happy that they were away from the border. He saw that his people all looked puzzled by Damien being on the Witches' side. Niculus then told his generals to follow him back to the castle, and that there were some things they need to know, but he told his fighters to stay behind to watch the border and to let him know if the Witches came back.

When all the Vampire generals were in the war room, Niculus started to explain to them, "Lilith's planning to start a war with Earth, and to kill off most of the Humans, and enslave the rest. Lilith also plans to force us to join her. We have to stop her from doing this."

"How do you know what Lilith's planning, King Niculus?" General Fire asked him.

"I know that this is their plan because I saw it with my own eyes through a vision that Trinity was having. It was bad, and I hope that we'll be able to stop it from coming true. Another thing you should know is that Damien is a betrayer, and he has been telling Lilith my plans. If someone finds him on our side, I want him captured and locked away forever. He is also the one who really killed my mother Jane." Niculus told them, and after he said that, a lot of Vampire generals were yelling, and asking he why Damien would kill his own mother. Niculus told them that Lilith has control over him, and he told them he thinks she talked him into it. And that he's been on her side since he was born.

"What's the plan, King Niculus?" General Dark asked him.

"We now have the girl that wields the Redfire on our side, and she will use the Redfire to block out the suns. After she does that, we'll attack the Witches and kill them all, to stop them from enslaving us." Niculus said, and his Generals seemed happy with the plan, the Vampires enjoyed a good fight.

After the meeting was over, Niculus didn't want to sleep that night, even though he could use a good night's sleep. He wondered around outside. He just wanted to be alone with his thoughts, but

Midnight found him, and she told him he should sleep, and he fell asleep next to her on the ground.

Chapter Forty-Two

Spell Room

When Dylana woke up, she had a killer headache, and she was thinking, what was in that needle, that she saw Trinity inject me with? She had a feeling she wasn't on Earth anymore, and that she must be back on Viterlea. She got out of bed and she went to look out the window. She wanted to see what the Vampire's side looked like, but she couldn't see much of anything. It was so dark, and it was weird to her to see that there was no sun in the sky at all, although there was this gray glow that looked almost like fog. She started to wonder how the Vampires see anything out there, because she knew that if she was outside, she'd be walking into things left and right. As she thought she heard someone knock on the door, she told them to come in, and she saw that it was Trinity.

"Oh, well you're up, Dylana I'm sorry about knocking you out last night, with a sleeping potion. It's just that Midnight has a problem with new people riding on her back." Trinity told her.

"So, there was a sleeping potion in that needle you poked me with. I woke up with a big headache, is that from the potion? And who's Midnight?" Dylana asked her.

"Yeah, sorry about the headache, that's one of the side effects of the sleeping potion. Midnight is Niculus' dragon. He likes to call her Night for short though. So, what do you think of Vampire's side of Viterlea?" She asked Dylana.

"It's gloomy, and I'd rather be on Earth, but it's still pretty." Dylana told her.

"I know and after you block out the suns, I'll take all back there." Trinity said.

"Okay, so when is the eclipse?" Dylana asked her.

"It's tomorrow, and if you want, I could show you around," Trinity said.

"Okay, yeah sure, I'd like to see what this place looks like. Hey, Trinity I thought we had two days before the eclipse?" Dylana asked her, and Trinity said that time goes faster on Viterlea

"Follow me," she said. The first room she showed Dylana looked like a giant closet, and she told Dylana that this was her favorite room in the whole castle. They went inside the room, and Trinity said, "I'm showing you this room first because Niculus wanted me to give you a gift for helping us. Wait right here I'll be right back." Dylana told her okay, as she watched Trinity go through a wall, and Dylana thought that was cool and she was wondering how Trinity did that. Dylana waited for a few minutes for Trinity to come back though the wall. She came though the wall with this beautiful dress in her arms.

"That's for me?" Dylana asked her, as she looked at the fiery red dress that had black flowers along the bottom.

"Yes, do you want to put it on now?" Trinity asked her. Dylana told her yes, and Trinity helped her put it on. Trinity then showed her to where the mirror was so she could see herself in the dress. Dylana was having second thoughts about Trinity; she didn't think she could kill her.

"So, are you ready to see the rest of this place?" She asked, and Dylana told her yes. Trinity showed her this room full of weapons. Dylana seen no weapons like these before. There were thirteen rooms just for training, and it was fun watching the Vampires training. It shocked her by how fast they could move, and at one point it was hard for her to see them at all. They stopped in a giant banquet hall, to get something to eat, and this room was so big it could fit at least a thousand people in it. After they ate, Trinity showed her around outside, and they ran into Niculus.

"Do you like the dress Dylana?" He asked me when he saw that I was wearing the dress.

"Yes, thank you, Niculus." She said to him, and he smiled at her.

"So, do you want to see what a dragon looks like?" He asked her.

"Absolutely," I said. They had to climb up a little hill to where she was. Dylana saw Midnight more and more with every step up the hill. Midnight opened her eyes as they got closer to her.

"Dylana, this is Midnight." Niculus told her.

"She's pretty, just like a starlit sky," Dylana said.

("Niculus, I how she described me. She's a sweet girl.") Midnight said, and Niculus told Dylana, that Midnight liked how she described her. Dylana said that she looked like a starlit sky, because Midnight looked black and blue, and some of her scales sparked like diamonds.

"Okay, Trinity, why don't you show Dylana, where she will be doing the spell from," Niculus said to Trinity, and she told Dylana to follow her. They went back inside, and Dylana followed her into a tower room. The room looked kind of weird, the walls were red, the floor was green, and the ceiling was blue. There was this white and yellow marble circle in the middle of the room.

"What kind of room is this? What is that?" Dylana asked, as she pointed at the white and yellow circle.

"This is the spell room. It's good for chanting the elements; we need the four elements for the spell to work. That in the middle of the room is a power stone. We use this stone to help channel power better." She said, and then Dylana asked her what the spell was.

"Well, you don't really need to say a spell. All you have to do is stand in the center of the stone and focus one thing and one thing only. The thing I want you to focus on is seeing the moons block the suns. You must call on the elements to help. After you do this, I'll bring you back to Earth." She said, and Dylana told her okay.

Chapter Forty-Three

Spy

Back to Niculus outside

After Dylana and Trinity left to go back to the castle, Niculus stayed outside with Night, enjoying the day before the battle. He hoped that after tomorrow this fighting witll be done with once and for all, and he thought about the prophecy again and if it comes true, he will lose Trinity, and he didn't know if he could handle that or not. Though if she doesn't die, he'll never be with his soul mate. As he was thinking this, he saw his Uncle Marcus walking toward him.

"Hello, Uncle Marcus. So, you found me, how's it going?" Niculus asked him, and Niculus thought if he came looking for him, it must mean that he has some bad news.

"My, King Niculus, you say that as if you were hiding from me? As I told you yesterday, there are some urgent matters I must talk to you about." He said, and Niculus knew somehting was wrong by just looking at his face, and he thought it was odd that his uncle called him by his title, because he's never called him King before, Marcus must have really wanted his attention.

"It must be serious, you've never called me King before, something must be worrying you." Niculus said, as he got up and walked toward him.

"Yes, Niculus, I know that I've never called you King before, but I needed your full attention and I knew that calling you that, I'd have it. If you would walk with me into the woods. There's something you have to see, and I'll explain on the way." He told Niculus.

"Okay, so what's going on, Uncle?" Niculus asked him, as they made their way toward the woods.

"Well some animals have been acting weird. Some Tigers have disappeared from our woods and they're on the Witches' side now." He said, and now Niculus was worrying too, because the Tigers help to keep the Witches away from the Nightspear flowers we used for healing, but the Witches steal the flowers to used them to make poison, that could kill us.

"Have they done anything else? Why would they be on the Witches' side?" Niculus asked him.

"Well at first, they were just acting weird, like they were guarding the Nightspear flowers, but they wouldn't let us go near the flowers to pick them. And then yesterday, before you got here, I was walking through the woods to see if the Tigers were still acting weird, and I saw that the Witches were in our woods and none of the Tigers were attacking them. So, I followed them, and they were heading to where the Nightspear flowers were. I watched as the Tigers led them to the flowers. The Tigers seemed to protect the Witches as they were stealing all the flowers. This morning, I thought I'd take another walk through the woods and now the Tigers are gone and the Nightspear flowers are gone." He said, and Niculus was anxious now, because without those flowers they can't make any healing potions.

"What, you've got to be kidding me, all the flowers are gone. Do we even have enough in stock to make our healing remedies? If you didn't see where the tigers went to, why do you think they're on the Witches' side?" Niculus asked him.

"We have little Nightspear in stock, but we'll be fine if we plant the seeds, and hope that the Witches don't steal them when they bloom. I think the Tigers are on the Witches' side, because I think they're being controlled by Lilith. I saw that the Tiger's eyes were all purple and not red." He said, as they were walking to where the Nightspear flowers were growing before the Witches took them all. As they got there, Niculus saw that the flowers were all gone. The Witches took every single one, and most likely all the Witches will have Nightspear poison on all their weapons, and that's a terrible thing for them. Niculus also thought if it wasn't for Dylana being on their side his hope would be lost, and at least the Witches can't see in the dark, their aim will suck.

"This is bad, Uncle Marcus. Do you know why they took the Tigers after they got what they wanted?" Niculus asked him as Niculus looked at the ground that once held her favorite flowers.

"I don't know why they took the Tigers, maybe Lilith's planning to use them to attack us tomorrow." He said. Niculus thought of his Tiger, Low, and he tried to call her to him, but nothing happened, and he got even more worried.

"That's possible. I think you're right about them being controlled. I tried to call Low and nothing happened. That bitch has my Tiger. I fear what Lilith may use Low and the other Tigers for something far worse." Niculus said to him.

"It's bad you can't contact Low. What could be worse than her using the Tigers against us?" he asked.

"Using them against people who don't know how to fight them, like the Humans for one." Niculus said to him, and Marcus nodded in agreement.

"My King, here you are," Niculus' royal messenger Delo said, as he ran up to them.

"What is it, Delo?" Niculus asked him.

"The Witch Prince, Fantos, has come here to talk with you, King Niculus. He's in the throne room waiting for you." He said.

"What, why is he here? Who even let him on our side?" Niculus asked him.

"Your sister let him come on our side, and she sent me to get you, My King, and she wanted me to tell you that Prince Fantos wants to talk to you." He said.

"Uncle Marcus, please come with me so I don't end up killing him?" Niculus said, and Marcus nodded his head. They followed Delo back to the castle and into the throne room. Niculus walked in the room and took his seat on his throne, and Marcus sat down in the chair next to his. Niculus looked at Fantos and his sister and Niculus saw that the two of them were holding hands and this worried him.

"So, what do you want, Fantos? Keep in mind that nothing you say will stop this final battle between the Witches and the Vampires." Niculus said to him.

"King Niculus, my mother thinks I've come here to get you to surrender to her, but that is not why I'm hereto see you." Fantos said, as he bowed, and Niculus thought this was odd because of how he acted the other day at the border toward him.

"Then why have you come here, Fantos?" Niculus asked him, but Fantos wasn't the one that answered, it was his sister, "Brother, there are some things I've been keeping from you, but Fantos has convinced me I should tell you this before it's too late and this battle destroys us all."

"What are you talking about Selene? Please don't tell me you're on the Witches' side too, like Michael?" Niculus asked, worried because he couldn't lose anyone else to the Witches.

"No, brother, don't be silly. You know that I'm loyal to you and no one else. Do you remember I told you we had a spy in the Witches' castle, but he was worried what would happen if the

Witches saw him talking to you? So, I was getting the information from him and reporting it to you?" She asked him.

"Yes, sister, I remember. Are you trying to tell me that Fantos here is our spy?" Niculus asked her.

"Yes, brother, Fantos is our inside man, but there's more that I have to tell you. Fantos and I are in love, and we're planning to get married, when Lilith is dead and gone." She said.

"We hoped that we could get your blessing, and I came here to tell you something that Lilith's planning." Fantos said.

"I just have one question first." Niculus said to Fantos.

"What would that be, King Niculus?" Fantos asked him.

"So, you've been on our side for a while, and yesterday at the border, were you just messing with me?" Niculus asked him.

"Yes, I had to act like that, because Michael was there, and Lilith ordered me to piss you off," Fantos said.

"If you don't mind me asking what made you betray your own mother? Why are you so worried about Michael?" Marcus asked Fantos.

"I don't mind you asking, and think moment I hated, and fearing my mother was the day she planned Jane's death with Michael. Back then, Lilith didn't let me leave the castle unless Michael was with me, because she didn't want me to near any Vampires, if had a chance I would have told King Dmitry what they were planning. Also, Michael had me worry a lot, because if he knew that I was thinking about betraying my mother, he would kill me, and I did not wish to die at his hands. So, that means I had to be careful around him. And so far, I've done a lot of bad things just to fool Michael, and the Witches and I regret all of them. King Niculus, I'm sorry about your mother. She was a kind woman." Fantos said as he shed a tear for Jane.

"I didn't know Lilith treated you like that. Just so you know, the only person I blame for my mother's death is Michael, and he will pay one day for what he's done. I have to ask, what did you have to do?" Niculus asked him.

"I bewitch your men so they would do whatever Lilith wanted them to do. And when you were all in the forest on Earth talking to Dylana, he was ordered to cast a spell to mess with your minds, to make it so you would act differently than you would have. I swear to you I will do whatever it takes to make it up to you, for the things I've done." He said, and Niculus saw how horrible he felt for doing those things.

"I forgive you. You were just doing what you had to." Niculus said understanding, and Fantos thanked him for understanding.

"Do you know what Lilith's planning to do with the Nightspear flowers, and Tigers?" Marcus asked Fantos.

"Lilith plans to use the Nightspear flowers to make poison, to coat all the weapons, and she will use the Tigers to attack Earth. There is something else that you must know about Dylana. She's been on Viterlea before." Fantos said.

"What, why was she here?" Niculus asked.

"Lilith wanted to talk to her and to come up with a way to fool you, and Michael came up with a plan to have Dylana fool you all and find out what you were up to." Fantos said.

"Well, I guess that plan failed, because she's on our side and she's agreed to do the spell to block out the suns." Niculus told him.

"That's good to hear. I'm glad that Lilith doesn't have the Redfire on her side," Fantos said.

"Another thing, do you know what happened to Misty's daughter?" Niculus asked him.

"I have bad news about her. She's on Lilith's side, but I haven't seen her in a few days, I think Lilith may have done something to her, why do you ask?" Fantos asked.

"I was just wondering, that's all. I know that she's powerful and it would have been nice to have her on my side too." Niculus said, and he thought Jade must think Trinity killed her mother.

"What did you think Lilith did to hear?" Marcus asked Fantos, and Fantos said that he doesn't know, but likely it's nothing good.

"So, brother, do we have your blessing?" Selene asked as she grabbed both of Fantos's hands in hers.

"Yes, and Selene, I hope that you and Fantos are thrilled together. Is there anything else you want to tell me?" Niculus asked, because he saw on his sister's face that there was something else that she wanted to say.

"Yes, there is one more thing. Do you remember that little girl was at my place on Earth about ten years ago?" She asked.

"Yes, I remember Danielle. You told she was the daughter of a friend of yours." Niculus said.

"Well, brother I lied to you. Danielle is mine and Fantos's daughter." She told.

"I see, and how did I not notice you were pregnant? Where is she now?" Niculus asked her.

"I stayed on Viterlea the whole time I was pregnant, and I avoided you the whole time. She's on Earth still with a friend of ours, who's keeping her safe for us. I had Fantos take away her memories to protect her." She said.

"Well, when we are at peace, I'd love to meet her." Niculus said.

"Yes, and you will, brother." She told him.

"Is there anything else we need to talk about?" Niculus asked his sister.

"No, brother, that was all I had to tell you, and I'm sorry for not telling sooner." She said, and he told her she has nothing to be sorry for, and then he looked at Fantos.

"Fantos, is there anything else that we need to talk about?" he asked him.

"Yes, there is something I didn't tell you about the tigers. Lilith's controlling them, and she's also bewitched the Wolves as well and they're as bad as the Tigers now, if not worse. She will use them to kill the Humans." He said.

"Well, hopefully after tomorrow we won't have to worry about that." Marcus said.

"Yes, sorry but I must leave now, before Michael thinks something's up." Fantos said, and Niculus said goodbye to him. When he left, Niculus left the throne room, and he went to bed to get some real sleep before the battle, and he thought to himself that he'll have to tell Trinity about what Fantos said when he woke up.

Chapter Forty-Four

Eclipse

Back to Dylana

For the rest of the day, Trinity just let Dylana walk around on her own. And that night when she went to bed, she couldn't sleep at all. She didn't sleep much, because she wasn't tired, and she was freaking out about what she would have to do tomorrow. Another reason she couldn't sleep was that anytime she closed her eyes, they were full of nightmares of Niculus killing her with his sword. She thought this nightmare was her seeing her death, and then she freaked out more, because in the nightmare she could feel his sword against her neck.

When she woke the next day, she saw that it was dark outside, and somehow, she knew that Trinity would come to get her to do the spell, and she tried to think of something she could say to her that would get her mad, so she could go through with killing her. As Dylana was getting out of the bed, Trinity walked in and said that it was time. So, she followed Trinity back up to the spell room.

When they got to the room, Trinity told her to stand in the center of the white and yellow power stone in the middle of the room. As Dylana did this, she looked outside and saw that the eclipse was starting. She started to focus on holding the moons in place. It took a few minutes for the eclipse to be in place. She put her hands up and closed her eyes. She started to see the moons blocking the suns in her mind. She felt the Redfire rise off her skin. Dylana called Fire to help, and she felt flames go through me. She called Water to help, and she felt waves go through her. She called Air to help, and she felt a breeze go through her. And then she called Earth to help, and she felt something hard go through her.

"With the power of Fire, Water, Air, Earth, and the power of the Redfire I wield the suns to block out by the moons." she said, and after that she felt something powerful come out of her hands, and then she fell onto the floor.

"Dylana, you did it. Are you okay?" Trinity asked her.

"I'm fine. I'm just a little drained that's all." Dylana said, as Trinity helped her up. Dylana looked outside, and all she saw was darkness. And now it was time to do what she told Michael she would do. It was time to betray Trinity and kill her. Dylana felt scared about it. She put her hands behind her back, and she wished for the blade that Lilith gave her to appear. She felt the blade in her hands, and then the Redfire fell off her. She knew that she died, that Michael would bring her back, so she didn't pick the Redfire back up.

"Okay, Trinity, there is something I have to ask you." Dylana said.

"Okay, what is it?" She asked, as she was smiling.

"I get that you wanted revenge, and you got it, but why did you have to make Misty suffer?" Dylana asked her.

"Who told you that Misty suffered?" She asked, and Dylana told her that Jade told her that.

"Jade knows how I felt. I wanted Misty to suffer, but I wasn't the one that killed her. Is this why you got so close to us? You want to get some revenge for Jade," Trinity said as she laughed. Dylana didn't believe Trinity when she said that she didn't kill Misty, and she started to radiate anger. It felt like her whole body was on fire.

Dylana tried to strike Trinity with the blade, as she ran toward her, but Trinity moved out of the way just in time for Dylana to miss the front of her. Dylana charged at her for the second time, and she stabbed Trinity in the back, and Trinity screamed in pain. Dylana pushed Trinity to the ground, and she heard Trinity scream more, as she stabbed Trinity, thirteen more times in her back with the knife.

Chapter Forty-Five

Betrayed

Earlier that day

Today is the day of the solar eclipse, and Niculus knew that it will be a superb day because today all the Witches will die. Niculus rolled over in bed and he saw that Trinity was still sleeping, so he quietly left the room to get some blood. He knew that he would need a lot of power today. He went downstairs to the kitchens, and on his way, everyone that passed him greeted him as Your Highness, or they would bow their heads to him. Even though he was King now, he wasn't used to this. I would rather they just called his name instead of his title. When he got down to the kitchens, he was the only one down there, because a lot of Vampires were getting ready for the battle, or they were still sleeping, because during the day the suns shining on the Witches' side were very strong. Even though the Witches' side was far away from outside, the suns on their side could still kill Vampires from that distance.

When he was full of blood, he ate some food, and then he walked into his private weapons room. As he walked in the room, he had the feeling that all my plans were coming together perfectly. He thought this will be fun. Niculus then started to arm himself with all the weapons he would need for the battle with the Witches.

In here, he had weapons of all kinds. There were blades, swords, and even some throwing weapons. The only things he didn't have in here were bows and arrows, because he liked to fight close and personal instead of shooting an arrow from afar. Niculus knew exactly what weapons he would grab before he walked into the room. he already had them lying out.

Niculus left the weapons room, with seven blades, two of them were in his boots, one on each arm, and one attached to each leg, and the last one was along his spine. He also had two swords, one on each side of my belt. Then he went to find Trinity to tell her about Fantos coming here last night and to make sure she had everything set up for the spell. He took a while to find her because she wasn't in our room like he thought she would be. He finally found her in the spell room, and he wasn't sure what she was doing.

"Trinity, what are you up to, lover?" He asked her.

"I'm calling the elements into the room." She said.

"How are you doing that?" He asked her.

"You know nothing about magic, do you?" She asked him, and he told her no. She told him she's calling the elements to go into the stone alter, so it will be easier for Dylana to call the elements to herself. As she said this, she pointed to the stone altar.

"Niculus, do you see that the stone is now red?" She asked him, and he told her yes, and she said it's like that to represent fire, and that she has four more elements to call, and then she would get Dylana to do the spell.

"Okay good, so nothing will go wrong today, right?" He asked her, and she told him to get out of here, so she could finish what she was doing on time, before he could tell her about Fantos being on their side. He then headed outside to join his army. He went to the front of the lines with Christopher, Marcus, and his generals, as they watched the eclipse start. The moons were going in front of the suns. He watched as darkness filled the sky, as the moons blocked out the suns. He was happy that his plan worked, but he had a sudden feeling that something was horribly wrong, and he knew that he had to find Trinity.

"Christopher, start the attack. I have to check something." He told him.

"What's wrong, Niculus?" Christopher asked him.

"Trinity. I can feel that something has happened to her upstairs, or something will happen to her. I'm just going to check. I'll be right back, brother, save me some Witches to kill." Niculus told him. As he walked back up to the spell room, Niculus could hear yelling. He got worried when he heard that the yelling was coming from the spell room. It sounded like Trinity and Dylana were yelling at each other about something. He didn't know what they were yelling about though, or why they were yelling at each other, if they're on the same side. When he heard Trinity screaming in pain, he investigated her mind and saw that Dylana was stabbing her in the back with a knife. Niculus rushed to the room as fast as he could and kicked the door down. He walked in and he saw that Dylana was still stabbing Trinity in the back with a knife, and he saw blood everywhere.

Dylana turned to look at him, and she saw that he had a furious look on his face. As she looked at him, she felt her eyes burning, as if his eyes were shooting a fiery blast into her eyes.

Dylana knew that he would kill her, and she knew that she had nothing to lose, so she thought why not fight him, so she just smiled at him?

"Your bitch here killed my mother. So, I killed her, an eye for an eye. I think the two of us are even now. What do you think, Niculus?" She said to him, as she got off Trinity, and stepped back a little from the body with the knife in her hand. Niculus looked at her with shock on his face, and then he looked at Trinity lying on the floor, as her spirit was fading away. Dylana just stood there mocking him and trying to get him madder, as he walked over to Trinity's dead body. Dylana watched as he kissed her for the last time. While he had his back to her, she came up from behind him, and she stabbed him in the back with the knife she killed Trinity with. He yelled from the pain that the knife caused him, and then she slowly backed away from him.

He looked at her, and he started to smile, as he pulled the knife out of his back and he threw it against the wall away from her, so she couldn't stab him again. he suddenly noticed that the knife was purple, and he knew that it belonged to Lilith. He knew that she always puts Nightspear in all her weapons to poison anyone with Vampire blood. That's why the cut from the knife hurt him so much, and the longer the knife is in a wound, the more poison gets in your blood and the more pain you fell.

He was so pissed off at this point because Lilith and Damien had Dylana fool him, so she could kill his love, and now he would kill her. He knew she was completely unarmed, and she looked at him with fear now, because she knew that this was it. He started to walk toward her, and she tried to run out of the room, but he grabbed her by the hair, and he threw her into a wall. She screamed in pain as he swung his sword at her, and then he took off her fucking head. as he was standing over her dead body, he felt that something good was happening, and he walked to the window, and he saw that the Vampires were pushing the Witches back to their side, and that the Vampires were winning. He started to feel the Nightspear poison from the knife affect him, and he fell to the floor and passed out, and he had a weird dream. In the dream, there was a beautiful girl.

To be continued